C000217635

About Face

Wendy Williams

First published 2016 by CompletelyNovel

ISBN 978-1-84914-992-1

Copyright @ Wendy Williams 2016

Wendy Williams has asserted her right to be identified as the author of this work.

All rights reserved. No part of this publication may be reproduced, stored in a retrieval system, or transmitted, in any form, or by any means (electronic, mechanical, photocopying, recording or otherwise) without the prior written permission of the author.

This book is a work of fiction. Names, characters, places, organizations and incidents are either products of the author's imagination or used fictitiously. Any resemblance to actual events is entirely coincidental.

Cover Design by CompletelyNovel

Back Cover illustration © Eleanor Broome

Editing by Eleanor Broome

Printed and bound by CPI

Follow Wendy via her blog: www.mylifewitheyecancer.com

For Geoff, Eleanor and Amelia

The loves of my life

Prologue

For the first time in her life, Soraya could not wait to shroud herself in the familiar comfort of her burqua. She wanted to take shelter in its folds, hide away from all that she was about to face. Her hands were shaking so much she could barely lift the heavy garment from the chair where it was carelessly thrown whenever she entered the house. Her lungs were crushed by a fear that made her fight for every whisper of air that she was able to drag into her body. For a moment she hugged the waterfall of blue cloth against her chest and took deep shuddering breaths, trying desperately to calm herself. Whether or not she survived what lay ahead, this night was to be the last that she would spend in her homeland.

Before she pulled the burqua over her head she clung to Ali one last time, feeling the bristles of his chin scrape against the soft curve of her cheek. She breathed in his masculine scent as if it were the last sweet aroma on earth. He put his arms around her and she felt his strength envelope her like the warmth of the fire on a freezing winter's night. She closed her eyes and wished that she could stay here, like this, forever. But too soon he pushed her away, gently but firmly. There was an imperceptible shake of his head before he spoke, his voice gruff with emotion.

'Now, Soraya, you must go. Now. It is time. The men are waiting.'

'Please, Ali,' she begged, clinging to his hands as if knowing that her life depended on never letting go. Her voice was encrusted with tears and her throat ached from the effort of keeping them captive. 'Please. Come with me.'

Ali shook his head sadly as she knew he would and she saw the pleading in his dark eyes. She had loved this man since the very first day of their engagement and not a single day passed without her giving thanks for her good fortune. She had so many friends whose lives were ruled by arrogant and bullying men. Sometimes, they said, it is the day when we do not get beaten which causes most surprise. But Ali was not like that. He treated Soraya with tender love and respect and in return, she happily followed the way of life expected of her. A husband with a rebellious wife was seen as weak and that was something that a man in Ali's position could not afford. Somehow, they had managed to find comfort and happiness amongst the ruins of their city and they had both been grateful for that. But things had changed.

Ali's voice was urgent.

'You must go now, for the sake of our child. For the sake of our future. I will not raise my family amongst the rubble that was once our life.'

He released his hand to hold it against the expanse of Soraya's abdomen, then bent to kiss the place where he thought the baby's heart might lie. She ran her fingers through his dark curls.

'Please come with me, Ali, please.'

Her voice betrayed the anguish in her heart.

'In six days, I will follow.' He kissed her tenderly on the lips, tasting her fear.

She shook her head. 'You can come now,' she begged.

'No,' replied Ali, resolve hardening his eyes. 'I must visit Kabul before I leave. It is the only way we can ever hope to be completely free.'

Soraya fought to control the tears that were stinging her eyes and nose. 'Husband, he will kill you!'

Ali was calm. 'No, Soraya. You share blood with his Chief Lieutenant. He will honour our wishes.' And if he doesn't thought Ali, I will leave with my insurance.

But Soraya shook her head. Hajji had always frightened her and even now, safe in the city of Herat, she trembled at the thought of the Talib policeman who laughed as he boasted of all those that he had raped and beaten and killed. She felt ashamed that her little brother worked for this man.

'I must know that you are safe if I am to look after myself,' said Ali. His dark eyes were pleading with hers and she saw his jaw stiffen as he fought to control the trembling of his lips. Soraya lowered her eyes. Her husband must not lose face in front of the friends who were waiting outside in the car. They were risking their own lives to help her and she knew that she must honour their gesture with her compliance.

She inhaled a ragged burst of air. 'Then I am ready.'

'Come,' said Ali, 'the men are waiting for you.'

Soraya grasped his arm and pulled him towards her as he moved to turn away. 'I love you,' she whispered.

'And I you,' said Ali, whispering into her hair. 'You are the breath that fills my lungs and the blood that flows through my veins. Without you, I would not exist. In six days I will come to you and our new life will begin.'

Soraya sighed with anguish but stood back proudly and did her best to smile.

Ali took the burqua from her arms. 'Come, I will help you.'

As he lifted the weighty folds over her head, he paused to look at her enquiringly, 'you have it safe?'

Soraya nodded and patted the pocket of her skirt.

He smiled as he lowered the burqua until only her soft, brown eyes were visible through the mesh of the headdress.

'In England, you will not need this, but for now, it will hide all of my most precious possessions.'

Soraya did not trust herself to speak. She was grateful to be able to conceal herself beneath the folds of anonymous blue for the very last time. She was determined that her husband's last sight of her would not be one of tears and misery.

She nodded and turned to the door. The cool, night air had settled the dust of the day and the first stars were sprinkled over the distant hills. Soraya wondered what the night sky would look like in England.

Outside the engine of a battered saloon car was already running, warming the interior for her, but even so, Ali tucked a large rug around her knees.

'The Khyber Pass will be cold,' he said.

He did not need to add that it would be dangerous. Soraya already knew that the narrow groove through the Hindu Kush Mountains had a reputation for being wild and lawless, but she knew also that the two men in the front of the car who would drive her to Peshawar in Pakistan were heavily armed and more importantly, well paid by Ali. Half now, and half when she was safely delivered. Ali had left nothing to chance. All she could do now was to try and calm her trembling limbs, close her eyes and endure the long, lonely journey ahead.

Chapter One

Thursday

The sleek, black Audi slid to a halt in a crunching tide of gravel that turned the heads of almost every team member already hard at work at the crime scene. The few that didn't bother to look up just muttered, 'Shaw's here,' and carried on working.

Detective Inspector Richard Shaw drove the way he worked, fast, focused, and totally in control. When asked what he was like to work with, his colleagues would say that he took no prisoners, but the truth was that he took more than most.

He stepped from the car and strode towards the yellow police crime scene cordons, his ID already held open for the constable on duty. He scanned the area as he walked and was relieved to find that the late hour and relative isolation of the disused warehouse had kept the usual crowd of morbid rubber-neckers at home. Nothing irritated him more than members of the public contaminating his crime scenes.

In his early thirties, over six feet tall and with the toned physique of the gymnast that he used to be, Richard managed to take up a lot of space in the vision of whoever happened to be looking his way. His dark suit and tie crisply ironed shirt and wool overcoat were immaculate as always. He was the only person in the squad, his DCI said, who could leave the filthiest crime scene with nothing worse than the shine taken off his beautifully polished shoes. Richard would reply that he didn't need to look like a villain in order to catch one. The portrayal of detectives in TV shows as scruffy slobs with drink problems infuriated him to the point where he had simply stopped watching. Professional, smart and dedicated to the job, his life was about making the streets safe for ordinary people. God knows he had suffered enough in his own life. Joining the force was the only way he knew of finding some retribution for himself and his family.

Richard was not a conventionally handsome man, his eyebrows were slightly too heavy and his lips could have been just a little fuller, but these minor imperfections were dwarfed by the most remarkable eyes. Two pools of caramel flecked with slivers of gold sharp enough to impale even an opinion against a wall. You could drown in those eyes the desk clerk at the station claimed. Not that she had ever been given a chance. DI Shaw always had better things to do than flirt with female staff. And they usually involved securing convictions.

Those same mesmeric eyes were now scanning the artificially lit crime scene as Keith Collins, a young Detective Constable hurried towards Richard carrying a white paper forensic suit and overshoes. He looks like an eager puppy, thought Richard.

'What have we got?' asked Richard. Collins was pink faced and sweating slightly as he read from his notebook. It had already been a busy night, his tie was crooked and DI Shaw had a way of making him feel untidy and nervous.

'Control received a call at 21:37 hours this evening, sir. The body of a woman was found by an elderly gentleman out walking his dog. Squad car reached the scene at 21:48 hours.'

'Walking his dog? Here?' asked Richard as he paused to remove his overcoat and suit jacket which he piled into Collins's arms so that he could don the sterile overalls that would prevent him from contaminating the crime scene. Collins folded the clothes carefully and placed them on the bonnet of the nearest squad car. Richard narrowed his eyes and Collins hurriedly picked them up again. 'I'll put these in your car, sir.' Richard nodded his thanks.

'So are you telling me that an elderly gentleman was wandering around a disused warehouse with his dog in the dark?'

'N-n-no, no,' stuttered Collins waving his arm to indicate an area of scrubby grass across the road. 'He was on the waste ground over there when the dog suddenly took off barking like crazy. Apparently, the dog never runs off so he knew something was up. The dog didn't come back when it was called so he followed it over here.'

Collins indicated the old, abandoned warehouse standing forlornly behind a bedraggled wire fence with its Keep Out signs ignored and askew. Originally part of a Victorian industrial complex, it was waiting to be demolished before developers began an ambitious project to develop a new campus of shops, restaurants and leisure facilities. For now, the damaged gates allowed entry to anyone who needed dark, dry shelter close to Worcester's town centre.

The concrete car park was cracked and crumbled with neglect and rubbish littered the ground. Damp cardboard, torn plastic carrier bags, empty beer cans, and enough broken glass to re-glaze every window in the building and more besides. The corrugated roof was mottled with rust and the fine red powder of disintegrating bricks had settled on the window sills like fallen snow. The thought made Richard grateful for the late Indian summer that graced the balmy September evening with unseasonal warmth.

As he walked towards the warehouse doors, Richard sidestepped to avoid a discarded packet of partially eaten fish and chips and paused for a moment considering its contents.

'Where's the chippy?' asked Richard.

'You hungry, boss?' asked Collins hopefully.

'Witnesses,' replied Richard. 'People obviously come this way with their supper. Someone might have seen something. And get them bagged in case our villains were peckish.'

'Course, boss,' said Collins as he scrabbled for his mobile to Google the location of the nearest chip shop.

'Lead on,' ordered Richard.

Their footsteps echoed on the temporary, metal walkway that had been laid up to, and inside, the doorway of the warehouse. As Richard approached, he nodded to the white-shrouded figures of the scenes of crime officers crouched beneath the arc lighting. They were picking carefully over the ground, occasionally pausing to place something into plastic evidence bags with tweezers.

'Where's the witness?' asked Richard.

'He's in the squad car with DC Spooner and the dog.'

'So what happened when he followed the dog?'

'The dog ran into the warehouse,' Keith continued. 'The witness said he couldn't hear it barking anymore so he wasn't concerned. He assumed the dog had chased a rat or something so he just peeped inside. He said the dog was eating something. He could hear it chomping.'

'Eating what?' asked Richard.

Collins consulted his notes again. 'He wasn't sure at first, there wasn't much light, but he had a small torch in his pocket. He switched it on and went inside. He went up to the dog to see what he had got. At first, he thought it was a piece of liver…'

Collins paused. His face was ashen.

'A body part?' guessed Richard.

'A placenta,' replied Collins. 'A human placenta.'

Richard stopped abruptly, just at the door of the warehouse and stared intently at Collins. 'How did he know that's what it was?'

'From the umbilical cord, it was dangling out of the dog's jaws.'

'Jesus Christ!' exclaimed Richard.

'The witness yelled at the dog to drop it and put him on his leash. That's when he saw the body.'

'A baby?'

'A woman. Stone cold dead was his description. He ran straight out and called us.'

'Did he touch anything?'

'Nothing, boss. Said he didn't want his DNA anywhere near that mess. He probably watches CSI,' added Collins with a grimace. 'It's a bit of a mess in there, boss.'

Richard closed his eyes and let out a deep sigh. No matter how many murders he investigated or corpses he saw, the first sight was always the worst. And it was always a mess.

Chapter Two

'Ah! There you are, Richard. Get those eyes of yours open. You're going to need them in here.'

The warm, energetic voice belonged to his boss, Detective Chief Inspector Diane Masterton. In her early fifties with grown up children, she was practical, efficient and very professional. All qualities that had gained Richard's respect over the four and a half years that they had worked together. The feeling was mutual.

'Nasty one this,' she said over her shoulder as she led Richard into the warehouse. He followed her neat figure inside the building where the flash of a camera was illuminating the scene like a lone strobe in an abandoned dance club. More than half a dozen overalled staff were busy beneath the temporary lighting examining the crime scene for evidence. Masterton touched Richard's arm briefly as she pointed to the side of the warehouse.

'Over there.'

The body of a woman lay alongside the wall. A maroon, velvet dress covered her swollen stomach beneath an unbuttoned, tailored trench coat. New clothing, noted Richard. Her stylishly cut hair hung neatly around her shoulders, not ruffled or tangled as often happened during a struggle and the carefully applied makeup around her frozen, bloodless eyes was mostly undisturbed. Just a few streaks of mascara beneath her eyes suggested that she had cried before she died. Richard saw that her shoes were placed neatly side by side just a few feet away, and a pair of tights were balled up next to them. Streaks of dried blood plastered her bare legs and she was lying in a pool of dark, sticky liquid.

Richard automatically put his hand up to his nose to ward off the offal like smell.

Masterton nodded in sympathy. 'Nasty, isn't it? Hope you're not having liver for dinner. Look over there.'

Richard lifted the corners of his mouth to acknowledge the rather bizarre sense of humour of his boss. He did not always approve of her comments but he knew it helped her to cope with unpleasant crime scenes. He moved towards the mangled lump on the floor that was being photographed from several angles.

'That's the placenta that the dog decided to sample,' said Masterton cheerfully. 'It's a bit chewed but there's plenty left for forensics to have a go at.'

'Probable cause of death?' asked Richard.

'We'll have to wait for the post-mortem on that one of course, but right now all the signs indicate that she gave birth and bled to death. She's pretty well exsanguinated. The two main questions for us are, where is the baby and why on earth did she give birth here? Nothing here is shouting foul play to me apart from the physical location but there are plenty of questions that need answers.'

Richard crouched down to study the body. He had a small dimple in his chin which he was now rubbing thoughtfully with his index finger. Masterton recognised the gesture.

'First thoughts?' she asked.

'I'm wondering why someone so well dressed should have given birth in an old warehouse when the Worcestershire Royal Hospital is barely a ten-minute drive from here. Look at her clothes. She was looked after, had money. Why didn't she go to the hospital? And if it was a simple robbery why was she left here?'

'What's making you think robbery?'

Richard pointed towards the woman's earlobes then her hands. 'No jewellery. A woman this carefully dressed and made up wouldn't go out without her rings and earrings. And where's her watch, her bag? Where's her mobile phone?'

'Maybe she was mugged and dumped here? The shock could have sent her into labour?'

Richard shook his head. 'There are no obvious signs of trauma and the blood is confined to this one area. If she had been moved we would see splashes or traces going to or from the door. I'll bet you a tenner she died right here.'

'A pint should do it,' smiled Masterton. 'Maybe she just left her bag and jewellery at home. You won't appreciate this but I promise you when you're in hard labour looking your best is not actually on your mind.'

'Then why the makeup?'

'Vanity or sudden onset of labour?' suggested Masterton.

'But would a woman in labour leave home without any bag at all?'

'Point taken. Probably not. Mine was packed after the first scan. Maybe she was brought here against her will? Could be a kidnapping that went wrong.'

'Are you thinking baby snatching?' asked Richard.

'I've seen stranger things,' mused Masterton, 'as have you.'

Richard stepped as close to the body as he could get without treading in the congealing blood spread across the floor. 'Look at that,' he said, pointing to the front of the woman's clothing.

Masterton also moved closer and crouched down to peer more closely.

'Blood, and some sort of white grease. What do you make of that?' asked Richard.

'You get that white stuff on newborn babies when they're premature,' remarked Masterton. 'My Tom was four weeks early and he was covered with it. It's called vernix.'

Richard called over his shoulder to the forensic pathologist who was making notes on his clipboard. 'Ok to touch?' he called.

'Be my guest,' came the reply.

The pathologist handed Richard a thin wooden spatula which he used to carefully turn one of the woman's hands. Traces of dried blood were clearly visible on the palm and there were smears of the same white substance that was on the front of her clothing.

'What can you give us?' Masterton asked the pathologist. He came over to them and regarded the body dispassionately.

'Female, late twenties, possibly from Pakistan, or somewhere of that origin. She's had a massive haemorrhage, probably post-partum. I won't know the exact cause until I've opened her up but I'll wager a pint on hypovolemic shock.

'Any sign of injury?'

'None so far, but that doesn't mean we rule it out until we've done the post mortem.'

'Estimated time of death?' asked Masterton.

'Recent, no more than a couple of hours. I'll know more later.'

'How soon can I expect the post mortem report?' asked Masterton with a pleading smile.

'Will tomorrow afternoon do you?'

'I owe you,' said Masterton.

'Constantly,' came the reply. 'Not that you ever pay your debts.'

Richard was still crouching down next to the body flicking at his lower lip with the tip of his finger.

'What's on your mind?' asked Masterton.

'It's these marks on her clothing. I think she held her baby,' said Richard. 'She gave birth here, held her baby, then she bled to death. The question is, why here? And why didn't she get help?'

'And where the hell is the baby?' added Masterton.

'And who else was here?' added Richard, 'because she certainly wasn't alone. Unless she walked here. I'm guessing that whoever brought her here took the baby away.'

'Ok,' said Masterton, groaning and rubbing her creaking knees as she stood up. 'There's nothing more that you and I can do here tonight. Go and get some beauty sleep, it's going to be a long day tomorrow. I'm going home to cook some dinner. Liver and onions I think.'

Richard grinned. 'You crack me up, you know that don't you, boss?'

Masterton waved a hand in the air as she walked away. 'Briefing at eight am.'

Richard was still staring at the body when Masterton turned back. 'Go and get some sleep. You're going to need it. There's a lot more to this than meets the eye.'

Chapter Three

Annie Collings lay in bed dreamily watching the late evening light drape itself across the sky. Summer was already starting to scurry away and Annie wondered how long it would be before the warm spell of weather ended and she would wake to frost and shivers. She had been trying to sleep without success for several hours and with a sigh of frustration, finally admitted defeat, hauled herself out of bed and headed for the shower.

Helen had called her just after lunch to say that she was experiencing niggling back pain. Or in Helen's words, 'my bloody back is killing me! Get over here with some bloody drugs.' Helen and Andrew had been close friends of Annie's since she had delivered their daughter two years before and even though Helen wasn't due for another six days, Annie remembered that this was exactly how Helen's first labour had started. She was pretty confident that she had a long night with her friends ahead of her and it would have been good if she could have banked some sleep.

By the time she was showered and dressed and had checked her midwifery bag the night sky had enveloped her little house. Annie was fond of her home which clung gamely on to the end of a long crooked terrace at the edge of Worcester City Centre. Close enough to walk to the shops and cafes, but far enough away to avoid the sight and sounds of revellers leaving the city's nightclubs and bars. On her days off she liked to stroll down London Road to Worcester Cathedral to marvel at its exquisite architecture and then wander along the banks of the River Severn. If she had stale bread, which wasn't often given her track record with grocery shopping, she liked to feed the hordes of swans bobbing expectantly beside the path.

But right now there was a baby on the way and Annie skipped down the stairs with her midwifery bag, pausing in the front room to look out into the street. Like many cities, most of its old terraces had been bulldozed years before and Annie's street was only saved because the Council ran out of money. The rent was low, the neighbours lovely and it was just a short drive from the maternity hospital. There was one big room and a kitchen downstairs and two bedrooms and a bathroom upstairs. Annie had decorated and furnished it cosily with warm colours and squishy sofas. She even had an open fire in the living room despite the pleas of all her visitors to get rid of it and install gas. And finally, the powers that be had begun to understand that new is not always better, that the concrete boxes that replaced the slums can be worse than the slums themselves and that some things are just plain worth saving.

Now Annie's street was protected and that was just the way she liked it. She was seriously thinking of asking her landlord if he would consider selling it to her. Providing the bank would give her a mortgage of course. Delivering babies was not the most lucrative way to earn a living but Annie loved it just the same. She couldn't imagine sitting in an office from nine to five with the only excitement coming from the occasional gossip around the water cooler.

Annie made her way through to the kitchen at the back of the house where she put the kettle on to boil before peering inside the fridge. It was depressingly empty. Annie was petite and slim which was partly down to her genes and partly due to the fact that she often forgot to buy groceries. She absent-mindedly ran her fingers through the thick dark hair which fell to her shoulders, still damp from the shower. She had given up trying to tame the curls that flew in every direction except the one that she wanted, and more often than not she resorted to pinning it up with whatever came to hand. Right now it was the broken end of a bamboo barbecue skewer from the cutlery drawer.

It was while she was trying to decide whether to call for a take-out or dash to the late night supermarket that she heard a noise at the back door. It wasn't a particularly loud noise, just a scrape, and a shuffle, but it was enough to make Annie start. She felt the acceleration of her heart and prickles of sweat worry between her shoulder blades. She quickly dropped down onto her hands and knees so that she could creep over to the door without being seen through the glass panel at the top. She crouched onto her heels pressing her ear to the door while she held her breath and listened.

A sudden meow from the other side of the door caused Annie to suddenly fall back onto her bottom. For a moment she was aware only of her beating heart and then she giggled and admonished herself for being such an idiot. Living alone was making her paranoid. Even so, she crawled back across the kitchen and grabbed the telephone handset before switching on the outside light. Only then, with the phone in her hand, did she pull back the kitchen curtains to look out into the yard where a stray cat was rubbing itself against the drain pipe and mewing plaintively. Against her better judgement Annie had got into the habit of feeding the cat during the evening. It was clearly well past its supper time, but tonight Annie felt angry with the creature for scaring her so she chose not to go outside and feed it. If she had, she might have caught sight of the human shaped shadow pressed immobile against the back fence.

Her pulse was just returning to normal when the shrill ring of the phone in her hand caused it to gallop off again and she dropped the handset with a clatter.

'Get a grip girl,' Annie scolded herself. 'This is not like you.'

She reached down for the phone. 'Hello?'

'Annie, it's Andrew.' Excitement rendered his voice an octave higher than usual. 'We're on the starting blocks.'

Annie kicked the door of the fridge closed as she spoke to Andrew and advised him what Helen should do and when to call again.

'Unless things speed up Andrew,' she said. 'Then you must call me on my mobile straight away.'

'Righty-o, Annie,' said Andrew. 'See you later, I hope.'

The line clicked and Annie's tummy rumbled into the silence. She looked at her watch. It was getting on for eleven pm and if she was going to be up all night she needed to eat. It would have to be a date with Dougie again.

Chapter Four

Richard usually left a crime scene with his head on fire with thoughts and theories. The challenge of the puzzle to be solved and the need for speed and precision would kick start the adrenaline rush of a new case. The first night of a new crime was usually a sleepless one. But something about the crumpled corpse of the mother who would never hold her child or see him grow had left him feeling bone tired, hungry and in need of some company. It was far, far too close to home.

Most of the time Richard was able to keep the past battened down in the far recesses of his brain. So far down and so securely caged that he could go weeks and even months without letting the horrors escape and invade his dreams so that he woke at night with his hands balled into fists and sweat soaking the sheets.

For once the thought of his peaceful, stream-lined bachelor flat did not appeal and he was anxious for some distraction. Any distraction would do. So when he saw the lights of the all-night café, its steamy windows running with delicate rivulets of water, he pulled into the nearby car park without a second thought. For someone who liked nothing better than his own company at the end of a long day, he was surprised to find himself drawn to the heat and chatter generated by the late night drivers and shift workers inside.

As he pushed open the door, he was overwhelmed by the fuggy warmth of the café and was taken aback at first by the level of noise until he glanced around and saw that virtually every table was full. Men in overalls and heavy boots were tucking into plates piled so high with cholesterol that it was a wonder they were alive to eat it, but eat it they did, and with such relish that Richard was almost tempted to try it himself. Groups of women in jeans and T-shirts laughed and gossiped over mugs of steaming tea while their forks darted towards the plates at the centre of the table as they sampled the cakes laid out in sacrifice before them.

Richard glanced at his watch. It was well after eleven and he guessed that most of the people in the room were relaxing after a long shift at the nearby chocolate factory. In fact, if he wasn't mistaken he was sure that he could smell traces of cocoa in the air. Then he smiled at himself as a middle-aged woman came towards him with a mug of steaming hot chocolate in her hand. She caught his smile and looked him up and down quite blatantly as she passed before tossing him a cheeky wink.

Richard wound his way between the tables and disorderly chairs towards the counter where, despite the tempting aroma of frying bacon and chips, he ordered a chicken panini and a pot of tea. There was only one vacant table left, pushed against the wall with two wooden chairs squeezed into impossibly small spaces on either side. Richard folded his tall frame into one of the chairs and sat with his back to the wall so that he could watch normal people leading normal lives while he half listened to a lady at the table next to him recounting in graphic detail to her neighbours exactly what had happened in the store room.

As the women shrieked with laughter the café door opened and a young woman walked in. Richard was immediately transfixed, not so much by her pretty face, but with the quiet confidence that made her appear still and tranquil amongst all the movement and chatter that surrounded her. As she made her way to the counter, she smiled at people as she passed their tables and he heard calls of, 'Hi, Annie!' She had an aura of something that gave her a presence and he was buggered if he knew what the hell it was. But he knew for sure that he wanted to find out. Richard suddenly felt himself an outsider, like a child with his nose pressed against the window pane while he watches the party going on inside, the party that he wasn't invited to.

'Hi Dougie, how are you?' Her voice was soft and warm as she greeted the man behind the counter.

'Busy, doll,' replied Dougie. 'You workin' tonight, Annie?'

'For my sins,' she answered with a smile that revealed perfect, small, white teeth.

'Do you want your usual?'

'Please, Dougie.' She handed over her money and then looked around the room for a seat. The only vacant chair was the one next to Richard and he silently thanked the Lord or the Gods or any other possible deity for smiling down on him that night. He caught Annie's eye and motioned toward the spare seat. She hesitated for a moment and he watched as her eyes examined him from top to bottom before she moved forwards. She took off her jacket and hung it on the chair before she sat down giving Richard a chance to see that although she was petite, she had curves in all of the right places. Her brown eyes, dark hair, and honey coloured skin gave her a European appearance. Maybe Italian, he guessed, late twenties, wild hair, no rings. He studied her full, moist lips and was suddenly aware that he hadn't kissed a woman for a very long time. She was watching him, watching her.

'So what clinched it?' asked Richard.

'I'm sorry?' Annie looked directly into his eyes, a small furrow between hers as she considered his question.

'You've just given me a thorough once over. What made you sit down?'

Annie was silent as if startled by the unusual eyes that held hers in a challenge.

'It couldn't have been my scintillating conversation, could it?' asked Richard.

Annie smiled. 'This was the only empty seat in the place,' she answered.

Richard shook his head. 'That wouldn't do it for you.'

'How do you know?'

Richard shrugged. 'Intuition?'

'That's a woman's prerogative, isn't it?' answered Annie.

'You asking or telling?'

'That was a rhetorical question.'

'Telling then.'

'Sharing.'

'Haven't you heard of equality?'

'Heard of it. Don't believe in it.'

'Ouch!' said Richard. 'Why not?'

Her gaze was direct and candid. 'Perhaps, because the world is full of women being hurt and exploited by men.'

Richard considered for a moment and then nodded. 'It grieves me to have to agree with you, but sadly, that is very true.'

Annie was momentarily silenced. It wasn't the first time a conversation with a man had started out like this. But it was the first time a man had actually agreed with her without argument. They normally jumped down her throat and accused her of being a women's libber. She appraised Richard again, his immaculate suit and overcoat, smart haircut and clean nails. The shadow emerging from his chin was the only sign that he might actually be human at all.

'Shoes,' she said.

'Shoes?'

'That's what clinched it. The reason I sat down.'

Richard stretched out his long legs so that he could take a good look at his polished lace-ups.

'You're serious about this, are you?'

Annie giggled and Richard thought it was the most gorgeous sound he had ever heard. 'You can tell a lot about a man from his shoes.'

Richard raised his eyebrows. 'Such as?'

'They're leather,' Annie pointed out, 'good quality, clean. They show me that you care about your appearance and that you probably have some sort of indoor or office job. Professional man. Intelligent, well educated. How am I doing?'

Richard was relieved that he hadn't stepped in anything that he shouldn't have back at the warehouse. What would she have made of a couple of bloody footprints? Or even a lump of placenta hanging from his shoelace?

His thoughts were interrupted by the arrival at the table of two identical chicken paninis and an enormous pot of tea. Annie and Richard looked at the food and then each other before laughing out loud.

'Thought you wouldn't mind sharing the pot Annie,' said Dougie as he unloaded the tray in front of them with a huge grin on his face.

'That's fine, Dougie,' said Annie, 'if you don't mind?' She looked at Richard.

'I don't mind at all,' he said and held out his hand across the table. 'Richard.'

'Annie.'

'I know. I heard'

They ate and drank in companionable silence until the paninis were gone and the teapot almost empty.

'So what about you?' asked Richard.

'What about me?'

Richard looked at his watch. 'It's almost midnight and you're sharing your supper with a stranger in an all-night café. There has to be a story there.'

Annie giggled and stretched out her legs to show him the comfortable trainers on her feet. 'You have to guess from my shoes,' she said.

One of the ladies at the next table turned around and stared as Richard burst out laughing. He had a warm, infectious laugh that transformed his serious features making Annie realise that he was remarkably attractive. She felt a little frisson of something that was exciting and scary at the same time.

Richard was still laughing as he shook his head and held up his hands in defeat.

'I don't do shoes.'

'So what do you do?'

He thought for a moment. He wanted to tell her that he did clues. Her presence in the café eating alone late at night and her ringless hands suggested she was single. She was clearly a regular so probably lived locally and her comfortable trainers indicated that whatever work she did involved her being on her feet. 'Hands,' he said, 'I do hands.'

He placed his right hand on the table, palm upwards. 'Give me yours.'

Annie placed the palm of her left hand on Richard's and tried to act nonchalant, ignoring the effect that the warmth of his skin was having on her. She stole a glance at him but he was engrossed in the examination of her hand. First, he studied the back before turning it over to scrutinise the palm.

'Don't tell me you read palms,' joked Annie.

He laughed. 'I only deal in facts.'

'You're not an accountant then,' she quipped.

'The tip of his thumb traced the lines on her palm and she felt as if a charge of electricity was surging from his hand to hers. She instinctively moved to pull away but he held her hand firmly. She forced herself to relax and tried to ignore her thudding heart.

'So what are the facts?' asked Annie, wanting and not wanting her hand to be released.

'Well cared for,' said Richard, 'and very clean. You use your hands for your work but it's delicate gentle work. Nothing rough or dirty. Nothing outside or in a factory. Your nails are cut short like a pianist's, but you're not a musician. Your fingers are fine and slim but too short for a keyboard. You almost have a beautician's hand.' He looked up at this point and examined Annie's face, causing her to flush slightly under his gaze. 'But not a beautician because you're not plastered in gunk. You have beautiful skin by the way.'

Like the detective he was, Richard searched for other clues. He looked at the jacket hanging on the back of the chair and saw a badge pinned to the lapel. It depicted a stork carrying a bundle emblazoned with her name.

'You're a midwife,' he said triumphantly.

Annie felt her jaw drop. 'You got that just from my hand?'

Richard laughed again, that lovely warm, joyous laugh that made Annie start to giggle too.

'The first part I did,' he admitted, 'but the last bit I got from that.' He indicated Annie's jacket with his eyes and when she saw the badge she began to laugh again.

'Ok, I'm going to try and have a go at you,' she said, then, 'oh damn and blast!' as her mobile phone rang. She took back her hand to fish the phone from her jacket pocket and Richard felt a rush of cool air flow over his abandoned palm.

'Hi Andrew, what's going on?' Richard tensed as she greeted the man on the phone with a familiarity that gave him a tug of something suspiciously like jealousy. For the first time in a very long time, Richard found himself attracted to a woman. He was slightly disturbed by that fact but was already considering the possibility that he could finally be ready to drop his guard. A boyfriend was the last thing he wanted Annie to have but as her side of the conversation unfolded he began to relax.

'How frequent are the contractions?' asked Annie. 'And how long are they lasting? Have her waters broken?'

She listened intently to the excited voice billowing out of the phone. 'Yes, it's time to go in. No, no rush. It's your second. Helen knows what she's doing. I'll meet you at the Unit. I'm on my way now, I'll see you there. Drive carefully.'

Annie switched off the phone with a rueful grin. 'Duty calls I'm afraid. A baby is on the way.'

She stood up to put on her jacket and then held out her hand to shake Richard's. 'It's been nice meeting you,' she said.

'You too,' he replied as he stood up, 'I'll walk you to your car.'

Annie waved goodbye to Dougie as she walked towards the door.

'See ya, Annie,' he called. 'If it's a boy tell them Dougie's a good name.'

'Not again, Dougie,' laughed Annie.

'And bring your friend back,' said Dougie, 'he seems like a decent sort.'

Annie chuckled as she stepped outside. 'He thinks we're together.'

'Easy mistake to make,' said Richard grinning broadly.

Annie unlocked the door of her car and was about to get in when Richard touched her arm hesitantly. 'Annie, will you give me your phone number?' He surprised himself by asking. He wasn't even sure why he was asking because women were simply not on his agenda. They hadn't been for a very long time. But even as he spoke he was already taking a small notebook and pen from his pocket.

She hesitated, considering. There was no doubt that she was seriously attracted to this man, but the fact was she knew nothing about him apart from his first name. He could be a serial killer or stalker, not to mention the fact that she had been burnt before by lies and deceit. Surely, someone like him had a wife and two kids at home?

'Are you married?' The question was abrupt, she knew, but she had nothing to lose except the heartache of getting mixed up with a married man. Again.

'No,' said Richard.

'Living with anyone?'

'No.'

'Children?'

'None.'

Annie nibbled at her top lip with her teeth while she considered. Her mobile rang again. Richard appraised her as she took the call. He noted the way small tendrils of hair were escaping from the barbeque skewer and curling into corkscrews around the sides of her face, the way her guileless eyes broadcast every thought and emotion. What a terrible villain she would make, he thought.

Annie closed her phone abruptly. 'I have to go or I'll be fielding this baby from the boundary,' she said.

Richard jotted down his mobile number in the notebook and tore out the sheet. 'This is me,' he said handing it to her. 'Promise you'll call. I have good references.'

She took the paper and he watched as she put it inside her pocket.

'I promise to think about it,' she said with a smile. And then she climbed into her car and was gone. And Richard was left wondering if she would call. How could he know that she wouldn't need to?

Chapter Five

Helen was gulping huge mouthfuls of gas and air through the mouthpiece and letting it out with a slow moan. She had been pushing hard for ten minutes and her face was red with exertion and damp with sweat. 'Christ, it bloody hurts,' she gasped. 'Get me an epidural.'

'Too late for that, Helen,' replied Annie. 'This little baby is almost here.'

Helen glowered at her husband. 'I told you I wanted an epidural. You should have got me an epidural. This is all your fault.'

'Not long now, honey,' reassured Andrew, 'It's almost over.'

'How would you know? Who made you the midwife?' she retorted.

Andrew grimaced and looked pleadingly at Annie.

'I am the midwife, Helen, and I need you to concentrate,' instructed Annie. 'Now put the gas and air down and focus.'

The baby's head had been visible for several contractions and with the last big push from Helen it moved right up against Annie's hand.

'Stop pushing, Helen, stop pushing, now!' ordered Annie. Her voice was purposely sharp so that she could get Helen's full attention. 'I want you to pant slowly for me. Listen to me, Helen, I want you to pant. Come on now, just pant.'

'Pant, honey,' encouraged Andrew but Helen told him to shut up and mind his own bloody business.

Annie always felt a little bit sorry for the poor hapless men who often got the sharp end of their wives' tongues, particularly during the transition between first and second stage. But at least Helen had not attempted to send her husband outside to finish the gardening as yesterday's labouring mum had tried to do.

Annie's left hand steadied the crowning head, slick with mucus, while she used her right hand to press firmly on the gauze pad that was keeping the baby's head flexed so that she could ease it past the paper thin tissue that was now the only barrier between the womb and the world. Annie was totally focused on the last few minutes of the birth and almost didn't hear the gentle tap on the door of the delivery room. The tap was repeated, louder, and Annie called out, crowning in here.

Andrew was holding on to his wife's hand as he repeated Annie's earlier words.

'Stop pushing, Helen, pant.'

'I am panting you bloody idiot. Why don't you try and give birth to a rugby ball?'

Helen was now taking fast, quick, guttural breaths as she tried to resist her body's desire to push away the pressure that was burning her skin.

'There's loads of hair,' Annie exclaimed, 'dark, like dad's.'

'Oh, I want to push.' Helen gasped.

'No pushing!' Annie's voice was sharp. 'Breathe this baby out. Or I'll still be stitching you up at lunchtime.'

Now, with each gasp of air, the head began to emerge, first the forehead, then the puckered eyes, the squashed little nose and with a small gush of liquor, the mouth, and chin.

Annie let out the breath that she always held at this crucial moment.

'Hello, baby,' said Annie, smiling at her first glimpse of another new life. And no matter how many times she witnessed this miracle, she always felt a few unshed tears sting her eyes.

Just then the delivery room door was pushed open and one of Annie's colleagues slipped into the room.

'Whatever it is, it can wait,' said Annie without looking up. Interrupting a delivery at this stage was a no-no in the unit and Annie would be bending someone's ear about it within the hour.

'But, but ...' stammered the young midwife.

'Get out!' snapped Annie.

'Annie there is a situation,' pleaded her colleague.

'Out!'

The woman blushed before turning away and leaving the room. As the door opened and closed Annie was vaguely aware of raised voices coming from the direction of the Unit Office but she immediately dismissed the disturbance to concentrate on the emerging baby.

Unperturbed, Andrew was grinning from ear to ear and kissing his wife repeatedly.

'I can see the head darling, I can see the head.'

'I'll see your bloody head in a minute if you don't let me concentrate,' was Helen's reply.

'Ok, Helen,' said Annie, 'we can have this baby delivered with the next contraction. Let me know when it's coming and this time, I want a nice big push from you.'

'The last one?' asked Helen.

'It could be,' agreed Annie, and as she spoke she saw the head begin to move as if the baby was turning to look at her. It was the sign she needed that the shoulders were rotating. Annie placed her hands on either side of the head.

'Contraction's coming,' said Helen.

'Come on then, don't waste this one, nice big push.'

As Helen pushed until her face was red and a groan rumbled at the back of her throat, Annie gently applied downwards pressure on the head to release the anterior shoulder, then reversed the direction to pull up the remaining shoulder which was quickly followed by a slither of baby, liquor, and umbilical cord. As Annie lifted the baby up onto Helen's tummy the little boy obligingly gave a croaky wail, weak at first and then stronger as Annie wiped him dry with a towel.

'Hello, sweetheart,' said Annie, 'welcome to the world.'

Helen and Andrew cooed and cried over their newly born son as Annie clamped the cord.

'Look at him, Andrew, just look at him,' she sobbed. 'Thank you, Annie, thank you so much.'

'Ready to cut the cord, dad?' asked Annie as she held up the cord scissors.

Andrew nodded and wiped his eyes on the sleeve of his gown before taking the spoon like surgical scissors with an embarrassed grin.

'Anywhere between the two clamps,' directed Annie.

Andrew cut deftly and handed Annie the scissors. 'Thank you so much,' he said, 'I'll never forget this day. Or you.'

'My pleasure,' said Annie.

And while mum and dad were counting fingers and toes and deciding whose nose and eyes had been selected, Annie focused on delivering the placenta and making Helen comfortable.

Within an hour, Helen was resting in a clean bed with baby Michael sucking contentedly at her breast. Already Helen was radiating the warm glow of motherhood.

'You're a natural,' said Annie.

Helen laughed. 'Let's hope the sleepless nights come as naturally.'

'So who do you think he looks like, Annie?' asked Andrew.

Annie studied the baby carefully. She was good with faces, always had been. It was names she forgot. Only last Saturday she had been browsing in House of Fraser when a woman had hailed her from across the counter.

'Annie! Annie! How lovely it is to see you.'

Annie had recognised the woman at once as a mum she had delivered the previous year. The black-haired, brown-eyed toddler who was now being thrust towards her was very cute, but the names were gone, lost somewhere in the archives of Annie's brain.

Annie took the toddler in her arms and used her failsafe mechanism of, hello gorgeous, haven't you grown? And turning to the mum, and you look so well, how are you? In fact, Annie had been known to conduct extended conversations without using any first names at all.

Annie managed to be updated on the first sixteen months of Rhiannon's life without discovering the mother's name, even though she remembered the labour and delivery with perfect clarity. Especially the part where Rhiannon's mother had vomited curry over the floor as she walked into the delivery room.

'I was hungry,' she had wailed, 'I didn't think I would get the chance to eat again for a long time.'

Annie, of course, was too polite to mention this mishap. When she was invited for coffee so she could be regaled with Rhiannon's progress through her developmental milestones, Annie claimed a prior appointment and escaped with relief. It was the babies that Annie adored. Helping to bring a new life into the world was a privilege that she treasured. And now she was looking at her latest delivery with an expert eye.

'Dad's chin, mum's nose and not sure about the eyes yet. They may not stay blue. Could go either way.'

'See,' said Helen, widening her eyes at her husband. 'I'd recognise that chin at a hundred paces.'

Andrew was now rubbing his own chin thoughtfully and trying to study his reflection in the metal bars of the bed. 'It's not that bad.'

Annie left them to it and went to complete her paperwork. It had been a long night and with a bit of luck, she would be able to snatch a few hours sleep before her nine o'clock clinic at the Asylum Centre. It was only as she was saying her last goodbye for the day that Andrew remembered the message.

'Did that guy find you?'

'What guy?' asked Annie.

'Some foreign guy. At least he had an accent. He looked a bit Arabic. He was at the desk when we checked in last night. I heard him ask the desk clerk if you were here.'

'Did he ask for me by name?'

Andrew nodded.

'And you didn't say that I was on my way?'

Andrew flushed red. 'I thought he might have a wife in labour too. We wanted to keep you to ourselves.'

Annie shrugged. 'You and Helen are my closest friends. There is no way on earth that I would let anyone else deliver your baby. Besides,' she added, 'I'm sure he'll find me if he wants to. Whoever he is.'

And she put the man from her mind completely.

Chapter Six

Friday

The Incident Room was a large open plan office on the second floor of the station. At one end a large whiteboard was already in place. Facing it were the team desks scattered with abandoned pens and files, laptops and empty coffee cups.

By the time everyone had arrived with their takeaway coffees and brown bags of morning sustenance DCI Diane Masterton had already covered a substantial part of the board with her neat handwriting. She turned to face her team as they gathered around the board, DI Shaw, DS McIntyre, DC Collins, and two female officers, DC Spooner and DC Palmer plus the usual admin staff. With the exception of DC Spooner, the core team had been together for two years and with their boss's efficient example and firm direction they were growing into a reputable and effective unit.

Despite her own late night, Masterton was as composed and fresh as ever. Dressed in her customary smart trouser suit and blouse and with her short, brown hair neatly styled, she looked ready for business.

'Ok, everyone, good morning. You will all know by now that a body was discovered late yesterday evening. Let's see what we've got.'

She pointed at the board with the tip of her whiteboard pen.

'One female, well-dressed, recently given birth, but no baby. Signs are that she may have held the baby before she bled to death. We are waiting for the post-mortem report but the indications are that the death was due to natural causes. We also have a chewed up placenta courtesy of a passing labrador.'

'They'll eat anything them labs,' said Collins. 'My uncle's dog ate two remote controls in one sitting. We had to call him in the house and make him jump up and down every time we wanted to change channels.'

'That is so not true,' said Spooner as several officers chuckled.

'Not the changing channels part,' admitted Collins. 'But the dog definitely ate two remotes. The vet's bill cost more than the telly. How come it didn't eat the whole placenta, boss?

'Thank you, DC Collins,' said Masterton. 'This is not helping.'

'Sorry, boss,' said Collins in a contrite voice but with the traces of a snigger on his face. Masterton gave him a hard stare but let the comment go. Collins was keen and conscientious. Sadly, time and a few murders would tone down his youthful enthusiasm.

'No signs of identification on the body, no mobile phone, no handbag and no jewellery but signs that jewellery has recently been removed.'

'Some women get swollen fingers when they're pregnant and take off their rings,' offered DC Spooner.

'Good point,' said Masterton, 'but her earrings were also removed and there were no neck chains, bracelets or watch.'

'Maybe she didn't wear them,' said Collins,

'A possibility,' agreed Masterton, 'although Richard thinks that she would have.'

A series of catcalls were directed at Richard until Masterton held up her hands and silence fell.

'Not helping, team. Richard?' she invited.

'She was very well dressed,' he began, 'and her clothing looked new. Certainly not your usual down and out or druggie.'

'You would know,' said Collins as he looked pointedly at Richard's smart, dark suit. Even though Richard had carefully removed the label from his nine hundred pound Armani Collezioni suit, the quality of Richard's clothes and his ability to afford them was a constant source of gossip. It was just as well that he didn't wear his Tom Fords to work but Masterton had long ago counselled him to dress down at work. That she meant him to shop at Marks and Spencer was totally missed by Richard.

'The point is,' said Richard, ignoring Collin's jibe, 'she was the type of woman that would go out looking neat and tidy. Even her nails were manicured.'

'So,' said Masterton, 'there may be missing jewellery.'

'Robbery?' asked Spooner.

'Or someone is trying to put us off the scent.' added Richard.

'Why?' asked Collins.

'Because her jewellery might identify her?' asked Spooner.

'Precisely,' agreed Masterton. 'Now, what else?'

'We can presume she was not alone,' offered Richard. 'The warehouse is in a non-residential area and given the fact that she was in labour it's unlikely she walked there. There was no vehicle on site so someone must have taken the woman to the warehouse and then removed the baby after the birth.'

Masterton added the word *Accomplice?* to the white board before turning to address her team. 'Not a lot to go on right now, but remember, we are still within the first twenty-four hours and fast progress is vital, so I need you all to listen up. That includes you, Collins.'

'Sorry, boss,' said Collins, closing the lid of the laptop that he had been looking at.

'Any evidence of a vehicle, ma'am?' asked Spooner.

'Unfortunately not. It was a warm, dry evening so no tyre tracks but light industrial units in the area operate during the day and it would not be possible to identify a single vehicle.'

'What about CCTV?' persisted Spooner.

'Nothing focused on this particular area but we can look at footage of the surrounding streets.'

'What about clothing?' asked Palmer. 'You mentioned that she was well dressed but if she had just given birth, what about underwear.'

'There were shoes and tights beside the body,' offered Richard. 'No sign of underwear.'

'Right,' continued Masterton, 'I want to know who this woman is, why she gave birth in a warehouse and who helped her. I also want to find that baby. Richard.'

'Yes, boss?'

'I want you and Spooner to start with the local maternity hospitals, clinics, doctors, and anyone that might give us a clue to who this woman is. I also want you to check for a newborn baby. Collins.'

'Boss.'

'Given that you seem so keen on screens this morning, you're on CCTV.'

Collins let out a groan at the thought of being confined to the small viewing room for the rest of his shift and probably more besides. He wondered how many energy drinks were stowed in his bottom drawer.

'Get everything within the vicinity of that warehouse and work outwards until you find something. And before you ask, I'll get you some help.'

'Thanks, boss,' replied Collins, immediately looking happier.

'I'll set up a press conference for this afternoon and appeal for any missing pregnant women and for whereabouts of the baby. And we'll get house to house underway in the vicinity of the warehouse.'

'There's nothing round there,' said Spooner.

'We'll take the nearest streets. Somebody somewhere must have seen something. Start with the chippie and off-licence.'

'What about forensics?' asked Richard.

Masterton nodded. 'Nothing positive as yet. The clothing has gone to the lab to see if we can find a source. The post mortem report should be with us this afternoon. We meet back here at four pm for a debrief and I don't want you showing your faces unless you have got something for me. Any questions?'

The team shook their heads, their brains already beginning to engage with the tasks ahead of them.

'Well, get on with it then,' said Masterton with a smile. 'I want this one cleared up by the weekend.'

Richard called over to Constable Spooner as he made his way back to his own desk which didn't have a chocolate bar wrapper or empty coke can in sight. His desk was orderly. Just like his approach to the job.

'Yes, sir?'

Spooner was new to the team and still nervous, but that fear of making a mistake made her conscientious and careful. Richard guessed she was in her twenties but with her blonde hair scraped back into a neat bun and very little makeup she looked much younger. Whether or not she was attractive, Richard had never noticed. Annie was the first woman that he had looked at properly for several years.

'I need a list of all ante-natal clinics, classes, doctors' surgeries, anywhere that a pregnant woman might go,' he explained.

'And shops, sir?' Spooner asked, 'you know, like Mothercare and places that sell baby gear?'

'Yes, good one, Spooner.' She flushed slightly at the compliment and began jotting things down in her notebook.

'We need to be on the street before nine so begin at the warehouse and work your way out. Get me the closest half dozen and ring ahead so that we can meet with whoever is in charge.'

'Yes, sir.' Spooner headed back to her desk and Richard beckoned to Palmer. 'Get some photos run off, please. We need to see if anyone can ID this victim.'

Palmer picked up on the word victim immediately. 'Are we treating this as a suspicious death, sir? I thought it was more about finding the baby.'

She meant murder and they both knew it.

'Until we hear otherwise, yes,' replied Richard. 'Otherwise bleeding to death in a warehouse would be a very unfortunate accident.'

Richard began jotting down notes himself, questions that he would ask, leads he would pursue. He had learned early on in his career that you needed to get the questions right first time, while the witness was still fresh. Contemporaneous evidence the lawyers called it. Plus there is nothing worse than failing to ask a vital question and having to go back. Good preparation was crucial.

Within minutes Spooner was calling. 'I've got something, sir.'

Richard hurried across to Spooner's desk. 'That was fast work, Constable,' he complimented.

She gestured towards the computer where a list of health facilities filled the screen. She was grinning with pleasure. ' The first one I found. There's an antenatal clinic not two miles from the warehouse.'

'Where is it?'

Spooner recited the address and Richard jotted it down.

'But it's better than that,' a huge grin now spread across her face. 'It's run at an Asylum Centre for refugees and people without GPs. And…'

She was enjoying this.

'You mean there's more?'

'The clinic starts at nine this morning.'

Richard grinned himself. This was almost too good to be true. 'You are a star, Spooner, but keep going. Just in case. Nothing is ever this easy.'

Spooner was already tapping at the keyboard making the most of every last minute before they left. Richard was soon calling to Palmer to get those photos pronto, he and Spooner were leaving in ten minutes.

Chapter Seven

Annie Collings was a popular midwife and as she settled Helen into the ward she was greeted by her postnatal mums who wanted to chat, show off their babies and ask for advice. Then just as she was about to escape she was called to the main office by the manager of the unit. As she entered the room Annie saw two other people seated in front of the desk. One was in a security guard's uniform and she recognised the young midwife who had interrupted her delivery. The girl looked as if she had been crying and for a moment Annie worried that she might be in trouble for snapping.

'Annie, come in and sit down.'

'What's wrong?' asked Annie.

The manager sighed. Linda Russell was approaching sixty and tired. Tired of working nights, tired of labouring women and screaming babies and very, very tired of the administrative burden imposed on clinicians by the NHS. Having to file an Incident Report after a long shift was not her favourite occupation and she wanted to get this done and get home to a hot chocolate and her own bed.

'During the early hours of the morning, an unknown male gained access to the hospital.' Linda glared at the security guard who had the grace to blush. Whoops thought Annie, someone wasn't on the ball. 'He found his way to the Delivery Unit where Staff Midwife Peterson asked if she could help. He said he was looking for you.'

'Who was he?' came the obvious question from Annie but Sally Peterson shook her head.

'He didn't say. He just kept asking for you.'

'He asked for me by name?'

'He had a foreign accent,' said Sally. 'He looked Arabic or something but he kept saying Collings, Collings, over and over again. I said you weren't available but he grabbed my arm and dragged me along the corridor opening doors.'

'Fortunately,' said Linda, 'I was doing my rounds and arrived just in time to see Sally being manhandled. I called security and the man was restrained. We hoped to fetch you from the room but I understand you were in the middle of a delivery.'

'I was,' agreed Annie. Then she threw a contrite 'sorry' in Sally's direction. 'I didn't mean to be abrupt but the head was literally crowning.'

'That's understandable,' said Linda.

'Where is the man now?'

'Unfortunately when security tried to remove him from the unit he became aggressive and managed to escape. We have no idea who he is or what he wanted. Given his appearance, accent, and limited English my first thought was that he was something to do with the Asylum Centre. Do you have any ideas?'

'Can you describe him?' asked Annie.

'He was taller than me,' said Sally. 'He had dark hair, brown eyes, a dark moustache. He was definitely foreign.'

Annie shook her head. 'Not a clue.'

Linda sighed. At least it would be a short report. 'Let me know if you can think who it might be or if he tries to contact you. And I don't think I have to tell you to be alert.'

'Of course,' agreed Annie. She was perplexed by the incident but not unduly worried. Despite the man slipping through main reception he had not got very far without being stopped and Annie had no reason to believe that the hospital was not a reasonably safe place to work. It was at home that she felt vulnerable. She often wondered who would hear her if she screamed, or who would find her if she fell and couldn't move. The hospital was always busy and she was never alone when she was at work. She felt safe there but right now she also felt unbelievably tired.

By the time she left the hospital it was almost eight in the morning and exhaustion was a lead weight behind her eyes. There was no point going home so she switched on Free Radio to listen to the cheerful voices of Hursty and Helen and headed for the Asylum Centre via a very strong takeaway coffee from Tesco. She could easily have called for someone else to cover the clinic but she felt possessive of her ladies there. What had started as a few ante-natal checks had become a full-blown health clinic for all of the women at the centre. It had taken an awfully long time to build up a rapport with the women there and she did not want to let them down. She would do her clinic and then go straight home afterwards to snatch some badly needed sleep. She silently prayed for an uneventful morning.

Driving with all of the windows of her car open helped blow away some of the cobwebs and the first thing Annie did when she arrived at the clinic was make herself another very large mug of strong coffee. She sipped the scalding liquid while she prepared for her clinic.

For decades Worcestershire had been a predominantly British White County with a small population of Asians from countries like India and Pakistan. During the summer months, Eastern European languages could be heard amongst the fruit and vegetable workers but as summer slipped into autumn the visiting workers would drift home until the next season.

All that changed in 2015 with the mass migration of refugees from Syria, Iraq, Afghanistan, parts of Africa and South East Asia. As a heaving tide of humanity half a million strong began to move across the Mediterranean, refugees fleeing war and persecution began to trickle into the UK. The numbers reaching Worcester were small in comparison to the crisis in mainland Europe, but that gave the Asylum Centre the opportunity to offer tangible support to those who arrived on their doorstep. The thirty room hostel was currently home to people from Syria, Afghanistan, Kosovo, Eritrea and Serbia and all of them had suffered to one degree or another. Annie was glad to be able to help at least a few of the dispossessed.

When the Asylum Centre first opened, many of Annie's colleagues had refused to work there. All the usual excuses were paraded, the UK is already over-populated, there aren't enough jobs for our own people, they are nothing but troublemakers, they are not genuine refugees, they are just here to have their babies on the NHS, why should the British taxpayer support them?

Annie ignored all of these comments. She had trained as a midwife to help bring new life into the world and that is what she would do. Who the women were and where they came from was not her concern. Let the politicians sort out the whys and wherefores. Annie was a genuinely kind person but she had a feistiness and resolve that had seen her through some unpleasant encounters in the past. When a volunteer was requested Annie had tossed her wild hair and offered to take on the clinic. And to her surprise, she had found the work to be the most rewarding of her career.

Malcolm, the Asylum Centre manager, had allocated Annie a room on the ground floor at the back of the red brick Victorian house that served as a sanctuary for the unwanted of the world. It was a small room, just large enough for an examination table, an equipment cupboard, a filing cabinet, a small desk and a couple of chairs, but Annie had been able to decorate the walls with bright posters and health messages in a dozen languages. On a good day she might have the use of an appropriate interpreter but mostly she got by with pictures, sign language and the limited English of her clients.

With everything ready and the second mug of coffee drained Annie found herself with fifteen minutes to spare. She leaned back in her chair and sighed with exhaustion. She would just rest her eyes for a few minutes and think about the gorgeous man she had met the previous evening. It was a long time since Annie had been seriously attracted to anyone and she was feeling more than a little surprised that a chance encounter had actually been enjoyable. She wondered if she would have the nerve to call…

'Annie!'

She jerked awake with such a start her neck clicked.

Malcolm was tapping sharply on her door.

'Come in, Malcolm,' she called.

Annie knew that she probably looked a mess but she also knew that Malcolm was grateful to have her there twice a week whether or not she needed a hairdresser and a good night's sleep. Not necessarily in that order. Even so, she rubbed the sleep from her eyes and smoothed down her crumpled shirt. Her hair was currently beyond redemption.

'There's someone to see you,' said Malcolm as he poked his head around the door. His shoulder length red hair and goatee made him look like a relic from the seventies but Malcolm had a Ph.D. in something complicated to do with race and victimisation and he ran the Asylum Centre with a startling competence and compassion.

'I'm about to start the clinic Malc...' she began, but he cut her off as he mouthed the word 'police' to her. Then, 'are you free?' in a normal voice.

Annie sighed. It was not unusual to be called upon by the local constabulary. If there was a spate of petty crime in the neighbourhood, the Asylum Centre was often the first port of call as locals pointed their fingers at the foreigners and transients that they saw as the source of all villainy in the area. And sadly, desperation did sometimes lead to the odd act of opportunistic behaviour that was strictly against the law.

Annie was wondering if Milinka had once again decided that the fruit displayed at the entrance to Asda was for people to help themselves when the door of her office was pushed open and Richard Shaw strode in.

Chapter Eight

Annie was on her feet in a flash, initially struck dumb with surprise. Even without looking at his face, she recognised his height, his beautiful suit, his polished shoes, even the scent of his aftershave. His male presence seemed to fill every corner of her small room and she felt a warm blush spread over her neck. 'Richard!' she uttered in surprise and instinctively took a step towards him. He stopped her in her tracks when he thrust an ID card in front of her face before she could speak another word.

'Detective Inspector Shaw,' he said, 'and this is my colleague Detective Constable Spooner.' Annie nodded politely at the female officer then turned back to Richard. His face was impassive, his beautiful eyes cold and expressionless.

'Do you two know each other?' asked Spooner as she glanced inquiringly from one to the other.

'We've met once, briefly,' admitted Richard, 'no more than a passing acquaintance.' The smile of sheer joy that had lit up Annie's face at the sight of Richard faded at once as his curt dismissal shot through her heart causing it to crumple against her ribs. Her long hair was once again escaping from the ponytail that she had roughly tied that morning and she had dark shadows of exhaustion beneath her eyes. 'Nothing like the cold light of day to turn a man's fancy,' she thought. It was pretty obvious that the attraction she felt for him was not reciprocated. So what was new? Weren't all men useless, thoughtless tossers?

When Richard saw her smile fade to be replaced by a look of bewilderment he felt sick to his stomach. As soon as the manager had told him Annie's name, he knew that it was the same beautiful woman that he had met last night. He also knew that one sniff of a female and Spooner would have the whole Department running some sort of sweepstake on him. He had a job to do and as always, he would do it with absolute professionalism and without distractions. He forced himself to focus as he addressed Annie. She looks tired, he thought.

'Thank you for seeing us,' he began. We're making some routine enquiries about an incident that occurred last night and we wondered if you could spare some time to answer a few questions.'

'Of course,' replied Annie. So he's a detective, she thought. Well, I didn't detect that one.

'Please, sit down,' he said.

Annie felt for the chair behind her and sat down carefully not taking her eyes from Richard's face. Richard tried to smile, wanting to get some message across to her that this was his job and he was still glad to have met her last night, but his mouth seemed firmly set in a straight line and his face ached from the effort of remaining impassive.

Spooner, sensing the atmosphere, looked again from one to the other, but there were no clues in the cold stares that were freezing the room. Richard took the seat across from Annie while Spooner leaned against the examination couch ready to take notes.

'Can you give me your full name?' asked Richard.

'Annie May Collings. Collins with a 'g',' replied Annie.

'Is it Miss or Mrs?'

'Miss.'

'And I understand that you're a midwife here.'

Annie nodded, her eyes still fixed on Richard's, while she wondered what she had done to deserve this cold treatment. Had she imagined the rapport between them last night? Didn't he remember that even now she had a small square of paper folded inside the pocket of her trousers that held the number of his mobile phone?

'I run a general health clinic here although my primary role is as a midwife. I'm actually employed by the local NHS Trust.'

Richard nodded. 'And how long have you worked here?'

'Two and a half years.'

'Now, for our records Miss Collings...'

Miss, she thought, what sort of cold hearted bastard is this?

'Please call me Annie,' she said.

His eyes narrowed as he asked the question, 'where were you early yesterday evening?'

She paused for a few seconds before answering. She wanted to say, 'I was with you. We talked, we laughed, we felt an attraction. Didn't you? Did I imagine it?' She shook her head imperceptibly before she answered with a slight edge to her voice.

'What do you mean by early, Inspector?'

'From six pm onwards.'

'I was at home.'

'Was anyone with you?'

'No, I was alone.'

'Do you live with anyone? Are you married?'

Annie shook her head. 'I live alone.'

'Do you have a boyfriend?'

'No.'

'When did your last relationship end?'

Spooner looked at Richard sharply. These were supposed to be routine enquiries. What was the DI playing at?

Annie caught the look. She didn't know what it meant but she knew that the young policewoman was starting to look uncomfortable. For the briefest moment, she wondered if this meeting was some sort of charade to get to know her better. But no, she already knew him well enough to understand that he wouldn't mess around like that. He had an intensity that demanded answers and she had no power to resist.

'Can you tell me what this is about, officer?'

She looked directly into Richard's eyes, demanding the truth.

Richard held her gaze without blinking.

Cold, thought Annie, ice cold.

'Were you at home all evening?'

You know I wasn't you bastard, thought Annie. But if this is how you want to play it, that's fine by me. At least we didn't get past the tea and panini stage. Even though I would have liked to. A rueful smile caught the corners of her mouth and Richard caught the tiny movement. He struggled to tear his eyes away from her face.

'I left around eleven pm. I went to Dougie's Café for some supper. Do I need an alibi, officer?'

The challenge in her voice was unmistakeable and Richard had the grace to smile sadly as he shook his head. 'No, you don't.'

He took his notebook from his pocket ready to take his own notes.

'And what is your address?'

Annie gave it, daring him to ask for her phone number. She looked away and glanced at the young police officer. Maybe that's his girlfriend, she thought.

'Telephone number?'

She delivered the numbers as a challenge and Richard heard it in her voice.

He jotted down the number in neat writing before closing the notebook and leaning forward to secure her attention.

'Last night, Annie,' began Richard, and Annie looked up sharply at the use of her first name. 'Last night, the body of a young woman was found in a warehouse at Shrub Hill. She had been dead for a matter of hours and she had recently given birth.'

Annie gasped. 'In a warehouse? On her own?' The shock in her voice was transparent as her mind created the scenario. She knew the area that Richard was talking about. Shrub Hill had once been a thriving area of small factories and commercial buildings surrounding the railway station. It was constantly fed by a bustle of lorries, vans, and assorted commercial vehicles.

Annie could remember passing by on the bus after school and the long queues of people at the bus stop waiting to go home for tea. Tired bodies would cram themselves onto the bus until the driver would shout 'no more' and close the doors against the groans of those left behind. Even then it seemed like a desolate life. Now the premises were used as light industrial units, offices and warehouses while a large corporation tried to get permission to develop the site promising shops, flats and even an ice rink. Still busy during the day, the site was empty at night encouraging antisocial behaviour, criminal damage, and even arson. After hours it was a creepy place to be avoided by decent people. What a soulless place to end up in.

'How did she die?'

'That is still to be determined but we believe it may have been a post-partum haemorrhage.'

Annie nodded. 'And what about the baby?'

Richard met her gaze square on. 'There was no sign of the baby. We are trying to find out what happened to it.'

'I guess the father took it.'

Richard shrugged. 'That's one line of investigation that we will be pursuing. Tell me, how well do you know your clients?'

'As well as I can given the secrets that some of them have.'

'What sort of secrets?'

'They are refugees and asylum seekers,' said Annie. 'They are all running away from something or someone.'

'How many of your clients are due to give birth?'

Annie turned to the computer on her desk and tapped at the keys. 'I don't have anyone due this week,' she said, 'although babies don't always appear on time. There are two next week and three the week after.'

'Are any of the residents here missing?'

'I don't think any of our resident mothers are missing,' offered Annie. That would have been the first thing that Malcolm told her. 'You can confirm that with Malcolm. But it's unusual for a pregnant woman to disappear. Most of them want help with their delivery.'

'The manager here has already confirmed that none of the residents are missing but I understand that you have visiting clients,' said Richard pre-empting her. 'We do have a photograph of the dead woman. We would like you to take a look and see if you recognise her.'

Richard indicated to Spooner with a nod of his head that she should show Annie the photo. Spooner stepped forward to place a brown file on the desk in front of Annie and opened it. Annie lifted a hand from her lap to touch the photo and Richard saw that her hand was shaking. It killed him not to reach out and touch that hand as he had last night but the truth was that she was a girl he chatted to in a café and this was his job. He must focus.

Annie studied the photo for some minutes before sitting back in her chair and looking at Richard. She had trained as a general nurse before she became a midwife and had seen her share of dead bodies. She had even laid out a few. But knowing that the beautiful Middle Eastern woman in the picture with her dead lifeless eyes was about to become a mother saddened her deeply. She met Richard's eyes and marvelled at the gold flecks that caught the light as he returned her gaze. Just the sight of him trapped the words in her throat and for a moment she couldn't speak. When she found her voice it was laced with exhaustion.

'I've seen her.'

Chapter Nine

The thrill of a lead surged through Richard and he leaned further towards Annie. 'What do you know about her?'

All he cares about is his job, thought Annie. He's the sort that walks right over people.

'She came to the clinic on Tuesday.'

'Is she a resident here?'

'No,' Annie was shaking her head. 'I mostly see residents but the clinic is open to anyone in need. We never turn anyone away.'

'Do you know her name?'

'I'm sorry, no.'

Richard visibly wilted in his chair. 'You saw her, but you didn't ask her name?' he asked, with disbelief stamped on every word.

'She gave me a name,' said Annie, 'but I doubt if it was her real name.'

'What makes you say that?'

'She gave her name at the desk when she came in to see me. But when I went to call her through she didn't respond at all. I called her twice and she didn't flinch. It was only when I walked right up to her and touched her shoulder that she heard me. That's not uncommon here. Most of my clients are refugees seeking asylum.'

'What name did she give?' asked Richard as he opened his notebook again.

Annie reached into a drawer of her desk and pulled out a bundle of slim folders that she proceeded to leaf through. She extracted a single sheet of paper from one of them.

'She said her name was Baseera.'

‘That’s all you’ve got?’ His disappointment was visible in the slump of his shoulders.

‘Inspector,’ said Annie, ‘you have to understand the type of people that come here. They are not respectable citizens with jobs and homes and money to buy nice clothes and shoes.’

Richard felt the dig like a stab wound in his heart but his face gave nothing away.

‘These people,’ continued Annie, ‘possess nothing. They have left their country of birth, many of them after being beaten, raped, tortured, practically starved to death some of them. They’ve probably lost their homes, their possessions, most if not all of the members of their family. Somehow, and sometimes we are better off not knowing how they make it here. I’m here to help them, not judge them. If they are illegal or have done something wrong there are authorities that will deal with that. When they’re here with me, they are people with needs and injuries that you could barely even imagine. These people come to me for care because they have nowhere else to go. Eventually, they might trust me. But some of them are too scared and damaged to risk even being seen in the same place twice. If they don’t want to answer my questions I know better than to ask them twice. Otherwise, I may never see them again.’

Annie tailed off as she thought of Baseera and acknowledged the reality of what she was saying.

‘I understand,’ said Richard. ‘Please don’t take our questions as judgements of you or what you do here. We’re just trying to do our job.’

Annie was caught by those caramel eyes again and had to force herself to look at the photo of Baseera. The contrast between the discoloured, lifeless eyes staring from the photo and those of Richard could not have been any more marked.

'The funny thing was,' said Annie thoughtfully, 'Baseera was different.'

'How was she different?' asked Richard.

Annie sat back in her chair and thought about the beautiful woman who had visited the clinic just under a week ago. Yes, she had seemed nervous and jittery, but at the same time, she had an aura of contentment about her. Pregnant women often seemed to be at peace with the world, finally fulfilling their natural urge to create life. It wasn't something that Annie saw very often at the Centre, but she had seen it in Baseera. Despite her nervousness, when she talked about her baby she was almost serene. Annie recognised Baseera as someone confident in the knowledge that they are greatly loved. She looked at Richard with sadness clouding her eyes.

'Most of the women I see here have reached the end of the line. They are weak, poor, desperate. Baseera just didn't fit the mould. She was healthy and well-nourished, well-dressed, and she had the most gorgeous jewellery.'

Richard was immediately alert. 'Can you describe the jewellery?' he asked.

'She had lots of gold bangles on both wrists. I didn't really pay much attention to those. She had gold hoop earrings with lots of small gold discs hanging from them, and she had a pendant. It had a large, red, oval stone in it.'

'Do you think the jewellery was genuine?'

Annie smiled faintly. 'I wouldn't have a clue. I've never owned a piece of decent jewellery in my life.'

'Was she alone when she came here?'

'Yes, she was.'

'Do you know how far through her pregnancy she was?'

'She wouldn't let me examine her. In fact, we hardly spoke at all. I asked her how I could help and she said that she needed to find someone to deliver her baby. I started to talk about doctors and hospitals but she seemed really scared.'

'I think I would be too,' said Spooner with a grimace which disappeared immediately as Richard looked over his shoulder to scowl at her.

'Was she scared of giving birth or do you think it was something more than that?'

'There isn't a pregnant woman on this planet who is not a bit apprehensive at the thought of labour and delivery,' said Annie. 'Even those who have already done it several times. But no, it was more than that. She just seemed jittery, as if she was about to scarper at any minute. In fact, that's exactly what she did. It's the main reason I can't give you any more information about her.'

'She did a runner?'

Annie nodded. 'There was a disturbance at the front desk. Some man had come in looking for his wife who he claimed we were hiding.'

'Does that happen often?' asked Richard.

'Not often, but we do get incidents from time to time. Malcolm called me to the desk to see if I could help calm things down and when I got back here she had gone.'

'How did she get past you?'

'She used the back door, most probably. It's always left open during the day so the residents can go outside for some fresh air or a smoke.'

'Was the man at the front desk looking for her?'

'No, I don't think so.'

'So you have no idea who this woman is or where she went.'

'I'm sorry,' said Annie. 'All I know is that she was scared and from the look of her the pregnancy was pretty well advanced. But she did look cared for like someone loved her.'

'Do you know if she went to any other hospitals or clinics?'

'I don't know for sure,' replied Annie, 'but I think it's unlikely. I can refer my patients into the NHS but an awful lot of the mums who come here can't deal with anywhere that smacks of too much authority. And if Baseera had been to the hospital she wouldn't need to come here to see me as well.'

Richard was closing his notebook and rising to his feet.

'Thank you for your time, Miss Collings.'

He held out his hand to shake hers. Annie placed her hand in his and she felt the gentlest pressure which made her stomach somersault painfully behind her ribs.

'We will probably need to talk to you again, but if you think of anything else that might be relevant please give me a call.' He released her hand and reached into his jacket pocket for a business card. Annie took the card and held it with both hands as she read it. 'Goodbye, Inspector.'

'Thank you, Miss Collings,' said Spooner as she left the room.

At the doorway, Richard paused and looked back.

'Get some sleep, Annie, you look exhausted.'

He turned to leave but Annie called him back. 'Richard.' She had so many questions for him, so much that she wanted to say but she was at once speechless. Maybe she just wanted one last look at him. Maybe she wanted some reassurance that he wasn't sorry they had met. And now she struggled for something to say.

He was at the doorway waiting for her to speak and Annie thought that she had never seen a more handsome man in her life. She shook her head. What was the point? Nothing would come of it that much was clear. Richard felt himself drowning as he gazed at her. Why this particular woman and why now? He read a biography once where the author stated that if you meet someone unexpectedly three times they would stay in your life forever. This was the second time but this was a live case and he would never compromise his work. He was wondering how he could explain to her but he didn't know where to begin. Instead, he smiled sadly. 'I'm sorry, Annie, it's my job. When this is over…'

That was all she needed. She smiled back. 'Just one more thing. About Baseera,' said Annie, 'I think she was an Afghan.'

Chapter Ten

With the positive identification from Annie, Richard was able to cut short his planned afternoon calls to maternity hospitals and doctors' surgeries so that he could get back to base in good time to update Masterton before the team briefing. He hated the smell of antiseptic anyway. Annie had given him a strong, positive lead and instinct told him that she was going to become an important witness in this case. If only he knew how important, he might not have been feeling quite so pleased with himself right then.

Shortly before four pm, he took his place at his desk in the office that also served as the Incident Room. Diane Masterton was already scribbling across the white board as the rest of the team drifted in, those with leads fired up for the chase, others with the dragging feet of the disappointed. Mostly it was dragging feet. By the time the shuffling and scraping of chairs had stopped there were nine officers seated around the room.

'Thank you all for getting back so promptly,' began Masterton, 'and I am not going to waste time with pleasantries. Now, what have we got?'

As she listened to the reports from her officers, Masterton paced backwards and forwards in front of the whiteboard pausing only when she needed to point at something as she did now. Her whiteboard marker was tapping at a photo of the dead woman.

'To summarise, we have the body of a young woman found in an abandoned Shrub Hill warehouse late last night. She had recently given birth but there is no sign of the baby. We have a name, Baseera.' Masterton paused to write the name beneath the photo before continuing,

'We think this may be a false name but we will use it for now. Baseera visited an ante-natal clinic at the Asylum Centre last Tuesday. She was looking for someone to help her give birth.'

'She didn't book the warehouse then,' muttered Collins, then added, 'sorry, boss,' as Masterton glared at him.

'This suggests,' Masterton continued, 'that she didn't plan to give birth unattended, let alone in a dingy warehouse. It also suggests that at this point at least she was operating within her own free will. However, the midwife that she saw, one Annie Collings, reported that Baseera seemed frightened. There was a disturbance at the front entrance of the Asylum Centre and when the midwife got back to the consulting room Baseera had gone. She left by a back door. Spooner, do you have something you wish to add?'

Spooner, who had been making kissing noises in Richard's direction looked sheepish and shook her head.

'Not funny, Spooner,' said Richard with a scowl.

Masterton narrowed her eyes but continued talking. 'The Asylum Centre is two miles from Shrub Hill. The hospital is two miles further on. This suggests that the woman was living in the locality. I want the house to house focused on a radius around the Asylum Centre and Shrub Hill. I also want everyone at the Asylum Centre interviewed. That includes staff, residents and anyone who went near the place last Tuesday. Collins, anything on CCTV so far?'

Collins shook his head wearily. After a day spent in a small windowless room staring at a TV screen, he was feeling sluggish and bleary eyed. The small mountain of caffeine and junk food that he had consumed during the day hadn't helped his concentration or his waistline.

'Nothing, boss. But to be honest, I don't know what I'm looking for apart from the dead woman. If I had a description of a suspect or a car or anything to go on it might have been a bit more use. I haven't found anything suspicious at all.'

'Palmer, anything?'

Palmer also shook her head. 'Since the identification of the dead woman I have been concentrating on trying to find the baby. I've called most of the clinics and surgeries in the vicinity of the warehouse and there are no missing patients or stray babies. No unusual activity. Nothing at all.'

'The fact that she went to the Asylum Centre looking for antenatal care suggests that she is outside the system,' interjected Richard. 'I doubt that we are going to find her registered with General Practitioners or hospitals. This woman wanted to keep under the radar. And it sounds as though she was easily spooked.'

'So where else might she have gone?' Masterton addressed the room and waited expectantly for a response. 'Come on you lot. I know some of you have got kids.'

'Pharmacies,' suggested Spooner. 'Self-medication for heartburn and that sort of thing.'

'Absolutely,' agreed Masterton. 'And anywhere that sells essential supplies. Nappies for one thing. This woman was preparing for birth and if she had only just arrived in the country she would need to go shopping. Focus on stores within our radius as soon as they are open tomorrow. Get that covered, Spooner.'

She paused to write on the whiteboard before turning to the team again.

'McIntyre, what do we have from the lab?' McIntyre was a plump, bespectacled officer who had long given up the rigours of the beat for a desk job. He had turned out to be surprisingly good at it.

'Her clothing was heavily blood-stained as we all know,' began McIntyre. 'The lab is still extracting the DNA but the type is O positive, maternal and baby blood are the same group. The front of the woman's clothes also had traces of liquor and vernix caseosa.'

'Vernix what?' asked Spooner.

'It's a white greasy substance that protects the baby's skin while it's in the womb. As the baby becomes more mature the substance is absorbed, but if the baby is born early there will still be traces in the creases of the body such as elbows, groin, and armpits. The more premature the baby, the more vernix there is. The amount on the woman's clothing suggests that the baby was at least a month early, possibly more.'

'So she did hold her baby,' said Masterton as she nodded at Richard.

'Also her clothing was all good quality and unlaundered,' continued McIntyre.

'Eeugh!' remarked Spooner.

'Not what you think,' McIntyre addressed her with a smile. 'Apart from the remnants of the delivery and particles from the warehouse floor, her clothes were all new with no residue from detergents or laundry products. Everything was brand new.'

'She had been on a spending spree,' said Spooner.

'But why?' asked Masterton. 'She was about to give birth, nothing would have fitted in a few weeks.'

'Because she had nothing else to wear,' said Richard.

'How do you make that out, Sherlock?' asked Collins.

'Annie Collings said that she thought the woman was possibly an Afghan. Those women don't wear Western clothes in their own country. Even with the Taliban overthrown some still choose to wear their burquas because they feel safe wearing them. They are not used to being looked at by men and some are afraid that they will be punished if the Taliban ever return to power. So, I think she had only just arrived in the country and the first thing she did was buy some Western clothes so that she could blend in.'

'Makes sense,' agreed Masterton. 'Spooner, I want you to start with the airports. Given that she was about to give birth we can assume for now that she didn't come across the Med in a leaky boat. Track down every heavily pregnant woman that has arrived in Britain in the last week. Start with Afghanistan and work your way out.'

'Pakistan might be a better place to start,' suggested Richard. 'It's unlikely that she would have got a flight out of Afghanistan. Most refugees get out via Pakistan.'

'Pakistan it is then,' agreed Masterton.

'How will I do that, boss?' asked Spooner.

'Most airlines request a doctor's note before they allow women in late pregnancy to fly. There should be CCTV as well. Get on to Border Control and see what they can do.'

'What other countries should I check?'

'Get an atlas,' said Masterton.

'There's one other thing, boss,' said McIntyre. 'The woman's underwear was found folded in her pocket but it was heavily blood-stained.'

'Suggesting?'

'Suggesting that she took them off because she had begun to have the baby or bleed or whatever happens and she put them in her pocket because there was nowhere else for them. They were put away tidily. It was as if she didn't want to lose them or forget them.'

'Maybe she was a tidy person?' offered Spooner.

McIntyre shook his head. 'She was lying on the floor of a filthy warehouse bleeding. Anyone else would have just thrown them somewhere and forgotten about them. She was tidying up. It makes me think she was consciously trying not to leave identifying evidence.'

'Good point, McIntyre,' agreed Masterton. 'It certainly fits with the concept of a woman trying to keep a low profile.'

Just then the phone in Masterton's office began to ring. 'Pick that up please, Richard.'

Richard chose to hurry through to Masterton's office rather than pick up at his desk so that he would not be disturbed by the feedback from the rest of the team. For some stupid reason, he was hoping that it would be Annie on the line. He shook his head before he answered the phone, furious with himself for letting himself be distracted by a woman. Even if she was drop dead gorgeous.

It was the pathologist and Richard began to scribble furiously as he listened to the report.

'Boss!' Richard uncharacteristically interrupted Masterton as she listened to the fruitless efforts of the crime scene team to find any further evidence that might be helpful to the case. He was almost breathless with excitement.

'Share it,' she said.

'Time of death,' began Richard, 'between eight and nine yesterday evening.'

'And what time was the treble nine?' asked Masterton.'

'Nine thirty-seven,' said Collins.

'So she had only just died when she was found,' mused Masterton. 'Go on, Richard.'

'The placenta,' began Richard, 'was apparently in a terrible state.'

'It was mistaken for a dog's supper,' interjected Masterton, causing a spate of sniggers from the team. 'All right settle down,' she said. 'It wasn't that funny.'

'Apart from the teeth marks,' said Richard. 'The placenta was in a bad way, infarcted was the word.'

'Pardon me,' said Collins.

'It means,' continued Richard, 'that the placenta was failing so the baby would have been badly nourished and suffering from...' He consulted his notes, 'inter-uterine growth retardation.'

'Small and weak,' added Masterton.

'Precisely. But listen to this. The post-mortem revealed that there was another placenta, just as ropey, which was still attached to the uterus. The woman gave birth to twins.'

A flurry of murmurs rippled across the room.

'Focus, please,' commanded Masterton. 'Go on, Richard.'

'The second placenta was still attached to the wall of the uterus and there was a blood clot the size of a small baby behind it.'

'I'm going to be sick,' said Collins.

'Save it,' retorted Masterton.

Richard consulted his notes again. 'The findings suggest that the woman had a severe post-partum haemorrhage due to a retained placenta. The presence of the placenta meant that the uterus could not contract and stem the bleeding. She would have been bleeding heavily and would very quickly have started to show signs of shock. There was no evidence of trauma to the birth canal suggesting that the twins were born quickly and easily. Given the size and poor state of the placentas, the babies would have been very small and very weak and unlikely to have survived the delivery without specialist care. The pathologist is also pretty sure that this was the first pregnancy.'

'Conclusion?' asked Masterton.

'Death by natural causes.' Richard replied.

‘That poor woman.’ It was Sarah Palmer who spoke, sitting with tears visible on her cheeks. ‘She must have been terrified. What on earth would make her go to that warehouse?’

‘But at least we can assume that she wasn’t alone,’ said Masterton. ‘Someone was there and they probably have two dead babies on their hands. They are going to turn up sooner rather than later.’

‘Does natural causes mean we are off the case?’ asked Collins.

‘Certainly not,’ said Masterton. ‘Death may have been due to natural causes but there is nothing natural about bleeding to death in an old warehouse and being left there. And we still have two babies to find. Both possibly deceased.’

‘Almost certainly,’ added Richard. ‘The pathologist estimates they were less than two pounds in weight maximum and would have immature lungs. The growth retardation due to the unhealthy placenta means that the babies would be unlikely to survive without medical help.’

‘Ok, team.’ Masterton clapped her hands together to signal the end of the meeting and allocation of tasks. ‘There’s still some daylight left and I have a press conference to go to. We are now looking for twins. Most likely deceased. Not so easy to hide. Spooner, you’re on airports. Palmer, finish up with any medical facilities and baby stores still outstanding and check all neonatal units for premature babies. I also want the stockists of all of the victim’s clothes by the end of the day. Collins, CCTV again. You’re looking for a car travelling towards Shrub Hill either too quickly or very, slowly. The driver would have been anxious. The female passenger may have been on the back seat possibly lying down out of view. We also need to check local taxi firms for any fares that terminated in or near Shrub Hill. McIntyre, forensics.

There must be something left at that scene. Find it. Richard, my office, please.'

Richard followed Masterton into her office and closed the door behind him.

'Is there anything you want to tell me?' she asked. One eyebrow was raised in enquiry and her jaw was set in a 'don't give me any crap' line.

Richard shuffled in embarrassment. How was it that the boss never missed a trick? Even on the first day of a major enquiry. He would be having words with Spooner later on. He feigned nonchalance.

'About what, boss?'

'About you, the midwife and those kissing noises out there. Is there anything that I need to know about?'

'No, boss.' Richard shook his head. 'I met her just by chance on Sunday. We sat together in a café and chatted. That's it.'

Masterton regarded Richard thoughtfully. He was the most professional detective she had met during the whole of her career and his drive and determination were unsurpassed. But since the death of his wife he had become focused on work to the exclusion of anything that might distract him from putting as many villains behind bars as possible. And while that was good for the team's results, Masterton was not convinced that it was good for Richard's state of mind. It would please her to see him getting some joy from life once again, but not if it was with a key witness.

'Is she pretty?'

Richard knew better than to be anything but straight with his boss.

'Very.'

Masterton saw the look on Richard's face when he thought of Annie and she chose her words carefully before she spoke. 'You're a good detective, Richard, and

I know that I can trust you to act with integrity, and God knows you of all people deserve to have a private life.'

'I'm fine, boss...'

'No, you're not,' she interrupted. 'Debbie's death knocked you for six and you have not been able to let go.'

'I've...'

'Don't interrupt. Your pregnant wife was brutally murdered and the perpetrator has not been caught. I know that eats away at you and I know you haven't given up trying to find out who was responsible. But it doesn't mean you can't find someone else to share your life with. It's certainly time you got back in the saddle so to speak. A good looking man like you shouldn't be going home to frozen dinners and a cold bed every night.'

'Are you telling me I should date a witness?'

'No, I most certainly am not. I'm telling you to be careful. I'm telling you that you need to make sure you don't do anything to jeopardise this investigation. I'm telling you that if you get involved with a witness you know that I will have to take you off this case. And you don't need to expose yourself to the sort of juvenile behaviour that I've come to expect from that lot out there.' She nodded her head towards the Incident Room as she spoke.

'Yes, boss.'

Masterton sat down and placed her elbows on her desk. She rested her chin in her hands as she contemplated her favourite employee. 'Do you know that you've had a sparkle in your eyes all day?'

'I haven't.'

'Richard, I sometimes think I know you better than you know yourself. Just keep a lid on things for a short while. We're going to crack this case quickly if it kills me. And right now Annie Collings is the only lead that we have. You'll have free rein when this is over.

Until then you stay well away. Now get back to work. We need to be in the Press Room in ten minutes.'

'Right, boss.'

'Oh, and Richard, one more thing.'

'Boss?'

'I need you to go back to the Asylum Centre tomorrow to specifically follow up on the disturbance. Let's see if there is any connection with Baseera's disappearance. Then you need to spend some time with the midwife. I want an ID on whoever caused that disturbance and I want sketches of the dead woman's missing jewellery.'

Richard's grin spread from ear to ear as he left the office with just a suggestion of jauntiness in his step. 'Good looking man, eh?' he threw back over his shoulder.

'Go.' smiled Masterton.

Chapter Eleven

Annie had been determined not to sleep right through the day and then spend a wakeful night watching each hour drag by more slowly than the last, so she had set her alarm for five pm. She loved her job but had never understood why so many babies insisted on being born during the night. Even so, it was almost six pm before she finally managed to drag herself out of bed and into the shower. She dressed in jeans and a vest top and brushed out her thick, dark hair. She peered into the bathroom mirror and wondered whether the dark circles under her eyes were ever going to go away. Downstairs in the kitchen she filled the kettle and switched it on before opening the door of the fridge.

Dammit, still empty. She poked around amongst some limp lettuce and a soggy tomato before deciding that she would have a black coffee and then go to the supermarket. At least there was a tin of opened cat food so the poor old stray wouldn't starve. She was feeling ridiculously guilty for not feeding him the night before. Annie retrieved a fork from the cutlery drawer and with the tin and fork in one hand she opened the back door.

She barely had time to cry out before she stumbled against something and found herself falling through the air and landing with a painful thud on the concrete slabs. She managed to put out her hands to save herself from smashing her face but although the fork skittered across the paving the lid of the opened tin can sliced into the palm of Annie's left hand with a piercing stab of pain. She grabbed her left wrist in her right as she rolled onto her side and untangled her feet from whatever she had fallen over before struggling to stand.

Blood was oozing into her stinging palm and it began to drip slowly onto the paving slabs in a random pattern of scarlet splatters. She gasped as she put her weight on her left foot then swore as she realised that she had probably sprained her ankle. The pain made her head swim and she closed her eyes until the world had stopped spinning.

It took her a moment to recognise that the object that had tripped her so cruelly was a large canvas sports bag sitting squarely on the back step. What on earth is that doing there, she thought? Then as she leaned over it, the blood trickling from her palm began to drip onto her jeans. Annie hurriedly hopped over the bag and limped into the kitchen.

At the sink, she momentarily let go of her wrist to turn on the cold tap allowing a surge of blood to fill the sink with a raspberry ripple swirl of water. She put her torn hand under the cold tap and gulped back tears as the cold water made the cut sting ferociously. She forced herself to look at the palm and was relieved to find that the cut was not too deep and could probably be sorted out with some steristrips. Even so, she wouldn't be delivering any babies for a day or two. She cursed again using the most unladylike language that she could think of. In truth, there were far worse words in the modern English vocabulary but even now she couldn't quite bring herself to use them.

She wrapped a cotton tea towel firmly around her hand using her teeth to secure a knot and rinsed out the sink before turning off the tap. Her hand was beginning to throb and Annie knew that she would need to get to an out of hours clinic sooner rather than later. First, though, there was the mystery of the bag on her back step.

Annie looked around before retrieving the bag. Her house was a standard terrace with a small back yard that led into an alleyway which ran the length of the terrace. She could see that the door to the alleyway was firmly closed and the bolt drawn across. Whoever had deposited the bag must have climbed over the gate and left the same way. Why would they do that? What was wrong with the front door?

She lifted the bag from the step and swung it onto the kitchen table with her good hand where it landed with a gentle thump. As she unzipped it she hoped that the contents might offer some clue to its appearance on her doorstep. She could only think that it had been left there by mistake.

Inside were two dark blue rolled towels. They were awkward to manoeuvre and Annie struggled to lift them from the bag with her injured hand. Only by putting the bag on its side on the kitchen table and tugging the bag away from the towels was she able to release the first bundle. As she unrolled the towel Annie's conviction that she would find wet swimming togs or muddy football gear prevented her brain from initially identifying what lay before her.

She stared in horror for what felt like minutes but was probably no more than seconds. She recognised what was in front of her but her horrified brain refused to accept the possibility that this was not some cruel joke. But as reality overcame incredulity she began to gasp out harsh sobbing breaths that tore at her throat and huge tears rolled down her cheeks. She pulled the second bundle from the bag and unwrapped that too, then she began to moan, 'Oh no. Oh, God, no.'

Two dead baby boys lay side by side swaddled in their blue towels. Their newborn skin was mottled and discoloured and their cold, motionless bodies were smeared with vernix. Their eyes were tightly closed but their mouths open as if gasping in vain for the oxygen and sustenance that would have kept them alive. Fine, downy hair typical of premature infants covered their stiff, twig-like limbs. They were far too small to have survived, registered Annie, and had most probably been dead for some time.

Annie backed slowly away from the table until she was hard up against the kitchen wall. The cold plaster pressing into her shoulder blades forced her to acknowledge that this was real. That she had to do something.

But why had they been brought to her and who had brought them? Annie's brain began running through her list of cases but she knew no-one who was expecting twins. She forced herself to look at the baby boys again and noticed their dark hair. They looked Asian and so very tiny. And then suddenly, inexplicably, she thought of Baseera. A strange woman, heavily pregnant, unexamined, scared and dead. And no sign of her baby. But Richard hadn't said anything about twins. Or about the possibility that they might be dead.

For a few brief seconds, she closed her eyes, wondering what to do, and it was Richard's face that she saw in her mind. She reached for the phone and tapped in the number from his card that she had pinned on her cork board.

He answered on the second ring.

'Richard Shaw.'

The sound of his voice was enough to unleash the anguished sobs that had gathered inside Annie so that she was unable to speak.

Still, in his office, Richard rose from his desk. 'Who is this? What's happening?' His voice was urgent and the few people remaining in the office became quiet as everyone watched and listened to the crisis that they knew was unfolding.

In between her sobs, Annie managed to say his name. 'Richard.'

He knew her voice at once.

'Annie, is that you? Annie, what is it? What's wrong? Where are you?'

Annie took several deep breaths so that she could speak. 'I didn't know who else to call.'

'Annie, tell me what's wrong.'

'I think it's Baseera's babies,' she gasped. 'I can't think of anybody else that it could be. I can't think of anyone that wouldn't have called me or gone to hospital.' It was all he needed to hear. Richard was already pulling on his coat as he motioned to Masterton through the glass window of her office while keeping his mobile pressed to his ear. She was at his side at once, her coat and bag in her hand.

'Annie Collings has the babies.'

'Dead or alive.'

Richard grimaced, 'I am assuming dead.'

'I'll drive,' replied Masterton.

They half ran to the car park while Richard was talking to Annie all the time, trying to calm her. He paused only to give Masterton Annie's address which he had already committed to memory.

'Annie, you must tell me exactly what's happened. Are you at home? I'm coming to you now.'

Annie gulped and forced herself to speak coherently. 'Someone left two dead babies on my back step. Two dead baby boys.'

'Shit!' Richard put his hand over the receiver to speak to Masterton. 'Two boys. They're both dead.'

Masterton cursed then immediately snatched up the radio and began issuing urgent instructions.

Richard pressed the phone to his ear and spoke calmly. 'Annie, are you listening to me?' he asked.

'Yes.'

'Stay where you are and don't touch anything. I'm on my way.'

There was a pause before Annie spoke. Her voice sounded small and frightened. 'Will you be long?'

'We're almost there, Annie, hold on.'

Chapter Twelve

Richard had the car door open and his feet on the pavement before the vehicle had come to a complete stop. He sprinted up the path to Annie's front door and pushed against the handle but the door was firmly closed. Without waiting he ran around the side of the house to the back alley. The door to Annie's yard was still bolted but Richard pulled himself up and vaulted over with ease. The door to the kitchen was wide open and the light from inside cast a trapezium of stark brightness onto the concrete outside. Richard registered a tattered stray cat licking the inside of an upturned cat food tin and faint splashes of blood on the ground.

His mobile was still open in his hand as he rushed into the kitchen, where he froze momentarily as he came face to face with the kitchen table. His expert eye took in all of the details in seconds. The canvas sports bag with its lightening logo lying collapsed to one side. Next to the bag were two navy blue towels laid out on the table and there, amongst the blackened stains of blood, were two tiny, naked bodies. Barely larger than the size of his open hand, they lay curled up as if they were still in the womb, each facing the other, their tiny fists clenched to their mouths. The remnants of their slender umbilical cords were crudely tied with blue nylon string. To Richard's untrained eye they looked perfectly formed. Only the mottled purple-grey skin and their icy stillness revealed that they were not just sleeping.

A movement in the corner of the room caught his attention and he turned to see Annie crouched in the corner sobbing quietly. Her face was buried in her arms, one hand still holding the telephone, the other wrapped in a bloody tea towel. Richard was on his knees beside her. 'Annie. Annie, it's Richard.'

She did not respond. She just continued to sob as if her heart were breaking.

Richard gently placed his hands on either side of her head to lift her face towards him.

'Annie, look at me.'

It was his touch that penetrated the grief and horror that had engulfed Annie. She had seen dead babies before. If you were a midwife long enough you would eventually deliver a stillborn or deformed baby. You would care for the baby as if it were living and grieve with the parents. But this was different. The horror of the abandonment was as great, if not worse, than the deaths themselves. And knowing that their mother was also dead simply compounded the tragedy. She turned her tear filled eyes to Richard.

'Two dead babies,' was all she could say.

'We think they're Baseera's,' said Richard. 'She gave birth to twins.'

Annie nodded. 'I guessed that.'

'I'm sorry I didn't get the chance to call you. I only found out an hour ago.'

Richard took the telephone from her hand and placed the receiver back on its hook. 'Just give me a minute,' he said as he left to open the front door to his boss.

'Thank you,' acknowledged Masterton as she pushed past Richard to the kitchen where she stood with her hands on her hips surveying the scene.

Masterton laid her hand on Richard's shoulder. 'Get her out of here. The squad's on its way.'

'Stand up, Annie.' Richard's voice and touch were gentle as he helped her to her feet, careful not to touch her injured hand. Annie cried out in pain as she put her weight on her ankle and she stumbled against Richard who caught her in his arms and with one swift movement had lifted her off her feet.

Masterton was ahead of him opening the door into the room next door and indicating a sofa where he laid Annie amongst a sea of cushions. Immediately she turned away from him and curled up, burying her face in her hands.

Richard covered her with a throw from the back of the sofa then left her for a moment to return to the kitchen where Masterton was standing looking down at the babies. Richard saw her dabbing at her eyes with a tissue.

'What a bloody shame,' she said now, her voice cracking with emotion.

Richard moved to put his arms around her and hugged her tightly. For a moment she clung to him and then stepped back with a sniff.

'Thanks, Richard,' she smiled.

'Anytime, boss.'

'It's the mother in me. You see a baby or child hurt and it always makes you think of your own.'

Richard stared at the two abandoned bodies not even as big as a baby doll. Their perfect fingers were curled into miniature fists and their little legs were bent and crossed. His face was passive and his body rigid as he struggled to fend off the memories of another little boy who had no opportunity to experience life. He sighed at the waste. 'Except we know these two were too small and badly nourished to survive.'

'Even so,' replied Masterton as she sniffed away the last of her tears, 'they deserved to be loved and cared for. No wonder it's been so hard on Annie. She dedicates herself to bringing life into the world. This must have been devastating for her.'

'She looks in a bad way,' agreed Richard.

Just then, the first blue lights began to flash outside in the street.

'Squad's here,' said Richard, turning his face away from the tiny corpses.

Masterton laid her hand briefly on his arm. 'Richard, forgive me. What am I thinking? You don't need to see this. Get yourself next door and see what you can find out. The ambulance shouldn't be far behind.'

Richard returned to the living room where Annie lay just as he had left her. He sat down in the space made by her bent legs and leaned forward to stroke her hair back from her face. Her sobs had subsided but she lay unmoving. He sat quietly, stroking her hair and caressing her with his voice as he repeated her name. Years spent dealing with victims of crime had taught him the power of voice and touch but this was different. He marvelled that even though he barely knew this woman, he felt an unbelievable attraction to her. Granted she was beautiful and alluring, but his feelings went far beyond the physical. Even now with her wild hair and red, tear-stained face he was drawn towards her. Richard couldn't define exactly how he felt, but he knew for sure that it was real, inevitable and potentially complicated.

The large room they were in would originally have been two rooms long since knocked together. It was unpretentiously furnished. The walls were painted in a pale, primrose yellow which suited the red and gold sofa that Annie was lying on. A plain carpet covered the floor, brightened by a scattering of rugs. Beneath the window at the front end of the house stood an ancient pine table with four assorted wooden chairs around it. There were two easy chairs placed either side of the open fire and on one wall was a computer sitting on what looked like an old sewing table. A small bookshelf held a collection of teddy bears. There was no real theme or décor to the room, not like Richard's modern colour co-ordinated penthouse apartment overlooking Diglis Water, which, the estate agent had assured him, presented a timeless ambience of neutrals, whatever that meant, but this home was warm and welcoming. Just like Annie, he thought.

Although she hadn't moved, Annie's breathing had become more regular and he continued to gently stroke her hair. Outside he could hear the clatter and footsteps of the team as they documented the crime scene and searched for evidence. There was a gentle tap on the door.

'Come in,' called Richard and rose to his feet as a paramedic entered.

'Hey, Dave,' Richard was relieved to see someone that he knew because although it was illogical, he thought that Annie would get better care that way.

'Hi, mate,' Dave grimaced as he greeted Richard, knowing better than to discuss the case in front of Annie. Richard nodded. Neither of the men needed to speak to convey their feelings.

Dave knelt down beside Annie. 'Hello, Annie. I'm Dave, a paramedic. Do you mind if I take a look at that hand?'

Annie rolled over onto her back and held up her hand, wincing as Dave removed the bloody tea-towel.

'Ouch, that looks nasty. How did this happen?'

Annie turned her head away. 'Cat food tin. It was in my hand when I fell. I tripped over the bag.'

While Dave cleaned the wound and applied a dressing Richard studied the pictures on the walls of the room. There were several photos of babies being held by smiling parents or older siblings. Annie's deliveries, Richard assumed. He was more interested in the artwork which was a stunning collection of techniques. There were several watercolour studies of plant life and woodlands which were exquisitely detailed down to the veins on the leaves of the wildflowers and a series of tropical flowers in acrylic which Richard was unable to identify. Interspersed around the room were a number of portraits carefully sketched in black pen and above the fireplace was a large picture depicting a scene that he recognised as Greece. As he studied the way that the shadows from the buildings fell across the terraces he saw the tiny signature in the bottom of the picture. Annie Collings. He looked back at the other pictures and saw that they were all painted by Annie. A low whistle escaped his lips. He was impressed.

He turned to Annie wanting to say something, to complement her but he realised that this was not the time. Dave was now examining her ankle.

'I'm done,' he said to Richard, and then to Annie. 'We need to take you into the hospital, Annie. That hand needs some stitches and you need to have your ankle x-rayed just to make sure there are no cracked bones. Probably a tetanus booster too unless you are up to date.'

Annie nodded.

'Good girl. Give me a minute and I'll be right back.'

He motioned for Richard to follow him into the kitchen where the white-suited photographers and finger printers were already hard at work.

'How is she?' Masterton addressed Dave.

'Pretty shaken up,' replied Dave. 'She needs stitches and an x-ray so she will have to go to A and E. I'd like to take the babies when you release them so I'll call a backup vehicle for Annie.'

'That's ok,' interrupted Richard, 'I'll take Annie. If you can get a lift back to the station, boss?'

Masterton considered this for the moment. She could almost feel the heat of Richard's gaze.

'There's not much I can do here,' Richard continued. 'And I haven't managed to speak to her yet. I need to get some sort of statement.'

'Ok, Richard,' she agreed. 'But be careful.'

'She's not at any risk,' said Dave, misinterpreting the exchange. 'I'll take her to the car for you.'

Dave returned to the front room to help Annie and as Richard turned to follow Masterton grasped his arm. 'Richard, I mean it.'

Richard turned to face her. 'I hear you, boss.'

'Good,' replied Masterton. 'Because I know you pretty well, Richard. This is turning into a bit of a nasty do and I need you on this. Don't give me any cause to turf you off this case.'

Richard shook his head. 'I won't. I want to solve this case more than anyone and I won't be flouting the rules along the way.'

'Go on then,' said Masterton. 'Don't let me down.'

Richard turned away. He knew what he needed to do to stay on the case and keep Annie safe. And he was confident that he could do it. What he didn't know was how much more complicated things were going to become and just how much his resolve would be tested.

Chapter Thirteen

Since training as a general nurse and then a midwife, Annie had put her hands in more human matter and tissue than most non-clinical staff even knew existed. It is true that sometimes she had physically gagged, and sometimes she had struggled to keep her face neutral but none of it had ever really bothered her. It was all part of the job and she had learned to breathe through her mouth and clear up quickly. Not like her friend Julie who would throw the vomit bowl at a patient and then run away and hide until order was restored.

That was until tonight.

As she lifted the bundles from the bag she had felt the firmness and weight of whatever was wrapped inside. As soon as she opened the towels she knew straight away that the babies were dead. The discoloured corpses were still and lifeless and she knew that their rigid limbs would be icy cold. But she didn't think she could have touched their marble skin if she had wanted to. Something about the horror of their abandonment had shaken her to the core. The two tiny bodies, so human, yet wrapped up like a pair of sweaty sports socks and thrown into a holdall. What a waste. What an appalling waste of two precious lives.

And then there was the blame.

Annie wasn't just crying for the babies. She was crying because she believed that they had lain on her doorstep for a day and a night. She clearly recalled the strange noise at her back door the night before that had made her switch on the outside light and peer out of the window cursing the stray cat. Then the call had come from Helen and Andrew and she had dashed off to deliver their son without a second thought. And now she knew for sure that Baseera was the mother of the two boys. Annie was devastated. Baseera had come to her in need and Annie had let her down. She had let the babies down. She said this now, to Richard, as they drove towards the hospital.

'I let her down,' she tried to say but her throat was still choked with tears and all she managed to do was trigger a coughing fit that caused Richard to pull into the side of the road and find her a tissue from the glove box. Annie dabbed at her eyes and then tried to blow her nose with one hand.

'I let her down,' she said again.

'Who?' asked Richard, already knowing the answer.

'Baseera. She came to me for help. She was lonely and scared and I let her down.'

'She ran away,' reasoned Richard.

'I gave her that opportunity. I should have stayed with her.'

'And what could you have done? Forced her to give you her real name? Tied her to the chair? Followed her home? Called the police?'

'No.'

'Then don't beat yourself up about this.'

'It's my job to earn the trust of these women so that they don't run away. That's the whole ethos of health care at the Asylum Centre.'

The tears began to flow again and Annie fumbled in the glove box for more tissues.

'Take the box,' smiled Richard, 'compliments of the taxpayer.'

He gently patted her arm and then pulled out into the traffic.

'Thank you, Richard.'

'For the tissues? You're easy to please.'

'For tonight. Thank you for coming. I didn't know what to do. You were the first person I thought of.'

Richard glanced at her before returning his eyes to the road.

'I'm glad you did,' he said.

They soon reached the hospital and Richard pulled the car into a parking space close to the entrance to the Accident & Emergency Department.

'How are you feeling?' asked Richard.

Annie shrugged. 'Guilty, shocked, incredulous. I can't really take it all in.'

Richard shifted in his seat so that he was half turned towards her. 'We still need to find out how all this happened,' he said. 'We need to know why Baseera was so frightened and we need to find the person that was with her, the person that brought the babies to you.'

'You want me to answer some questions,' said Annie.

'Are you up to it?'

Annie nodded. 'I know it won't bring any of them back, but it might help to understand.'

'Tell me what happened.'

Richard fished his notebook and pen from his pocket and began to write as Annie related the events of the last twenty-four hours of her life. The twenty-four hours that would change it forever. She told him about hearing a noise outside her back door and dismissing it as a stray cat. He smiled when she talked about stopping at the café, where I met a handsome stranger she said but frowned when she talked about being interviewed by 'a tall detective.'

That was the only time he interrupted. 'I'm sorry, Annie. I had a job to do and a colleague breathing down my neck. I can't get involved with a witness during an investigation. They'll take me off the job. That still applies.'

'I understand,' she said. It was enough for her to have him there with her. He made her feel safe.

Annie continued with her story, delivering Helen and Andrew's baby and then being called by her manager just as she was leaving the hospital. Richard felt the hair at the back of his neck tingle as she described the incident with the intruder. 'And your colleague said he was an Arab?'

Annie nodded as a dawning realisation gripped her. 'Do you think there could be a connection? Do you think he was the father? Do you think he was coming to tell me about the babies?'

Richard saw the horror in her face and chose his words carefully.

'I can only work with evidence, Annie, police work is not guess work. But it's one hell of a coincidence and I will be interviewing all the people involved last night.'

'But tell me what you think, please?'

'What time did you hear the noise outside your back door?' asked Richard.

'Some time after ten, I think. I left the house about a quarter to eleven and I had probably been on the phone talking to Helen for a quarter of an hour. Yes, between ten and ten fifteen.'

'The pathologist thinks Baseera died between eight and nine pm last night, so whoever brought the babies to you must have come virtually straight there.'

'If I'd only opened the door,' said Annie, and the tears began to roll down her cheeks again. 'I might have been able to save them.'

Richard leaned across to lift her chin with his hand so that she was forced to look at him. 'Annie, we have the pathologist's report. The babies would not have survived. They were two small and weak. The placentas had packed up and the mum had a huge haemorrhage.

There was nothing you could have done to save them. You saw how small they were. And I would hazard a guess that they were already dead when they were left on your back door step. I feel confident that the pathologist will confirm that.'

'But I didn't have to leave them all alone, did I?'

'You didn't know, Annie. You have done nothing wrong. What we need to do now is try and find out why Baseera gave birth in a warehouse in the first place, we need to know who was involved and we also need to know why the babies were brought to your home and left on your doorstep.'

'Well, the why is easy,' said Annie. 'Baseera came to the clinic and met me there. I am probably the only member of health staff that she knew. When she realised her babies were in trouble she must have sent them to me. I don't know how she got my address, though.'

'That's easy enough with Google,' answered Richard, not wanting to add that she might also have been followed.

'But the babies were wrapped up in towels and carried in a bag. They *must* have already been dead, mused Annie. 'Perhaps the father didn't know what to do with them.'

'Or perhaps he was trying to steer clear of the authorities.'

'And when I wasn't at home, he came to find me at work.'

'If it was him.'

Annie paused before looking into Richard's eyes as she delivered her question.

'You will find out for me, Richard, won't you?'

'Come on,' said Richard, 'it's time to get you inside. I'll go and get a wheelchair.'

'Richard?'

‘I’ll sort this Annie, believe me.’

Chapter Fourteen

While Annie was being stitched and x-rayed, Richard strolled back to his car to call Masterton on his mobile phone. He gave her the pertinent facts from Annie's statement.

'Good work, Richard. We haven't got anything from the bag but we'd better get fingerprints from her tomorrow for elimination purposes and we will still need her statement about the disturbance at the Asylum Centre to rule out any connection.'

'I can bring her in,' said Richard.

'No, Richard,' said Masterton. There was a sharp edge to her voice that Richard had no intention of ignoring. 'You've done a good job tonight and you were the best person for her, even I can see that. But I don't want you getting too close. You do understand, don't you?'

'Yes, boss.'

'Just find out where she will be first thing in the morning and I'll arrange transport for her. Now go and get some rest. Briefing is at eight am.'

'Ok. Goodnight, boss.'

'Night, Richard.'

Back in the hospital Richard showed his warrant card and asked to be taken through to Annie. He was met at the door to her room by a young female doctor. She was brisk and confident.

'Annie Collings,' she said, consulting her clipboard. 'Laceration to the left palm which has been stitched and a sprain to the right ankle. We've strapped that up and she should be fine. She needs to rest and we'll give her a referral for physiotherapy. We're keeping her in overnight, though. She was very distressed and showing some signs of shock. We've given her a sedative and we'll keep her in our observation room. We're not too busy so she should get some rest.'

'When will she be discharged?' asked Richard.

'She can go home whenever she likes, to be honest. But hopefully, she'll get a good night's sleep and can leave in the morning.'

'Thanks, Doctor,' said Richard. 'Can I see her before I go?'

'Of course. Just give us ten more minutes to get her settled.' He's cute thought the doctor, pity I'm engaged. 'Oh, and Detective, one more thing. She kept talking about dead babies.'

'She's a midwife,' was all he said as he shook the doctor's hand and thanked her.

Before he went through to see Annie he made his way to the foyer of the main hospital where he was pleased to find a Costa Coffee just about to close. He grabbed a latte and a reduced price flatbread and sat amongst the empty chairs and tables while a young Indian woman pushed a mop half-heartedly around the floor.

The foyer was cavernous, all white metal supports and glass that usually echoed with the bustle of visitors hurrying through bearing worried faces and bags of fruit. Beneath the vaulted ceiling, there would also be a motley assortment of dressing-gowned patients sneaking outside for a crafty cigarette, fags and lighter in one hand, a drip stand in the other. Tonight, the empty space was both a relief and a comfort.

Richard had been living and working in London when his wife had died and he remembered sitting in a similar foyer after identifying her body. One hospital was very much like another, he thought. They were usually over-heated, unnerving and almost always bad news. He supposed Annie's job was the exception to that but as Baseera had demonstrated so graphically, pregnancy and childbirth did not always have a happy ending. But then he already knew that.

Richard didn't believe in God or spirits or fate. He just believed that life happened. Sometimes it was good and sometimes it wasn't. At the age of twenty, he was in his second year at Oxford, studying, socialising and having the time of his life. Oh, it was so good. The good ended when he was called into his Professor's office to speak to a policewoman. He waited to hear if he was in trouble for relocating a rather bloated statue from its plinth at the front of his College to the chapel entrance but the rather unattractive woman looked far sadder than the statue deserved.

She told him that his parents were both dead. They were boat builders and were delivering a boat to the Mediterranean. The boat had been boarded and sunk in the Bay of Biscay and their bodies, and boat were never recovered. The news was devastating and Richard was angry for a long time. His parents had employees who delivered boats. They had no need to go themselves. And whoever heard of pirates in the Bay of Biscay? Didn't these people steal the boats, not sink them? But although their deaths were recorded as manslaughter, the investigation was closed due to lack of evidence and his parents were denied justice.

But the good was that Richard and his brother became the owners of the modest company. The bad was that the company had been running at a loss for several years prior to their parents' death and their home had been heavily mortgaged to prop up the ailing company. Add to that the fact that neither of the brothers had any interest in boats despite a lifetime of cajoling from their parents. Richard would even go so far as confessing to a touch of seasickness at times. So the company and family home were sold and with the small amount of money left to them after debts and lawyers' fees were paid the boys found themselves facing a very different future.

Richard remembered shaking the policewoman's hand and thanking her for coming to see him. No, Professor, no assistance required, I just need some time, thank you. Time to hang up his hard-won scholar's gown, pack his rucksack and walk away. That was the start of Richard's lost years as he made his way to Heathrow and boarded the first plane with an available seat.

Almost two years later, his brother found him dossing on a misshapen sofa in a Cairo flat reading Sartre in the original French.

'Time to go home,' said his brother expecting a fight.

'I think so too,' was the measured reply.

By the time their plane had landed Richard's brother had failed to persuade him to go back to University, to start a business or train for a career, perhaps in the City. His two years backpacking around the world, taking odd jobs and sometimes sleeping rough had given him the education that had been missing from his previously privileged life. He was going to join the police, become a detective and catch the villains who destroyed the lives of their victims and their families. There was even a notion that he could find out what had happened to his parents.

His brother was horrified. 'Richard, you can do anything you want. Do you seriously intend to spend your life dealing with drunken yobs and petty criminals? Do you know that they vomit on your shoes? You can do better than that.'

'You can do better than the Army,' countered Richard.

'That's different and you know it. I joined up before mum and dad died. I love it. The Army is my family.'

'Would you have joined up if you had known mum and dad were going to die?'

His brother thought for a while before answering. 'Of course, I would, more than ever. I'm not a nine to five guy and I don't have your brains. If I wasn't in the military I probably would have squandered my life on dead end jobs and petty crime.'

Richard looked at his extremely fit brother and shook his head, 'No you wouldn't. You are much too solid for that.'

His brother shrugged. 'Do you have any idea what mum and dad were doing delivering that boat?'

'None at all. But it was a strange thing for them to be doing. Maybe they weren't delivering it.'

'What are you getting at?'

'Well, we know now that their business was failing financially and the house was heavily mortgaged. Maybe they were running away?'

Patrick looked horrified. 'Seriously? You seriously think they would have done that to us?'

'Maybe they couldn't see any other way. Maybe they couldn't face us.'

'You could be right. I suppose joining the police could be a good thing. Not sure how long you will last mind. But it could be a good thing.'

Yes, thought Richard now. It was a good thing. Every time a conviction was secured he felt a groundswell of satisfaction that could not be beaten by anything he had experienced to date. And now his job had brought him Annie. The thought of her drew him to his feet and he made his way back to casualty.

There were four beds in a line against the wall. Three of them were empty and Annie was lying in the fourth bed next to the window. Richard approached quietly for fear of disturbing her but he saw that her eyes were open.

'How are you?'

She gave the ghost of a smile as she waved her bandaged hand towards him. 'I'm ok,' she said. 'Stitches out in five days.'

'They're going to keep you in overnight.'

'That's ok, I don't fancy going home anyway.'

'They probably wouldn't let you just yet. It's still a crime scene.'

'What will happen now?'

'We'll take DNA samples to confirm that the babies were Baseera's and the pathologist will conduct a post-mortem to confirm time and cause of death. Our next step will be to try and find whoever helped her. If you're up to it, we'll need you to come into the station tomorrow. We'll take a formal statement and we'd like to talk to you about the disturbance at the Asylum Centre and the incident here in the hospital.'

'Do you really think those things had something to do with it?'

'We won't know until we've investigated but it might be the reason she did a runner. We can assume that someone brought her to the Asylum Centre and we can also assume that whoever it was drove her to the warehouse.'

'That's what I can't understand,' said Annie. 'Why some grotty old warehouse?'

'I suppose there was no chance of them being seen,' said Richard. 'Everything that we have learned so far suggests that Baseera was scared of something or someone.'

'But the hospital was so close. She must have known how early her babies were.'

'Or,' suggested Richard, 'she could have been on her way to the hospital when she realised that she wasn't going to make it.'

'That is a possibility,' agreed Annie. 'Premature babies can be born very quickly and easily. They could have been on the way before Baseera realised the delivery was so close.'

'And that's what we are going to find out,' replied Richard. 'But right now, you need to get some rest and I will see you tomorrow.'

Annie closed her eyes. 'Can you stay for a few minutes?' she asked.

'Until you're asleep,' said Richard. He leaned across to stroke her hair and within minutes she was fast asleep. Richard didn't leave straight away. He stayed where he was with his hand on her hair committing every detail of her face to his memory. This woman was affecting him in a way that he had never believed possible but her connection to the case had created a tangle of emotions that he was finding difficult to keep in check. Fatigue wasn't helping either and as Richard rose from his seat by the bed he leaned across to kiss Annie lightly on the forehead. He left the room quietly without looking back. If he had he wasn't sure that he would have had the strength to leave, but if he had, he would have seen the smile that crossed Annie's face as she stirred in her sleep.

Chapter Fifteen

Saturday

At eight am the following morning the Incident Room appeared to be in chaos with officers, administrative staff, and detectives scurrying around with papers, mugs of coffee and half-eaten slices of toast. A muffin was tossed from one officer to another and several staff were staring at computer screens and tapping at their keyboards. Following the press conference the telephone lines had been ringing since dawn and DC Spooner had been at her desk for an hour and a half ploughing through the messages. So far nothing of significance had been called in.

Masterton sat in her office with the door firmly closed. She had suffered a restless night thinking about the poor little mites stuffed into a sports bag and dumped on a doorstep. She thanked God that her own three were grown up and out in the world. There were just so many damn dangers out there these days. She remembered telling her children not to take sweets from strangers or get into cars with people they didn't know, scolding Tom when he was an hour late from football practice because he had spent his bus fare on sweets and had had to walk, and grounding Alice for a month for pretending she was studying with a friend whilst actually going to a party. How petty those things seemed now compared to parents dealing with underage sex, drug abuse and knife crime.

There had been nothing in her parenting vocabulary about drugs, knives and child abuse and all the other crimes that she dealt with in her job. Away from the station, she led an ordinary life with an ordinary husband who miraculously still loved her despite her frequent, unplanned absences from no end of family gatherings, school events and even much needed but rarely experienced weekend breaks. Scrumping apples was the worst crime committed in her family and that had been carried out by her father when he was eighty-four. What sort of world left a young mother to deliver premature babies on the cold, concrete floor of an empty warehouse?

Masterton thought about her first delivery and remembered how disturbing it was when her contractions started. Her excitement at the thought of finally meeting her baby was tempered by the fear that she wouldn't be able to cope with the pain or that something might go wrong. But she never once imagined that she might die. And never in a million years could she envisage a scenario where she would give birth anywhere other than in a hospital with midwives and doctors and her husband beside her.

The more Masterton thought about the circumstances of Baseera's death, the more convinced she was that there had to be something significantly wrong with her situation. Every indication was that the young woman was well looked after and financially comfortable. Her difficulties with the English language masked her educational status but she knew enough and was confident enough to access health care at the Asylum Centre.

Whatever the reason for her premature labour, surely whoever was with her would have tried to make it to the hospital, call 999 or even just stop at the side of the road and flag down a passing car? Why had they left the road and hidden? And why had her body been abandoned? Who or what on earth could have made them so afraid? There were still far too many questions without answers and Masterton had a very, very bad feeling about this case. And now her best officer was mooning over a witness. That was odd too. Since his wife had died Richard hadn't looked at another woman. What the hell was going on?

She sighed wearily as she got to her feet. It was time to face her team and get this case moving. She surveyed the bustle of activity in the Incident Room with satisfaction as she stood in the midst of the throng with her hands on her hips.

'Is it too much to ask that you lot feed and water yourself before you get to work in the morning?'

'I did, boss,' called McIntyre from his desk as he dabbed at the splotch of marmalade on his tie. 'But that was three hours ago. This is elevenses.'

'So what were you doing up at five am this morning?' she asked with genuine interest.

'Forensics,' he replied, with a grin that almost split his face in two. 'We have strands of human hair from the warehouse.'

'Hallelujah!' cried Masterton clapping her hands, which was all that was needed to bring the team to attention.

'Right, update. First of all, thank you to all of those who have come in on their day off. We are still in the critical first forty-eight hours of the crime and your assistance is greatly appreciated. There may even be muffins at coffee time.'

'It's always coffee time here, boss,' called a voice from the back of the room.

'Not for me it isn't. Now, listen up. For those of you who don't already know, and if you don't where the hell have you been for the last few hours, twin baby boys were abandoned at the home of the midwife Annie Collings last night. We have already been able to confirm that they are the children of the dead mother found at Shrub Hill. At this stage, it looks as though the babies died of natural causes i.e. the complications of extreme prematurity and poor growth in the womb.

We have the holdall that was used to carry the bodies of the babies. There are only one set of prints on it. These are probably the midwife's and we will confirm that later this morning. We also have two towels which look brand new. Palmer, work on those, anything you can get. The bag also looks new and both towels and bag were probably purchased locally. Spooner, stay on airports. Collins, CCTV in the vicinity of Annie's home. We have a date and time so it shouldn't take you too long. Also, CCTV from any stores selling the bags and towels in the vicinity of the crime scene. And McIntyre, do you have something for us?'

'I do,' said McIntyre triumphantly. 'Several strands of hair found on the dead woman's dress. They're not hers.'

'So if we find our accomplice,' said Masterton, 'we can use DNA to put him or her at the scene. All we need to do now is to find him. Get to it. Debrief at 4pm.'

'Boss, can I have a word?' Richard was at her shoulder. He looked tired and worried.

'Come into my office and sit down. Is it Annie?'

Richard nodded. 'I called the hospital this morning to arrange her transport but she had already left. I've tried calling her but there is no reply.'

'Where do you think she's gone?'

'Not far with her ankle injury, that's for sure.'

'Is she at work?'

Richard shook his head. 'I rang her manager. She isn't rostered to work today although she is on call for deliveries. She hasn't arrived at work nor has she called in sick but they wouldn't expect to hear from her unless anyone is in labour. I've sent a text asking her to call in and left a message on her home phone and mobile.'

'Ok, call her manager back and find out if anyone knows where she would normally be on a Saturday morning. Does Annie know that we need her in here?'

'I told her.'

'Well, don't worry. I'm sure she'll turn up. If she hasn't arrived by noon send a uniform round to check her house. When she does get here I'd like to interview her.'

Disappointment caused Richard's shoulders to sag just a little.

'Sure, boss?'

'Yes, I think it's for the best. And make sure those Asylum Centre statements are in by lunch time.'

Chapter Sixteen

In a leafy suburb just a few miles from Annie's house, an anonymous grey car had been parked in the same place for several hours. Inside were three men. Their sallow skin was scarred in places and their faces unshaven. Their black hair was unkempt and their alert, dark eyes were ringed with a bloody history. They were the sort of men that would make law abiding citizens avert their eyes and cross the street to avoid a stare that could chill you to the bone.

A few minutes away, Masood sat on a bus clutching his Tesco carrier bags stuffed with groceries. His English was excellent and he had managed to find the store and buy what he needed without drawing attention to himself. But even after six weeks in the country, he was still overwhelmed by the massive shop with shelves piled high with every type of food imaginable. Masood had seen supermarkets on TV but had no concept of just how enormous they were until he had stepped inside the land of plenty.

Masood's attention was drawn to the road ahead as the bus came to a halt and a collective groan travelled to his seat near the back. He peered through the window and could see that two cars had collided in front of them. Both drivers were out of their cars inspecting the damage and the bus driver poked his head out of the window and called to them to move their vehicles to the side of the road.

The lady sitting next to him muttered something about a hairdresser's appointment but Masood kept his head down and pretended not to understand. It was only a matter of time before the body was found and he needed to make himself invisible until Ali arrived and told him what to do. Masood had let his brother down and his arms and legs began to shake as he thought of everything that had happened. He prayed that Ali would understand and would forgive him. And he prayed that they would not all be thrown into a British prison.

He believed now that when the blood came he should have taken his sister-in-law straight to the hospital to get some help. But she became too afraid. She insisted that she would only see the lady midwife. It had been easy to find the midwife's address on the internet. Masood thought that these English girls should be more careful but in the end, it had been of no use. Masood could not find her.

So, Masood had driven towards the hospital without informing his sister-in-law of their destination. Then the pain had come and she had screamed for him to stop the car and in his panic, he had swerved off the road. He had no idea where he was. He just saw a dark place without people. He had helped her inside where she lay down and her frightened eyes and groans told him that the baby was coming. But when it arrived, the baby was so tiny and so very, very still. The baby did not breathe and while he had tried to offer comfort another tiny boy had arrived. He too was still and silent.

He put his head in his hands and tried not to cry. His sister-in-law had been in such a panic about her boys, begging Masood to do something, to help them. But they were so tiny and he was just a man. He tried to comfort her and pray with her to keep her calm. But in the dim light of the old warehouse there was nothing he could do and in their distress, neither of them noticed the pool of blood that was growing around them until she became pale and cold and her eyes had closed.

It was then that Masood ran. He ran to his car and drove frantically to the nearest supermarket. At Asda in

Lowesmoor he bought towels and a sports bag, scissors and string, then hurried back to carefully cut and tie the cords and wrap the little boys in their makeshift shrouds. It was too late to help any of them but he wanted the boys to be properly looked after and buried with dignity. The midwife was the only person that his sister-in-law had met and he knew that it was her job to care for mothers and their children. He had to trust that she would look after these boys. He knew that she helped other Afghans and God willing, she would help his brother's sons.

He was relieved to see that lights were on in her house and her car was on the drive. He had quietly scaled the back fence then held his breath as the outside light came on and he saw the midwife look outside and then turn back to the room. He laid the bag gently on the back step and hurried away before she came out. All the while he muttered a prayer for the dead mother and her baby sons. How could he know that Annie would not open the door for a night and a day?

The lady next to him began to complain about the delay and Masood excused himself and left the bus. He did not want to be remembered by anyone and it would be best to walk the rest of the way. The rented house was close and away from the main road. Perhaps once he was there he would feel safer and the shaking would stop.

He turned into his street still deep in thought. The incident on the bus had shaken him and he forgot to be alert as he neared home. He failed to see the grey car or the small movement from inside it as the men gave him their attention.

'There.' the man in the passenger seat pointed across the road where Masood was hurrying along the pavement. He was dressed in jeans and a non-descript dark jacket and was carrying a supermarket carrier bag in each hand.

'He does the woman's work,' said the driver. The other two men chuckled.

Masood turned into the driveway of a large detached house where he deposited his shopping on the front door step. The waiting men saw him look around carefully before he put his key in the lock, opened the door and took his shopping inside. From the front of the house, the grey car was partially screened from view by the sycamore trees planted in the verge and there was now no chance for Masood to see it. Without speaking, the three men left the car and walked quickly across the street. There was little to distinguish them apart from slight differences in height. Same crumpled jeans, T-shirts and unshaven faces below short, dark hair. One of them hurried around the side of the house where he crouched by the side fence. Through the gaps in the wood, he could see into the kitchen window where Masood was unpacking his groceries. The third man was already over the fence and in the garden where he crept to the back door. He gave the signal by raising his hand. The driver of the car rang the front door bell.

Inside the kitchen, Masood dropped a bag of sugar which fell to the ground and spread across the grey tiles like a spilt shovel of sand. Ignoring it he ran to the back door which he thrust open, ready to run. His legs crumpled beneath him even as he saw the gun and the hand that was holding it. Before the assassin had even begun to shout his obscenities, Masood had drawn his last breath.

Chapter Seventeen

Annie had been woken early that morning by the sounds of the Accident & Emergency Department, telephones ringing, voices handing over the shift, trolleys being cleared, the clatter of something dropping to the floor. She had dozed fitfully during the night, disturbed by the strangeness of the hospital. She sat up in bed and tested her left hand. It was stiff and sore but, much to her relief, she could wiggle her fingers. She had been afraid that more severe damage could have put an end to her career. Her clothes were on the locker beside her bed and she removed the hospital gown to slip them on, grateful that she was still wearing her undies. She had no idea how she would fasten her bra with one hand.

Once she was dressed she reached down for her trainers. The strapping on her foot and ankle made it a tight squeeze but by loosening the lace completely she was able to push her foot in. The effort caused her ankle to throb and for a moment she had to lie back on the bed and take deep breaths until the pain had subsided.

Tentatively, she put her weight on the ankle. The pain caused sweat to trickle down between her shoulder blades but Annie forced herself to hobble to the door. She had calls and a clinic that morning and she needed to get home to sort out some cover. It never occurred to her to call in sick and let someone else sort it out. Resources were stretched at the best of times and Annie knew that if she had a telephone and a comfy seat she would be able to manage the bulk of her workload. And it also never occurred to her that the previous evening's shock and the effect of the sedative might have clouded her judgement.

At the desk, she picked the youngest nurse she could find in the belief that she would ask the least questions. Annie told her who she was and that she was ready to leave if a taxi could be called. The nurse checked Annie's notes before agreeing that she could go. She called the taxi and handed Annie some written instructions for follow-up care.

Annie had a front door key in her pocket but no money and as it turned out, she was very glad to be able to lean on the arm of the taxi driver as she hobbled up to her front door. After she had tipped him generously and closed the front door she hopped cautiously to the kitchen.

From the kitchen doorway, Annie could see that everything had been left clean and tidy and the back door was firmly locked. Her tummy was grumbling slightly but breakfast meant venturing further into the kitchen and Annie was not sure that was something she wanted to do just yet. Besides, she was pretty sure there was still no milk. At least there was no sign of what had happened there and she breathed a sigh of relief. She sat down on the bottom stair and carefully removed the trainer from her left foot. The other one she practically threw off.

She crawled up the stairs on her hands and knees before pulling herself to her feet and limping into her bedroom. She would just have a quick lie down before she got going for the day. Putting all of her weight onto her good foot she hauled herself onto the bed where to her surprise, she fell quickly and easily into a deep sleep. As she slept soundly, the awful events of the last twenty-four hours slipped away from her consciousness. How could she possibly know that the horrors had barely begun?

Chapter Eighteen

Diane Masterton was updating the whiteboard which had now been joined by a second when the phone in her office rang. Her mind was still on the case as she hurried to her desk and answered automatically, 'Masterton.'

She listened for a few minutes, then shook her head angrily. 'Why us, boss, we're right in the middle of a case?' She was instantly alert at the answer, listening intently and writing copious notes.

Ever alert, Richard left his desk at the change of tone and went to stand in the doorway of Masterton's office. She acknowledged him with her eyes and indicated that he should stay.

'Bloody hell!' she said as she put down the phone and grabbed her things. 'Thank God you're still here, Richard. Get on your mobile and delegate the Asylum Centre interviews. You're coming with me.'

Richard grabbed his coat from the back of his chair and strode out beside her.

'What is it, boss?'

'Another body, Richard. They're piling up on my desk like pancakes at an American breakfast.'

'Why us? We've already got a full workload here.'

Masterton grimaced. 'Uniform thinks he's an Afghan.'

Richard raised his eyebrows. 'Could it be the father?'

'That's what we need to find out.' Masterton tossed him the car keys. 'You drive please, I need to make some calls.'

'How did he die?' asked Richard as they reached the car. Masterton formed her right hand into the shape of a gun and mimed a shot to her forehead.

'Right between the eyes.'

'Suicide?'

'Professional kill,' said Masterton. 'And in Worcester, for God's sake. This is not gangland Britain, but it is starting to get interesting.'

While Richard drove across town on blue lights Masterton was on the phone re-allocating the morning's work. He heard her ask Spooner to go and find Annie and he heard her calling Headquarters to plead for more resources.

'This is not someone abandoning a woman to die alone, this is a professional killing, sir. Two Afghans dead in as many days. It can't be a coincidence. This is going to be high profile and I need more manpower.'

Richard heard the agitation in her voice.

'I can't pass it on, I think they're connected and I think this is going to get bigger before it's sorted out.'

She listened again and said, thank you, before snapping shut the phone.

'Any luck?' asked Richard.

'He'll see what he can do,' she shrugged. 'Look, we're here.'

The flashing blue lights and yellow crime scene tape were clearly visible as Richard and Masterton turned into the street. Richard parked with his usual flourish and held the yellow crime scene tape for Masterton to duck under as they both showed their IDs.

'Nice house,' said Richard as they walked up to the front gate where they were handed their coveralls, shoe covers, and gloves.

'Nice area,' said Masterton as she dressed. 'There's some money here. I bet the neighbours won't like this.'

They showed their IDs again at the entrance to the house before being directed through to the kitchen.

'Holy shit!' exclaimed Richard as he stopped dead in the doorway. Masterton peered around him. 'Bloody hell,' she added.

The body of the dead man was lying half in and half out of the kitchen's back doorway. There was a single bullet wound between his eyes and a congealed pool of blood beneath his head. But it was the kitchen itself, and not the corpse, that had caused the shock.

Every cupboard and drawer in the room had been ransacked and every item torn apart.

'What the hell happened here?' asked Masterton. 'Who was first on the scene?'

A young uniformed constable stepped forward. 'I was, ma'am.'

'Tell me what you know,' commanded Masterton.

'We had a treble nine from a neighbour at nine twenty-nine. She heard voices which she said were unusual. Not the voices so much, just the fact that there were any at all. The tenant here is unusually quiet she said. And then she heard a loud bang.'

'Tenant?'

The constable nodded. 'The lady next door owns both houses. She rents this one out.'

'Go on.'

'She looked out of her window and saw three men walking away along the pavement.'

'Walking, not running?'

'Definitely walking, I asked her that.'

'So why did she think it was suspicious.'

'She said the three men looked shifty and out of place. She knows most people in the street having lived here for thirty-two years. She didn't recognise any of the men.'

'What did they look like?' asked Masterton.

'Dark-skinned and foreign. Oh, and they all needed a shave.'

'What sort of foreign?' asked Masterton even though she was sure she already knew the answer.

Middle Eastern, she thought. 'She said they looked like the Taliban off the telly. She decided to call round after she had finished her laundry and found her tenant flat on his back in a pile of cake mix. She dashed home and called treble nine.'

'Ok, I'll go and talk to her in a minute. Thanks, Constable.'

Masterton followed Richard into the kitchen along the metal plates that had been placed across the floor to protect the crime scene.

'I just think this case might have got a whole lot bigger,' she said.

'Might be the fancy of a bored old lady.'

'I wish I could believe that,' she replied. 'What do you really think?'

'Definitely a professional hit,' said Richard, 'but ballsy. No attempt to conceal the body and the shooter walks calmly from the scene.'

'If it was them.'

'If it was.'

'What about the mess?' she asked.

'Apparently, the whole house is like this,' said Richard.

'What for?' asked Masterton. 'They've killed their target, why trash his place? Is it some sort of warning to someone else or do they just get off on it?'

'Neither,' replied Richard. 'I think it was a search.'

'For what?'

Richard shook his head. 'Don't know boss, but it's not your usual trashing. There's no tagging, no graffiti, nothing has been smeared around. Things have just been emptied on the spot.' He pointed to a small mound of biscuits and breakfast cereal on the kitchen floor. They haven't spread anything or thrown it around, they've emptied everything systematically. And look at the sink.'

Masterton saw that the draining board was covered with empty bottles. Inside the sink was a blue colander smeared with the remnants of what looked like sauce.

'They sieved all the liquids. They emptied every bottle in the house through the sieve.'

'Bloody hell. What could they have been looking for?'

'Well, it's certainly small,' said Richard looking around the kitchen, 'but not small enough to fall through this sieve.'

'Ok, Richard, you work things here. I'm going next door to talk to the neighbour.'

Chapter Nineteen

After two cups of tea and a slice of lemon cake, Masterton was feeling very pleased with herself. She waited at the front of the house for Richard to emerge.

'Any luck?' he asked.

'No, not really. She only saw the three men briefly from the side and then from the back so she can't describe them very well. The guy that rented the house paid cash up front. He paid three months in advance and has been a model tenant. Exceptionally quiet, no visitors that she is aware of and kept the place tidy.'

'Until today.'

'Ha!'

'References?' asked Richard.

'She took them but can't find them. She will try and hunt them out for us. I imagine they were forged, though.' As she spoke, Masterton struggled to conceal the smile that was playing at the corners of her mouth.

'So why are you looking like your Lotto numbers have come up?'

'Ooh, you're just too good you are,' she said playfully.

'I do my best,' smiled Richard.

'Our dead man, Masood, was waiting for his brother and pregnant sister-in-law to arrive from Afghanistan?'

'And?'

'The sister-in-law was supposed to arrive last week but our landlady hasn't seen sight nor sound of her.'

Richard had removed his overalls while they were talking and they made their way to the car. He was rubbing his chin. 'So, we have a third man, probably a brother. Does she know anything about the brother?'

Masterton shook her head. 'No sign of him either.'

'So we need to find him before the baddies do.'

Masterton nodded. 'What about you?'

'Get in the car,' said Richard with a cheeky grin.

'What have you got?' she asked.

Almost with glee, Richard reached inside his jacket for a clear evidence bag. He handed it to Masterton. Inside was a colour photograph. It was creased in several places and a corner was torn but the picture was as clear as day. It was the face of a happy smiling Afghan man cheek to cheek with Baseera.

Masterton grinned and was on her mobile as Richard pulled away.

'Get everyone back in,' she shouted into the phone. 'Now! And you can put your foot down, Detective.'

The office was buzzing with news of the murder as Masterton and Richard walked in. A third whiteboard had already been set up. Masterton began talking as she walked through to the front of the office and everyone was silent.

'Thank you all for getting back in so promptly,' she began as she scanned the room. 'We have two new members joining our team, Sergeant Eddie Craven, and Sergeant David James. Welcome to the team.'

There was a round of applause from the rest of the personnel scattered across the office. Extra heads and hands were always appreciated.

'You've all heard,' she began. 'We have a murder on our hands. Male, mid-forties, believed to be of Afghan origin. Shot between the eyes at close range. Three suspicious looking strangers were seen in the street outside shortly after voices were heard from the house where the shooting took place. Ballistics still to come but it has all the marks of a professional execution. And,' she motioned Richard to come forward, 'we have a piece of evidence from the scene.'

Richard stuck the evidence bag onto the board with a flourish.

'A photo of our dead mother with an Afghan man. However,' she held up her hand to stem the flow of questions that were already beginning, 'this is not today's murder victim. As yet his identity is unknown. We do however have the name of the victim from his landlady.'

Masterton turned to write on the board. 'Masood. Apparently, it means lucky.'

'Not in his case,' said Collins.

'Is there a last name?' asked Spooner.

'Apparently not. The landlady tells me that Afghans traditionally only have one name, and if they do have two names it's more of a double barrelled first name rather than a surname and forename as we know it.'

'She's well informed, this landlady,' commented Richard.

'Well, she did try to check him out when he came to rent the house. It had been empty for a while and she was just thinking of dropping the rent when Masood appeared on the doorstep with good references and a bucket of cash. He told her that he was waiting for his pregnant sister-in-law and brother to arrive from Afghanistan. The sister-in-law was supposed to have arrived last week but wasn't actually seen by the landlady. Although that does not mean that she wasn't in the house. No sign yet of the husband who we can assume is still on his way.'

'Shall I put a watch on the airports, boss?' asked Spooner.

'Thank you, Spooner. I want this man's mugshot circulated to every port of entry on mainland Britain.

Make sure that everyone knows this man is not to be approached. He may well be armed.'

'How would he smuggle a firearm in, boss?' asked Palmer.

'If we knew the answer to that we would be able to stop it happening. And if he has a network already established in this country he has access to anything he needs. Just assume for now that he is armed and dangerous. We are dealing with professionals here.'

She ran her fingers through her hair, the nearest that Masterton ever got to showing pressure.

'So, a recap. A young woman pregnant with twins gives birth in a disused warehouse. We know that she must have had someone with her, and we can now assume that he was our dead man Masood. McIntyre, I want that confirmed before the sun rises tomorrow. There were hairs recovered from the warehouse. See if they match our corpse.'

'On to it, boss.'

'And make sure the lab check his DNA against the babies. I want to be able to eliminate him as the father. Collins.'

'Telly,' nodded Collins with resignation.

'Telly it is. We now know who we are looking for this time. I want to place this man at the scene. Until now, we've been looking at nothing more than what appeared to be panic and neglect without knowing why. We know the woman was scared enough to do a runner from a clinic when she needed help and it now looks as though that fear was justified. The unanswered questions?'

Masterton indicated that Richard should write on the whiteboard as she reeled them off.

'Who were Baseera and Masood? Why were they here in Britain, and what were they scared of? Who killed Masood and what were the killers searching for?'

'Could it have been a revenge killing, boss? The Taliban and all that?' asked Collins.

'The place had been turned over,' Richard interjected. 'Searched from top to bottom. All we know is that they were looking for something that would fit into the palm of your hand.'

'And we know that it's important enough to kill for,' added Masterton. 'Do we have anything from the Asylum Centre disturbance?'

'Nothing, boss,' said Palmer. 'Just some guy who came in looking for his wife. It happens all the time apparently.'

'Ok. We will have to assume that the raised voices were enough to spook her into running, we need to know why.'

'And why she didn't go for help when she started to haemorrhage,' said Richard.

'Richard I want you to get on to the National Crime Agency. See if they can shed any light on this for us, and see if they can identify that photo. Craven, I want you to lead on the house to house. Carter, witness statements from the crime scene and neighbours.' Spooner, I want to know if there is any trace of a woman at the house. Get on to it team, we've got three armed assassins loose in this city and none of our loved ones are safe until they're caught. Back here at five, please.'

Chapter Twenty

As detectives scurried from the office like bees deserting a burning hive, Masterton went into her office and closed the door. She needed to think and she needed peace and quiet to do it well. She sat down behind her desk which was covered with papers relating to the case and yellow hand-shaped post-its scrawled with her notes. On one side of her desk was a framed photo of her husband and three children. Two sons and a daughter, all grown up now and her daughter married and pregnant. Masterton was hoping that she would have more time to spend with her grandchildren than she had with her own kids. She imagined what it must have been like for Baseera delivering her twins in that filthy warehouse. What could have frightened her so much that she had to hide? Unless she was hiding something herself?

Masterton grabbed a pen and began to write, repeatedly crossing out and scribbling as her ideas formed on the paper. She was deep in concentration when the door to her office burst open without even a knock. Richard and Collins almost fell into the room together.

'Boys!' Masterton was irritated at having her thoughts interrupted but knew her team well enough to realise that they both had a lead.

'You first, Collins.'

'You have to come out to the screen, boss.' Perspiration had soaked the back of his shirt and droplets of sweat were still visible on his forehead.

Masterton hurried to the flat screen hung on the far wall of the main office and waited while Collins fumbled with the buttons on the remote. Richard was impatient besides her. Finally, a hazy image filled the screen.

'This is the Asda supermarket just off Lowesmoor,' said Collins, 'less than a mile from the Shrub Hill warehouse where Baseera's body was found. Time,' he pointed to the screen, '20:42.'

The camera was directed at a check out. A teenager with backcombed hair and too much cleavage on show was slumped in her chair, idly swinging backwards and forwards while she examined her nails. As a customer approached the girl sat up and began scanning the items without even looking at the man who was nervously shifting from foot to foot.

'She'd make a good witness then,' observed Richard sarcastically.

'Why are the cameras always pointing at the back of their heads?' asked Masterton with exasperation. 'What are we supposed to get from that.'

As if startled, the customer half-turned to look around and scan the area behind him. Collins paused the screen so that they could examine the fuzzy image of the customer.

'Bingo!' breathed Richard. 'Our man, Masood.'

Collins restarted the recording and they watched as the check out operator struggled to try and fit the canvas sports holdall into a large carrier bag. A short conversation ensued following which she unzipped the bag and placed two blue towels, a pair of scissors and a ball of green string inside. Masood handed over some cash, waited for his change and receipt then walked through the checkout, looking behind him again as he left.

'Why couldn't we have found this two days ago?' asked Masterton. 'He might still be alive.'

'We didn't know what we were looking for boss,' Richard pointed out.

'Even so,' replied Masterton, 'I can't help thinking we might have been able to do something.'

'Now watch this,' demanded Collins.

Richard and Masterton returned their attention to the screen. The checkout operator was now engaged in a detailed examination of the ends of her long hair. She completely ignored the three dark-skinned men who strode past her. Once again Collins paused the picture and although the image was fuzzy, there was no doubt that the three men were of Middle Eastern origin. And they were not in the store to do their shopping.

'Bloody hell!' said Masterton. 'Well done, Collins. Any more where that came from.'

Collins was already pressing buttons on the remote. They were now looking at a view of the car park and watched as Masood got into a blue Ford and drove away.

'So what's happened to the three goons?' asked Richard.

'Can't see them, boss,' replied Collins. 'But we can assume that they're following.'

'So that's how they got to Masood. They were on to him all the time.'

'And the time, boss. Masood must have gone back for the babies and then taken them to Annie's place.'

'Where is she by the way?' asked Masterton.

'Home,' said Richard.

Masterton raised her eyebrows. 'Good to know you are keeping tabs on her.'

'Spooner called the hospital and spoke to the nurse who discharged her and ordered the taxi to take her home.'

'Have you spoken to her?'

Richard shook his head. 'Her answer phone is on and she's not answering her mobile but Spooner did speak to the taxi driver. He helped her into the house and said she seemed fine.'

Masterton nodded.

'So what are you so excited about?' asked Masterton. 'Spill the beans.'

Richard consulted the notebook in his hand. 'Masood rented the house on the 26th of last month, the same day the advert appeared in the local paper. The landlady said he turned up in a blue Ford with a Hertz sticker on the back window.'

'You've got the car?' asked Masterton.

'Not yet, boss. It's not at the house. But we've got the reggo, it won't take us long to find it, we've got uniforms out there now.'

'Go on.'

'The car was rented at the airport on the 25th in the name of Masood. A Masood arrived on a flight from Pakistan at four pm that day. Presumably, he holed up somewhere overnight before going to rent the house the next day. Now Baseera was found dead last Thursday on the 23rd, almost a month later. We've checked all arrivals from Pakistan for the last month. A pregnant passenger calling herself Soraya Haq arrived from Pakistan last Monday, the 20th. I think she may be the woman who visited the Asylum Centre clinic on Tuesday. The rest we know.'

'Right,' Masterton was already plotting timelines in her head. 'I want that car found today. Collins, find where it went on Sunday. Spooner, interview the check-out girl. Richard, send Palmer to bring in Annie Collings. She's our key witness.'

The three of them scattered like greyhounds from the trap.

Chapter Twenty-One

Shortly before lunch, Palmer approached Richard's desk with a sheet of sketches and several pieces of typed paper.

'Witness statement typed up from the interview with Annie Collings, boss, and sketches of Soraya's jewellery from her visit to the Asylum Centre clinic. She's a good artist.'

Richard turned the pages of the sketchbook, examining each picture in detail. Annie had used a pencil to provide detailed drawings of two earrings, a stone on a chain and a wrist of bangles. Each item was drawn with meticulous detail.

'We could do with her on the team,' said Richard, before adding casually, 'how is she?'

'Shattered, I think,' said Palmer. 'After Masterton had finished interviewing her I took her to the canteen for a cup of tea and a hot meal. I will take her home when she's eaten.'

'Thanks, Palmer,' said Richard handing back the sheets of paper. 'Log these for me, will you? I want a quick word with her before she goes.'

Palmer smiled to herself as she watched Richard leave the room. Mr. Cool, calm and collected was looking a little ruffled, she thought.

He saw her at once, her lemon T-shirt standing out amongst the uniforms like the sun bursting out after a summer storm. She was sitting in a corner with her foot up on the next seat so that she could rest her injured ankle and perch her sketch pad on her knee. She glanced up as he joined the queue for tea, and smiled as if expecting him. He motioned to the tea and mimed a drinking action with his hand. She nodded and returned to her sketching trying to calm the turmoil that raged inside her at the sight of him. She had been disappointed to find that it was a woman officer dragging her from the bed that morning and her spirits had sunk even further as the morning progressed and the realisation dawned that she might not see him. She had jumped at the chance to go to the canteen in the hope that she might at least catch a glimpse of him.

Richard remembered how she took her tea from the café, a splash of milk, no sugar, and he made sure that it was perfect before he headed over to her. He could see the curious glances that she was getting from the male officers in the room and he felt proud to be sitting down with her.

'I was hoping I would see you,' he said as he sat down.

'I thought you were going to interview me,' replied Annie without looking up from her drawing.

'I have to do as I'm told,' remarked Richard.

'Well, it's nice to see you now.'

'They've told you about Soraya?'

Annie nodded. 'I didn't think Baseera was her real name. She was so shifty when she said it. Soraya. That's pretty.'

Richard watched her mouth as she talked and found himself imagining how it would feel to kiss those lips. She still looked pale and tired but when she glanced up at him he saw that the sparkle was returning to her extraordinary brown eyes

'How are you feeling?' asked Richard.

'My palm is quite sore,' she said, holding up her bandaged left hand and wiggling her fingers, 'but I'm hobbling well.'

'What are you drawing?' he asked trying to peer over the top of her pad, but she pulled it sharply to her chest and smiled at him again. He was finding it hard to breathe.

'Uh-uh,' she said shaking her head, 'I don't like people peeping until I've finished.'

'Fair enough, but don't let your tea go cold.'

Richard sat back in the chair watching as her hand moved across the paper. He had spent the last fifteen years of his life watching people, memorising their features, observing their characteristics, their tics, and habits. He reckoned he could profile most people within an hour of meeting them. But not this woman. Annie was an enigma that he couldn't crack. She had something indefinable that drew him to her like a magnet. He felt like he was home when he was with her.

'Why do you live alone, Annie?'

'Why do you?' asked Annie.

'Witness is not answering the question, your honour,' smiled Richard.

'I don't like having lodgers,' replied Annie. 'They invade your space and steal your milk. Not to mention the phone bill.'

'That's not what I meant.'

'So, are you trying to confuse the witness?'

He placed his cards on the table.

'I'm trying to find out if there is a man in your life,' then added as an afterthought, 'or woman.'

'Plenty of women,' said Annie. 'That's the trouble. I'm on call to my mums, I work long hours, that's enough.'

Richard laughed. 'So, who hurt you?'

'That's a cliché,' said Annie.

'Clichés are based on truisms.'

'Touché, Inspector.'

'So, what's the truth?'

Annie sighed and stopped sketching to look at him. Her private life was something that she liked to keep private but she suddenly found herself wanting to open up to this man. 'I had an affair with a married man,' she said.

'Don't tell me,' said Richard, 'he promised to leave his wife for you.'

'Oh no,' disagreed Annie. 'I wouldn't fall for a line like that. I didn't even know he was married.'

'How long did it last?'

'Two and a half years.'

Richard whistled. 'Didn't you guess?'

Annie shook her head. 'Not a clue. He worked for the European Commission in Brussels so he travelled a lot. Whenever he was home he spent most of his time with me. I stayed at his flat, cooked him meals, we went away for weekends together.'

'And where was his wife?'

'In Brussels. She is a very beautiful French national working in the same Department. They had been married for four years.' Annie returned to her picture with a shrug.

'Any children?'

'Not then.'

'So how did you find out?'

'I didn't. At least not on my own.' Annie stopped drawing for a moment to push her hair back behind her ears. 'He sent me a letter.'

'What?'

Annie shook her head again.

'His wife became pregnant so he decided to settle permanently in Brussels. He sold his flat, shipped his furniture and got rid of all the excess baggage he didn't need. That included me.'

'Annie, I am so sorry.'

She shrugged. 'It's old news now. He's been gone two years.'

'Did you ever contact him?'

'What was the point? Besides, I didn't want to give him the pleasure of thinking I cared.'

'But you must have done at the time?'

'No.' Annie returned to her sketch. 'I think I was in love more with the idea of him. I liked the fact that he didn't have a boring, predictable life and I enjoyed the time I had to myself. I think if I had really loved him I wouldn't have been able to bear even a day without seeing him or speaking to him.' Annie looked up again and held Richard's gaze. 'I would have got goose bumps every time I thought of him and turned to jelly whenever he entered the room.'

Richard held her gaze, feeling himself flushing. Annie dropped her eyes. 'In the end, I realised he was a super-sized prat who didn't deserve me. I returned his letter marked, Not known at this address. After I had steamed it open and resealed it of course.'

She closed the sketch book with a flourish and picked up her mug of tea.

'Mmm, perfect,' she said. 'So, what about you? How come you're alone?'

Richard stared at her thoughtfully as if making up his mind about something.

'Very few people know my story,' he began, 'so if I share this with you…'

'You'll have to kill me?'

Richard laughed. 'Wrong movie.'

'But you would like me to keep it to myself?'

'Exactly.'

'On my mother's life,' said Annie.

'Is your mother alive?'

Annie grinned. 'Actually, no.'

'So, try again.'

'On my life,' said Annie. 'You can trust me.'

Richard pondered for just a few seconds. 'Yes, I think I can.'

He sighed and looked down at his hands which were clasped together so tightly his knuckles were white. Annie wanted to reach over and touch them but feared that she would break some spell.

'I was married,' he said. 'For three years. My wife was murdered.'

Annie's face froze and her eyes widened with horror. 'Richard, I am so sorry.'

'Thank you, but it was almost five years ago. At the time it was pretty dreadful and I suffered from guilt as much as sorrow but the pundits are not far off when they say that time heals. It leaves a bloody, nasty scar but the pain eases.'

'Why guilt?' asked Annie, still upset at what she had just heard. Murders were something that she read about in the newspaper or saw dramatized on TV. She had never knowingly had contact with anyone close to a murder victim. Now this handsome, calm and slightly aloof man was sharing his personal horror with her.

Richard sighed. 'We had been talking about divorce for almost a year. It wasn't a great marriage and we had both had enough. I deliberately took night duty so that I wouldn't have to spend too much time with her. If I had been there, she might still be alive.'

'You can't know that.'

'I know that a man entered the house and stabbed her right through the heart before leaving her to bleed to death. She was alone with no-one to protect her. I should have been there.'

'Was the man caught?'

Richard shook his head. 'A man was arrested but there was insufficient evidence and he was released.'

'God, that's awful.'

Richard ran his hands through his hair and leaned towards Annie.

'I have spent the last five years going over every detail of the weeks leading up to her murder. I feel sure I'm missing something that is right underneath my nose but I have no idea what it is. However I felt about our relationship, I never wished Debbie any harm and she didn't deserve what happened to her. We were both bloody miserable at the time and just wanted the marriage over so we could move on and find some happiness. I won't give up until someone is brought to justice for denying her that.'

'Do you think the man might be re-arrested?'

Richard shook his head. 'I don't think it was him.'

'What makes you say that?'

'He was a gardener, handyman. He did lots of small jobs for us so his DNA and fingerprints were all over the place. But he was a nice guy, harmless. And Debbie definitely had her secrets.'

'What do you mean?'

'She was pregnant.'

'What?'

Richard grimaced. 'Oh, it wasn't my baby. We hadn't slept together for a very long time. I only found out at the post mortem. But, like you, I had no idea that she was seeing someone else.'

'Did you find out who it was?'

'No. I have a few suspicions but she was careful. I can't help wondering if whoever she was seeing had something to do with her death.'

'Did you tell the police?'

Richard shook his head. 'It's all supposition and no-one has any idea who her lover was. So what was the point? It wouldn't have changed anything.' Richard shrugged. 'Like I said, it was a long time ago.'

'Have you dated since?'

'Half-heartedly,' he admitted, 'but quite honestly it's more trouble than it's worth.'

'We're in agreement on that one then,' said Annie.

'Only up until now.' His eyes were searching hers. Annie began to tremble and her face flushed. He watched her lick her lips as if her mouth was suddenly dry and she cleared her throat.

'What do you mean?'

'Well, I'm willing to do an about face if you are?'

'Change my mind, you mean?'

'At least enough to have dinner with me when this case is over.' Richard held his breath, preparing for her refusal.

She answered without hesitation. 'I'd like that.'

Her smile was radiant but before Richard could reply Collins came scurrying through the canteen towards them.

'Boss, boss, you've got to come.' His voice was loud in Richard's ear.

He turned with a scowl. 'What is it, Collins?'

'We've got the car, boss.'

'Where was it?'

'Not far from the house,' said Collins.

Richard scraped back his chair.

'Sorry, Annie, I've got to go.'

'Wait, Richard.' She leaned forward and handed him the sketch pad. He took it with a smile and a wink that warmed Annie's heart. 'Go home and get some rest,' he said.

In the lift, he opened the sketch pad to find a perfect likeness of himself smiling from the page. She had signed it in the bottom corner, to Richard love Annie.

'Blimey, boss,' said Collins, looking over his shoulder, 'she's made you almost good looking.'

'Get to work,' ordered Richard with a smile as the lift doors opened.

Chapter Twenty-Two

It was gone five pm and several members of the team were already at their desks as Masterton positioned herself in front of the whiteboards. She was pleased with the progress they had made that day but saddened that they had not been fast enough to prevent another death. She had left the Met and moved to Worcester so that she could spend more time with her children while they were at school. The move had been a good one and twelve years later with her children flown from the nest she nurtured a vision of a gentle amble towards retirement. Three days ago that bubble had been cruelly burst. She addressed the team.

'We're getting new information in all the time and we're making good progress. So, well done all of you. Now, listen up. We have found Masood's rental car parked two streets from the rented house even though he had access to a garage and driveway. He was obviously being cautious. The front passenger seat was heavily blood-stained. Forensics are on to it but we are expecting them to confirm that it is Soraya Haq's blood. Soraya's jewellery was in the glove box. There is also evidence that Soraya was living at the house with Masood. Collins. CCTV, please'

Collins came forward and attached a street map to the board. He pushed in pins as he spoke. The room was silent as the team absorbed the briefing they were being given.

'We picked up the car on Sunday evening, heading towards Warndon, here.' Collins pointed to one of the pins on the map. 'Time is 19:30. At 19:40 the car changes direction and heads out towards Shrub Hill.

There is no CCTV actually in Shrub Hill Road and we don't see the car again until it reappears at the Asda supermarket. At 20:42 Masood is seen leaving the supermarket and heading back towards Shrub Hill. At 20:59 we pick the car up again heading towards Annie's address. This line,' he said, pointing to a dotted line drawn on the map, 'shows the route from Shrub Hill to the Asylum Centre.'

'Thank you, Collins,' said Masterton. 'What we now know is that Masood arrived in Britain on the twenty-fifth of last month when he rented a car at the airport. The following day he rented the house, paying cash and informed the landlady that he was waiting for his pregnant sister-in-law and his brother to arrive. Soraya Haq arrived in the country from Pakistan last Monday, the twentieth. She had medical clearance to travel in late pregnancy. We believe she is the woman known as Baseera. On Tuesday, she visited the clinic at the Asylum Centre seeking obstetric care. Unfortunately, a disturbance spooked her and she ran. On Friday, she left the rental property with Masood. They were driving towards Warndon when something happened that made them stop. Evidence from the recovered car and the body suggests that Soraya had started bleeding. She was probably in pain and would have been scared.'

'Poor sod,' said Collins.

'The route taken,' continued Masterton, 'suggests that they were heading either for the Asylum Centre or the hospital. Wherever they were going they were almost certainly hoping to find medical assistance there. They never made it. On the way, Masood stops at the warehouse. The babies were born there sometime between 19:40 and 20:42. We know that Masood left Soraya to buy towels and a holdall, presumably because by this time the babies were dead. At 20:59 Masood is on his way to Annie's house with the babies. We know that he was being followed from the supermarket and presumably the tail had been with him all evening. Forensics puts Masood and Soraya in the car and puts Masood at the scene of Soraya's delivery and death. DNA has confirmed that Masood was not the father of the twins.'

'Is there any evidence to suggest that the three tails went into the warehouse?' asked Richard.

'None,' replied Masterton. 'We can assume that Masood and Soraya were followed from the house but whatever they were after, it wasn't Soraya and her babies.'

'Where does that leave us, boss?' asked Spooner.

'It should leave us with a closed case,' said Masterton.

Cries of 'What?' and muttered groans swept around the room. Masterton held up her hands to silence them.

'There is nothing here to suggest that this woman's death was anything more than a tragic accident. We have two immigrants, chased and terrified who do nothing worse than fail to get medical help. The mother and her children are now dead and there is no-one else involved. We don't need to waste any more of the taxpayers' money chasing ghosts.'

The mumbles continued.

'However!' she said, pointing to the board again. 'On Saturday morning, Masood was executed in cold blood and in broad daylight. His house was searched from top to bottom. We now have three suspects loose in this city and our job is to find them before anyone else loses their life. Questions.'

She began to write on the board.

'Why were Soraya and Masood here? What was Masood hiding? Who and where are our gunmen?'

Masterton rapidly allocated jobs sending Richard back to his desk research and scattering the rest of the team. He had barely begun when his phone rang with a call from one of the constables on house to house.

He put his hand over the receiver and called to Masterton while he continued to listen. 'Boss!' She hurried to his desk. Richard said his thanks to the phone and replaced the receiver. 'The landlady came up with one of the references that Masood gave and uniform have paid him a visit. He's a hairdresser in the shops nearest to Masood's house. His name is Kambiz. Apparently, he is a distant cousin of Masood. He's been living in Britain since he was twelve years old and hadn't seen Masood in all that time. Masood stayed with him his first night in the country and Kambiz helped him find the house. This could explain why they came to Worcester in the first place.'

'Anything else?'

'Nothing that connects Kambiz to the shooting. But, we do have a confirmed name for the man in the photo. One Ali Haq, Soraya's husband, and Masood's brother.'

'Any reason why anyone would want to shoot Masood?' asked Masterton.

'Nothing specific, according to Kambiz. He hasn't had much contact with his cousin over the last decade and thinks Masood was a guy just looking out for his brother and sister-in-law. However, Kambiz gave us another name, Hajji. Kambiz described him as some sort of big cheese and warlord. He is big trouble, anyway. Kambiz reckons he is rumoured to be in the country but he doesn't know why. He thought that if anything was going down in the Afghan community this Hajji would have a hand in it. Kambiz said that his family still in Afghanistan believe that Masood was involved with Hajji in some way.'

'OK, Richard. Follow this up and see what you can find.'

Masterton addressed McIntyre at the adjacent desk. 'Anything back from ballistics?'

'Browning nine millimetre,' offered McIntyre. 'We've run the marks through the computer. It's never been used before.'

'Well, let's make sure it's not used again,' she replied.'

Within the hour Richard was tapping on Masterton's door.

'I've got something. My desk, boss.'

He sat down and tapped at the keyboard. A picture of the man from the photograph with Soraya rolled down the screen. McIntyre swivelled his chair across to Richard's desk for a better look. Richard considered the face of the man with life and light in his eyes. How would he look when he heard that his wife and twin sons were dead?

'From the NCA,' said Richard. 'His name is confirmed as Ali Haq from Afghanistan. They have no photos of Hajji but they certainly know of him. Hajji is a top level Taliban police officer and master criminal. He is currently on the wanted list in eleven countries including the UK. It seems he slips into a country and organises a few lucrative illegal activities before disappearing as quickly as he came. He never stays anywhere long enough to get caught. As far as public records go, this man is a ghost.'

Masterton stood up and massaged the small of her back as she listened to Richard. She was aware that the office had gone quiet as the team members still working at their desks listened to the conversation.

'There is no official record of Masood or Ali being directly involved in illegal activities but Masood has been confirmed as a frequent associate of Hajji's so there is an assumption that Masood is on the payroll. They have no convictions recorded and no arrests. Ali seems to have kept himself respectable, to the point where he left his native Kabul to set up home in Herat. He has been resident there for three years and has become a respected leader in the community. He is known only because of his brother, Masood, hangs out with Hajji.'

'How does he earn his living?' asked Masterton.

'Ali is a pharmacist, all above board. But this is the good part,' continued Richard. 'Six weeks ago the NCA received intelligence that a man was claiming to have enough evidence to bring down Hajji for good. They are taking this seriously.'

'Why are the NCA so interested in an Afghan?' asked Masterton.

'Child pornography amongst other things. Hajji has a crime network that stretches across Western Europe and the Middle East. Drug trafficking, human trafficking, prostitution, pornography, you name it if it makes money he probably has a department to deal with it. The caller offered the evidence in exchange for new identities and UK citizenship for himself and his immediate family.'

'Comprising?' asked Masterton.

'Comprising, two men and one woman.'

'So if we assume that the snitch is Ali Haq, we can assume that he was going to shop Hajji?'

'One of them was. What we don't know is who actually made the contact. It could have been Ali or Masood. What we do know is that one of them was bringing the evidence to Britain.'

'Do we know what evidence?' asked Masterton.

'Everything needed to bring down his organisation. Names, dates, contacts, trafficking routes, bank accounts, enough to smash the whole European network. Someone has made a copy of Hajji's laptop which allegedly never leaves his sight.'

'So how could they have accessed it?'

'Ali and Masood are brothers remember, and Masood may have been working with Hajji. The NCA are not sure what the connection is between the three men but for some reason the two brothers want Hajji convicted.'

'I wonder why they would be doing this?' mused Masterton. 'I can't see that money is the motive.'

'We might not be able to establish the motive without finding Ali, but maybe with twins on the way he wanted a better future for his children. Freedom, a life in the West? He would need money for that.'

'How was the evidence going to be delivered?' asked Masterton.

'In person, and on a USB.' Richard smiled as he held out his open hand to his colleagues. 'Small enough to fit in the palm of the hand.'

This revelation was greeted by murmurings from around the room as another piece of the puzzle slotted neatly into place.

'And we can assume they haven't found it yet.'

'No.' Richard shook his head. 'Masood's house had been ransacked from top to bottom. If they had found it they would have stopped searching and scarpered. We should get the bodies of the babies re-checked and we need to talk to Annie again to see if she knows anything about it.'

'And we need to find Ali,' said Masterton.

'Before the bad guys do,' agreed Richard.

Chapter Twenty-Three

Annie woke with a start, still fuddled from painkillers. She had gone straight home after the interview and lain down in her pretty bedroom to rest her ankle. She must have drifted off. All she seemed to do lately was sleep and she was starting to get annoyed with herself. The sun was streaming through her bedroom window and she blinked at the clock beside her bed. It was just gone four and she hadn't been asleep for long so she closed her eyes wondering what had woken her and whether she could drift away again. Being awake meant thinking about the dead baby boys and that was something still too tragic and raw for Annie to deal with right now. She would think about Inspector Richard Shaw instead. She tried to conjure up his startling eyes and confident smile and the way she felt when he smiled at her. She was beginning to regret leaving him her sketch pad.

A faint thump from the room below made her open her eyes and sit up in bed, tense with anticipation. She listened intently in case she had been mistaken while her brain sifted through possible options for the noise: stupid cat, postman, a knock on the door. There was nothing. Annie began to relax when something at the periphery of her vision moved. The scream of terror that began to escape from her throat was strangled as a rough hand clamped itself over her mouth and an arm came around her neck to choke her cries. She tried to claw at the arm around her neck but her bandaged left hand was useless and the arm that was holding her too huge and strong.

Adrenaline cleared Annie's head as she was dragged from the bed by her neck, fear draining the strength from her legs even as she kicked and struggled to try and free herself. A second man appeared and Annie was held on either side unable to run. She had no time to think or analyse what was happening. She wanted to speak, to ask what this person wanted but it was all she could do to drag oxygen into her lungs through the stinking, rancid hand.

As she was pulled to her feet she saw another man approaching her from the bedroom doorway. He was not much taller than Annie herself but he was strong and wiry. She could see the outline of his biceps through his too small shirt. He brought his face so close to Annie's that his breath soured what little air was reaching her lungs. Annie was helpless and she knew it. But even in her terror, she remembered that she was good with faces. She should commit this face to memory so that she could draw it for Richard. Richard! How she needed him now. She stared at the cruel face before her, the unshaven skin pocked with scars, the damp, fleshy lips that were parting to reveal crooked teeth stained almost to blackness. Dark, bushy eyebrows were hooded over vicious eyes and they were staring straight into Annie's.

The man must have given some signal to her captors because they suddenly released their grip on Annie. With her head down, legs trembling and gasping for breath as she held her throat with her good hand, Annie failed to see the blow. With all her weight on her good leg, she was knocked flying from her feet by a stinging pain across her mouth. As she struggled to her knees, she tasted blood and when she looked up she saw that the wall was sprayed a bright, bleeding red. The second blow caught her beneath the eye and sent Annie sprawling as her head burst into a thousand fragments of pain. She lay gasping, struggling to breathe while she tried to fight off the waves of nausea rising from her stomach.

An order in a language that Annie did not understand was barked out and she was hauled to her feet. Her arms were held firmly behind her back, bruising her skin, blood dripped from the split that had opened up her lower lip and the pain in her face and head made her certain she would be sick. As Annie's legs threatened to collapse, the man holding her lifted her up to stand and face those bleak, black eyes.

The man was smiling now, enjoying himself. He looked at Annie for a long time before he reached out a hand and caressed her breast through her clothing. Her instinct was to flinch and pull away but she was already too battered and bruised to do even that. She closed her eyes as tears began to roll down her face to mingle with the blood and saliva on her T-shirt. She wanted to cry out but had only the strength to keep breathing. As long as she was breathing she was alive. They could do what they liked with her as long as she stayed alive.

The three men were laughing.

She was suddenly jerked upright and her eyes flew open. The man in front of her addressed her.

'Where is it?' he demanded.

It took Annie several attempts to form the one word.

'What?'

This time, the man's balled fist thudded into her abdomen. Annie fell forwards, hanging from her captured arms, retching and choking as pain and nausea overwhelmed her. All she could see was a storm of stars and blackness and her legs could barely support her weight. Annie knew then that she was going to die. Once again she was jerked upwards.

'Where is USB?'

Even if Annie knew what to say, she was unable to speak. How many more breaths left, she thought? She closed her eyes and began to count, one, two… The next blow was to Annie's head. It was the last. As her head jerked to the side, her arms were released and she crashed into the corner of her dressing table and into merciful blackness.

The interrogator kicked Annie twice to make sure that she was finished then began to harangue his accomplices for letting go of her. How could they be so stupid? Now she was no use to them. They would have to search themselves. Had they forgotten already how long such a search would take?

Two of the men began with Annie's bedroom, quickly and methodically searching every space in the room, slashing pillows and emptying cosmetics to find the elusive flash drive. The third man left to search the sitting room.

A shout from downstairs halted the search and without speaking the two men in the bedroom ran downstairs leaving Annie crumpled beside her bed. A red stain crept stealthily around her head. The man who had been searching downstairs was at the window talking hurriedly. A blue light could be seen in the distance. Without another word, the three men slipped from the back door and out to their waiting car.

By the time the squad car was outside the three men had vanished.

Chapter Twenty-Four

Richard was still browsing the NCA file when a sudden thought sent torrents of ice down his spine. He grabbed his mobile phone and sprinted to Masterton's office. His face was white.

'Richard, you look as if you've seen a ghost. What's wrong?'

'Masood was followed by the men who killed him.'

'Yes?'

'They followed him home *after* he had dumped the babies. So it stands to reason they must have been following him *when* he dumped the babies. And they didn't find what they were looking for.'

'Annie.' she said. 'They know where she lives.'

They were in the car in minutes. Richard was in the driving seat and Masterton already on the radio as she called for back up to Annie's address. The reply she received drained any remaining colour from both their faces.

'Officers and ambulance already at the scene,' was the response.

Richard pressed down even harder on the accelerator and with blue lights and sirens he tackled the city traffic as if they were stragglers at Silverstone.

'What information do you have?' asked Masterton into the radio.

'Triple nine received seventeen minutes ago from a neighbour stating robbery in progress. Three men were seen breaking and entering.'

'Shit!'

Masterton glanced at Richard. His mouth was set in a firm line as he concentrated on getting them through the traffic as quickly as humanly possible. She returned to the radio and requested an update.

'No sign of the suspects but a female has been assaulted.'

'Oh God!' was all Richard said as he swung the car into Annie's street.

'Don't contaminate the scene, Richard,' warned Masterton. 'If she's been hurt we need to get these bastards.'

Richard was in his overalls and running before Masterton had removed her jacket. He flashed his ID at the sergeant at the door and raced into the house. He groaned as he saw the rubbish tip that used to be Annie's beautiful home. He took the stairs two at a time, panting with fear as much as exertion as he flew into Annie's room. He saw at once that it was empty and trashed and amongst the debris, he saw Annie's blood staining the walls and carpet. He turned and headed back downstairs.

At the front door of the house, Masterton was talking to the constable on duty. She held up her hands to halt Richard and when he stopped in front of her she put her hand on his arm.

'She's been taken to the hospital,' said Masterton. 'She's been badly beaten but she's alive.'

A moan escaped Richard's lips as he slumped back against the wall in the hallway. Masterton patted his arm.

'Do you know where she keeps her car keys?'

Richard looked confused. 'I think I saw them in the kitchen by the phone,' he said.

'Watch how you drive,' she said.

Richard understood at once. He grabbed Annie's car keys and headed for the hospital still wearing his forensic suit.

At the by now very familiar hospital Richard ran straight through to the Accident & Emergency Department's treatment area. A large central nursing station was surrounded by curtained cubicles. Richard thrust his ID at the first nurse he saw.

'D I Richard Shaw,' he said. 'I'm looking for Annie Collings.'

'Oh. I need to check.' The nurse seemed flustered and Richard hopped from one foot to the other as she shuffled through notes on one of the desks.

'I'm sorry, Inspector, she's already gone to theatre.'

Richard felt himself deflating as if all the air was being sucked from his lungs.

'I need to speak to someone about her,' he demanded.

The nurse looked at him nervously, sensing his agitation. 'Wait there.'

She disappeared through a doorway and Richard waited impatiently.

Hospitals are like another country, he thought. If you have been brought up in them, trained in their language and culture, then you can slip into them like an old pair of shoes, comforting, close-fitting and familiar. Richard thought of himself more as a tourist, someone who visited often during his days on the beat, collecting drunks on a Saturday night or interviewing victims and villains. He couldn't claim to understand everything that went on there, but he felt reasonably comfortable in the Accident & Emergency Department as well as the canteen and he was on more than nodding terms with some of the staff. Today, though, he felt like an outsider, completely out of his depth, struggling to find his way in unfamiliar territory. He wondered why it was that simply knowing Annie could have affected his equilibrium quite so badly.

When the door reopened a smiling man in a white coat came forward with his hand outstretched. He was in his fifties with greying hair and a network of laughter lines around his face. Richard felt relieved that Annie had been cared for by someone who looked experienced and kind. He shook the doctor's hand.

'I'm Doctor Latham,' he said. 'Why don't you come through?'

He directed Richard back through the doorway into a cramped office. A desk and chair were against one wall with a low seat and a filing cabinet against the other. The desk was piled with patient notes and paperwork which the doctor pushed aside.

'Sorry about the chair,' he said as he indicated that Richard should sit. 'We have to be grateful for what we're given these days.'

Richard lowered himself down. 'I understand you can tell me about Annie Collings,' he began.

The doctor held up a hand. 'Do you mind if I see some identification first?'

'I'm sorry,' said Richard, reaching into his pocket to show his ID.

'We get all sorts in here,' apologised the doctor.

'I understand,' said Richard. 'It was my error. 'About Annie Collings?'

'Ah, yes.' The doctor was searching for a sheet of paper on his desk which he consulted briefly before he spoke. 'She was brought in by ambulance unconscious and badly beaten.'

'How bad?'

The doctor consulted his paper again. 'She has multiple bruises and contusions on the face and arms, broken ribs, and a suspected ruptured spleen.'

Richard felt the colour drain from his face and he was forced to clasp his hands together to stop them from shaking.

'She was taken to theatre just a few minutes before you got here,' said the doctor. 'She will almost certainly need a splenectomy.'

'How would she have sustained that injury, Doctor?'

'I can't be sure of course, but looking at the state of her I would put my money on a boot. She looked as if she had been kicked.'

Richard felt a tingling in his nose that suggested tears. He hadn't cried since his wife was killed. He wasn't going to give in now. He took several deep breaths while the doctor again consulted his notes.

'Fortunately for her,' he continued now, 'she received a head injury.'

'Fortunately?' asked Richard.

The doctor nodded. 'It would have knocked her straight out. The bruising to the central torso was all on one side. Her injuries suggest that she was kicked while she was on the floor. If she had been conscious she would have moved around trying to protect herself.'

When Richard was eleven years old, he climbed the fence at the bottom of the garden with his older brother and younger sister. Their mother had berated them repeatedly about leaving the safety of the garden, but the green meadow behind their house was as tempting as the apple in Eve's hand. They had run away quickly before they were spotted and called back, giggling and whispering about who could climb the highest in the oak tree at the end of the meadow.

Richard's brother was taller and stronger than him, but as Richard climbed his weight caused the branches to creak and sway until he lost his nerve and stopped, claiming that he was too tired to continue. Richard was smaller and lighter and laughed delightedly as he reached Patrick's waist, then his shoulders and was soon passing him so that his knees were level with his nose. As he climbed above Patrick's head, his brother and sister began to worry and call him back. If anything happened to Richard, they knew that they would be for it. But Richard ignored his siblings. He was invincible. He would climb to the very top and make them all swear that he was the king of the castle. The branch beneath his foot cracked and fell away beneath the sole of his shoe so that for a brief moment he dangled, scrabbling with his feet to try and regain a foothold. His sister, Emily, squealed from the ground below where she was standing with her hands thrown back, watching every move.

'Be careful, Richard,' she cried.

Richard looked down to grin at them, still sure of himself, but the branch to which he was clinging could no longer bear his weight and it gave way, sending Richard tumbling between the branches while he tried his best to break his fall.

As he hit the ground with a thud, his left arm, which arrived before the rest of him, fractured in two places. The air was forced from his lungs and he lay motionless apart from the heaving of his chest as he tried to recapture the air that he needed to answer the anxious questioning of his siblings. As the oxygen finally reached his lungs, the pain in his arm sprang to life, draining the colour from his face and making him tremble with shock. His older brother ran to the house for help while his sister stroked his hair and begged him not to die. Richard remembered lying helplessly on the ground unable to move. It was the first and last time in his life that he had experienced such overwhelming physical pain.

Until now. Now his whole body screamed with anger and distress.

He turned his attention back to the doctor.

'And the head injury?'

'Not too severe at present. She was certainly considered stable enough for an anaesthetic. We will, of course, be hoping that there is no bleeding to the brain but at the moment it looks like a straightforward concussion.'

'Will she recover?' asked Richard.

The doctor put down his piece of paper to address Richard. 'I can't guarantee anything. She is critical and currently undergoing life-saving surgery. But she is in the best hands and I feel confident at this stage that she will pull through. Physically, at least.'

Fingers of relief began to pluck at the fear encasing Richard's heart.

'How long will she be in theatre?'

'It depends on what they find,' said Doctor Latham, 'but probably an hour or two and I suspect she will be ventilated for a while afterwards to give her body time to recover. If you're hoping to interview her it may be a day or two I'm afraid.'

Richard cleared his throat which was clogged with the debris of emotion. 'And what is the impact of having her spleen removed?'

'She will be more prone to infection so will need to keep her immunisations up to date and will have to take care to avoid infections as far as she can. But the liver takes over most of the functions of the spleen when it has been removed. She should recover well.'

Richard nodded his thanks. 'I'll leave you my card, Doctor. I will be grateful if you could get someone to call me the minute she wakes up.'

'Of course,' replied Doctor Latham.

'We will also be arranging some protection for this patient. We believe that the men who did this to her have already murdered. They were disturbed tonight by a vigilant neighbour but there is a risk that they will come after her again.'

'What sort of protection?' asked the doctor.

'A protective cordon of armed officers plus one officer at every entrance to the building,' said Richard as he tried to calculate the cost and hoped the budget would stand it.

'I'll need to refer you to the duty manager.'

'That's fine,' said Richard. 'I can do that now.'

While Richard waited at the nurse's station for the duty manager to arrive, Masterton appeared closely followed by four armed officers. Richard actually found himself smiling with relief. Masterton followed his gaze and interpreted the look.

'You didn't think I would leave her to the mercy of those sadistic bastards, did you?' she asked.

'Of course not,' said Richard, 'I was just worried about your budget.'

'Bugger the budget,' she replied. 'Apart from anything else, Annie is our only living witness. If that doesn't get it past the Super nothing else will. So, tell me what you know.'

Richard filled Masterton in on all he had been told.

'Ok. Now go home.'

Richard was flabbergasted.

'I'm not going home, boss.'

'That's an order, Richard.'

He opened his mouth to complain but the look in her eyes made him close it.

'There is nothing you can do here and if you want to keep a vigil you can do it at home.'

'Boss...'

'I'll see that she's kept safe, Richard, you can be sure of that. But you need to go home now.'

Richard felt too angry to reply. He turned and left the Department and headed outside to slump in Annie's car. He started the engine and drove out of the car park but before he had even left the campus he had to pull over and park because he could no longer see through the tears that were streaming down his face. He rested his forehead between his hands which were still clenched around the steering wheel and he surrendered to the shuddering sobs that wracked his body.

When he could finally breathe normally again he searched around in the car for some tissues and found them in the glove box. He blew his nose noisily and wiped at his face. His anger at Masterton had evaporated with the first sob. She had seen what he didn't realise was there and had protected him in the only way she could, by sending him away. But when he thought of Annie being punched and kicked the anger inside him was enough to kill a man with his bare hands. They would not escape justice. He would make sure of that.

Chapter Twenty-Five

Richard lay on his sofa staring at the television screen as he flicked from one channel to the next. His flat was modern and minimal. He had taken very little from the marital home, not wanting to be surrounded by reminders and memories of the past. Over the last five years, he had added nothing more than the bare necessities of daily living. Right now, he was glad not to be distracted by furnishings and fripperies. He lifted his head to sip absent-mindedly at the can of beer in his hand and could think of nothing but Annie's face as she walked into the café. When the buzzer sounded he ignored it, wanting to stay where he was, with Annie. The buzzer continued insistently but Richard took another sip of beer and closed his eyes. Only when his mobile rang did he reluctantly take the call.

'I'm freezing my backside off down here, do you mind opening the bloody door.'

'Sorry, boss,' said Richard, still conditioned to follow orders.

He was waiting at his open door as Masterton emerged from the lift carrying a brown carrier bag. She noted his swollen eyes but pushed past him into the flat without comment.

'What were you doing?' she demanded.

Richard shrugged. 'I was thinking, boss.'

'We're off duty now, you can call me Diane,' she instructed as she handed him her coat. 'Where are your dishes?'

Richard opened a cupboard to show her his sparse collection of crockery.

'Never mind,' she said. 'We'll eat out of the containers. Got any chopsticks?'

Chopsticks were something that Richard had plenty of and he retrieved four from a drawer.

'Can I get you a drink?' he asked.

'I'll have what you're having,' she said, indicating the beer can in Richard's hand.

'Don't bother with a glass. No need for washing up.'

Richard went to the fridge for the beer and motioned to Masterton to sit down. He switched off the television. Masterton removed the tin foil containers from the carrier bag and placed them on the coffee table and Richard helped to remove the lids.

'Get stuck in,' said Masterton. 'Chinese. And I don't want any waste.'

Without much appetite, Richard reluctantly helped himself to some noodles and then discovered that he was hungry after all.

'So, how are you holding up?' asked Masterton.

Richard regarded her gravely.

'I know why you're here, boss.'

'And why is that?'

'You're wondering if I'm up to the job.'

Masterton captured a wayward piece of pineapple and chewed it thoughtfully before she spoke.

'I know you're up to the job, Richard. You're the best detective I've got and I think you know that.'

Richard responded with an imperceptible nod.

'That's why I need you to be performing at one hundred per cent,' she continued. 'We've made amazing progress on this case in just a few days and I know that we can crack it. But I need to know that you can keep a lid on your personal feelings.

Richard's jaw tightened as he spoke. 'I'm up for this. You know that. I've got more reason than anyone to get the bastards responsible for this. Beating up an innocent woman and killing in cold blood? They're not even human.'

She observed him as he spoke. Nothing more than a rigid set to his face indicated that he was seething with pent up anger. Talk about control, she thought.

'You've really got it bad, haven't you? Want to tell me about it?'

He placed his chopsticks on the coffee table and sat back in his chair. He raised his eyes to the ceiling and took a deep breath before he spoke.

'I met Annie on Thursday night, as you know,' he began. 'I stopped at a café on my way back from the job. I don't know why I just couldn't seem to settle. It's like I was drawn there.'

Richard went on to describe his meeting with Annie.

'When she walked into that café, it was like she brought summer in with her. And everyone there felt it. I could feel the affection in the room and it was all for her. And she was so… so…' He struggled to find the right word. 'She was so together. There was one empty seat in the whole place and it was opposite me. I prayed to every deity known to man that she would not order a takeaway. And she didn't. She sat down right next to me.'

'What if she had ordered a takeaway?' asked Masterton.

'I think I would have followed her outside,' he said. 'When she drove off that night I felt as if my world had shifted. It looked the same but I knew that I would never feel the same about it ever again. Now, what's that all about?'

'It's called love, Richard,' smiled Masterton. 'Haven't you ever been in love?'

He shook his head vehemently. 'Not like this. Not that wham at first sight thing. I barely even know her.'

'Then it's about time. Wasn't it like that with Debbie?'

'Not even close. Debbie was beautiful. She could have been a model. Everyone thought she was stunning but she chose me for some bizarre reason. I think I married her because everyone else wanted to. I suppose she was a bit of a trophy. But it was always hard work with her. I had to think about everything that I did and said so that she didn't blow up and scream at me. But even in the very beginning, it wasn't the overwhelming attraction that I feel for Annie. Is that how it was with your husband?'

'It still is, Richard. I still happen to love my husband very much. Even after three children. I couldn't do this job without any of them.'

'What do you mean?'

'I do it because of them. I do it for them. I don't spend my days chasing bad guys for the sake of it. Or for the fantastic salary. I do it to make this world a safer place for my children and grandchildren. And I do it knowing that at the end of a day full of shit like today, I can go home to the company of my loved ones. They revive me.'

Richard nodded as he took up his chopsticks again. 'I'm beginning to understand.'

'Does she feel the same?'

Richard shrugged. 'To tell you the truth, I don't know for sure. I have been trying to keep my distance. And let's face it, I've only known her a few days.'

'But it feels like you've known her forever?'

'I feel like I've been waiting for her all my life. And then today happens.'

'And then today,' agreed Masterton.

Richard chased a piece of chicken around one of the containers before he gave up and stabbed at it, skewering it on the end of his chopstick.

'If I had been having a relationship or prior friendship with Annie, then I know that I should have declared that and been taken off the case. I also know that a relationship with a witness is considered a no-no. But none of these apply to me. I met her once in a café full of customers.'

'That's all it takes,' replied Masterton.

'That's not fair, boss, and you know it. I can't be disciplined for having feelings. If I acted on them, that would be a different matter.'

'I'm putting my own neck on the line here, Richard,' she pointed out. 'I am actually taking a risk.'

'The risk is,' he mused, 'that she will forever associate me with what's happened.'

'Won't you?'

'I don't care. Except that she's hurt.'

'Then neither will she.'

Richard rubbed his eyes with his hand.

'God, I hope you're right.'

Masterton leaned forward and placed a hand on his knee. 'I know I am.'

Richard moved his hand to cover his nose and mouth and she saw the effort it was taking him not to break down.

'It's going to be all right, Richard.'

His shoulders shuddered before he lifted his head and looked her straight in the eyes. 'I can do this, boss. I will do it. For her. I want to make the world a safer place for Annie. And I just want this to be over so that I can take her to dinner, get to know her better and act like a normal person.'

Masterton blew out a puff of air as she began to gather together the remnants of their meal into the carrier bag.

'Richard, you will never be normal.'

Richard feigned hurt but Masterton flapped her hand at him. 'That's what makes you an astoundingly special person and a bloody good detective. For God's sake, don't ever wish to be anyone other than yourself.'

'Sometimes, it would just be nice not to have to deal with scum every day of my life.'

'So, how was she the last time you phoned?'

Richard was caught and he knew it. He managed a smile. 'No change.'

'But stable?'

'Yes.'

'Then that's good news, isn't it?'

'I hope so. If she doesn't make it…' His voice trailed off.

Masterton stood up. 'She will make it. Now, I want you to get some sleep tonight and I'll see you back in the office at eight am.'

Richard closed his eyes with relief. 'Thank you.'

'But, Richard,' she began.

'I know,' he replied.

'I'm going to say it anyway. I want you better than your best. One slip and you're off my team. I can't do you any favours on this one.'

'You won't need to. You have my word.'

'Well, get me my coat,' she said. 'I have a family waiting.'

Chapter Twenty-Six

Sunday

There was a subdued hush when Masterton strode into the office at seven am the next morning. Although the team briefing was not scheduled until eight am, she was pleased to see her full team already hard at work at their desks and no-one was complaining about overtime. That included Richard who was as smart and well groomed as ever in a dark grey suit and tie. She caught his eye as she passed his desk and acknowledged his brief nod of thanks with one of her own.

Masterton hung up her coat and dropped her bag onto her desk. She took a few moments to scan her messages and order her thoughts before she went outside to call the team to attention. 'You're all here so we might as well make a start.'

She wrote 'Annie Collings' at the top of the board.

'Late yesterday afternoon, Annie Collings was viciously attacked in her own home and the place turned over. The three men responsible were disturbed by a treble nine from a neighbour.'

'How is she, boss?' asked Palmer.

Masterton looked at Richard as she spoke. His face remained impassive.

'She has been badly beaten and she has undergone surgery to remove a ruptured spleen.'

'Ruptured spleen? How did that happen?' asked Palmer.

'She was probably kicked while she was unconscious on the ground.'

Mutters of 'bastards' came from around the room.

'At this stage,' continued Masterton, 'we are assuming that they are the same men that murdered Masood.'

'But why, boss?' asked Spooner.

'I'm coming to that. Richard, would you like to fill us in?'

Richard strode to the front of the room as professional as ever. There was no suggestion that he had any emotional involvement in the case. His voice was steady as he spoke.

'Information received from the National Crime Agency yesterday suggests that the three men are searching for some sort of USB.'

Richard reached into the pocket of his trousers and pulled out a small metallic object which he held up.

'It's probably no bigger than this.'

'What do we think is on it, boss?' asked Palmer.

'Enough to bring down the empire of one of Europe's most wanted criminals,' replied Richard.

Richard took the whiteboard pen from Masterton and wrote the name 'Hajji' on the board.

'This guy has got a multi-million Euro empire stretching from Afghanistan to Ireland. If there is a profit involved and it's illegal he is into it. The NCA have been tracking him for several years now but this man is clever and powerful. He holds a senior Taliban position and has a loyal private army that he pays well. He is also as elusive as a wisp of vapour. There are no known photos of him and he is yet to be associated with any permanent physical location.'

'If he's so elusive, how do we know he is behind all this?' asked Spooner.

'Fair question,' replied Richard. Six weeks ago, the NCA were contacted by a man offering to trade the contents of Hajji's laptop for UK citizenship and new identities. He didn't give his name, but he did say that there would be two men and one woman. We are assuming that those three people were our dead woman Soraya, her brother-in-law Masood, also dead, and Ali Haq, Soraya's husband, and Masood's brother, whereabouts unknown. This photo,' said Richard stabbing at it with his forefinger, 'which was recovered from Masood's rented house shows Soraya with Ali Haq. We have reason to believe that Ali Haq is either already in the UK or will be arriving shortly. Meanwhile, we have got three armed thugs razing the ground before them.'

'So they must think the USB is already here,' offered Palmer.

'Which means that Masood or Soraya carried it into Britain,' agreed Richard. 'Given that Masood's home has been thoroughly ransacked, nothing has been found in his rental car and Annie's home has been partially searched, we can assume that the USB is still missing. That leaves our dead woman, Soraya.' Richard paused to tap the photo of the dead woman before continuing. 'Nothing was found on the dead woman's body or at the warehouse where she died. Her only known contact in the UK was with the midwife, Annie Collings. In the light of yesterday's events, we can assume that our three thugs think Annie may know something or may even be in possession of the USB. Unfortunately, we are not likely to be able to question her further for a day or two. We also know that the three men were disturbed by the 999 call so we can assume that if the USB was in Annie Colling's house, then it hasn't been found. Are there any questions?'

No-one spoke so Richard nodded at Masterton to indicate that he had finished and returned to his seat. Masterton took his place.

'Right, I want every man and his wife on CCTV. Those thugs must have been tailing Masood and Soraya for most of Thursday at least. I want their vehicle identified before anyone goes home tonight. Collins, see if there is anything we can do to enhance the tape from the supermarket. I know it's only a rear view but we should be able to get a description of their clothing and hair if nothing else. Spooner and Palmer, I want you two to get onto car hire companies, stolen cars, flight records, anything that might help us identify where and when these murderers came onto our patch. Richard, stick with the NCA. I want every known associate of Masood, Ali, and Hajji. Mug shots, vital statistics, shoe size, you name it, we're interested.'

'Question, boss,' said Collins.

'Go ahead, Collins.'

'If these villains,' he said, pointing at the incident board with his pen, 'are as bad as we think they are, you know, killing everyone that gets in their way and everything.' He paused as if trying to order his thoughts.

'Spit it out, Collins,' said Masterton.

'Well, the thing I don't understand, is why didn't they kill Annie Collings?' He looked around the team as if trawling for answers. 'Why leave her alive? Especially when she could identify them.'

'Good question, Collins,' said Masterton. 'Any ideas, team?'

Richard shifted in his seat before he spoke. 'Because they want her alive,' he said. 'We know they were beating her badly enough to try and get her to talk. But she was knocked unconscious. I am sure that was an error on their part. We also know that they were disturbed. That kick to the abdomen…' He paused and swallowed.

'Go on, Richard.' Masterton's voice was gentle.

'The kick was like one of them lashing out in temper. They hadn't finished with her. It was a sort of 'we'll be back' kick. They think she has the USB.'

'Maybe she does,' Spooner pointed out.

'I hear what you're saying, Richard,' said Masterton, 'and it is a good theory. Unfortunately, we won't know anything further until Annie Collings wakes up. Meanwhile, she'll have round the clock protection and I'll get a search warrant for her house. If the USB is there, we'll damn well make sure that we find it first.'

'Boss,' said Palmer, 'Annie Collings is a fantastic artist. When she regains consciousness we could get her to sketch her attackers.'

Richard's eyes swivelled to the sketch pad on his desk. Had it been moved? Damn! He should have locked it in his drawer but in the panic of yesterday he had run out of the office and left it in full view of the whole team. Everyone must have looked at it. He stared hard at Palmer but if she felt his eyes on her she refused to acknowledge them.

'Good thought, Palmer,' said Masterton, 'but I don't think Annie Collings will be picking up her paint brush for a while yet. Now, I have a press conference to prepare for and it looks like we are getting interest from the nationals so I don't want to be disturbed unless you have some information that will move this case forward. Get to work.'

Everyone complied without a murmur. The drudgery of criminal behaviour, violence, and sexual offences were a dim and distant memory as the team knuckled down to tackle the most serious crime of many of their careers. They needed to work well and work fast and they had no intention of letting their boss down. Against all the Health and Safety rules, Richard trawled through NCA files until his eyes were sore. Only when his vision began to blur did he leave his desk and go out to the car park at the back of the building. He went and sat in Annie's car while he called the hospital on his mobile.

'She's doing well,' said the nurse in charge. 'She's been stable overnight and is showing signs of regaining consciousness. The good news is that she underwent a partial splenectomy so she still has some functioning spleen left.'

Richard was smiling broadly as he flipped his phone closed. She was going to be ok. Suddenly the world seemed right again. He closed his eyes to savour the moment.

'Sleeping on the job, Inspector?'

Richard's eyes sprang open and he saw Masterton looking at him.

'I just needed some fresh air, boss,' he said.

'That's ok, Richard, so did I.' Then she added, 'You're looking happy. Good news I presume?'

Richard's smile lit up his face. 'She's doing well. Showing signs of waking up, and they only took part of her spleen.'

'Good,' Masterton smiled. 'Is this her car?'

'Yes, boss, I thought I would leave it here for now. This seems to be the safest place for it.'

'Yes, good idea. Has it been searched?'

'Yes, it's clean.'

Masterton's thoughts were already back on the case. 'Take your time,' she said. 'I'll see you inside.'

Richard pulled the lever to open the boot before he stepped from the car to check whether there was anything in it that Annie might need. It was empty apart from her black leather midwifery bag. He unzipped the main compartment and stared for a moment at the sterile packs of instruments inside. He saw Annie's face again, in the café and remembered her laughing when he had told her she was a midwife. He zipped the bag closed and locked the car securely before transferring the bag to the boot of his own car.

He made his way back to the computer. His short list of potential candidates for the three thugs was already nine files long and he expected it to be much longer before the day was over. If only Masood and Soraya were alive to tell their tales, things would be so different. If only the dead could talk. Above all, he knew that they needed to find Ali before anyone else did.

Chapter Twenty-Seven

'Boss. Boss.'

Collins burst through the office door with several members of the team in hot pursuit. There was an orange stain down the front of his tie where his energy drink had missed his mouth and sweat stained his armpits. He rushed over to the screen shedding cheesy wotsit crumbs from his trousers and began pressing buttons on the remote control while still calling for the DCI She was joined by Richard and the two WDCs who all waited, immobile with anticipation.

The disc began to play. They were watching the corner of a busy suburban street where a set of traffic lights was holding and releasing the cars like cows in a cattle race. As the traffic stopped and started, Collins slowed the film. The time said 20:46. Collins pointed to a blue Ford Fiesta, 'Masood's car after leaving the supermarket on Thursday, presumably on his way to Annie's address,' he said. He let the tape run and they watched the car turn the corner and disappear. Collins grinned at his audience as he traced it with his finger, anticipating a response, but they all knew better than to play guessing games. Collins rewound the film and ran it again, slower this time. As the Ford approached the lights, Collins pointed to a different car. 'Watch the grey Honda three cars behind,' said Collins. 'As it approaches the traffic lights they turn amber, the car speeds up and, watch.'

'You drive like that all the time,' joked McIntyre.

'Ah, but,' said Collins, wagging a finger at McIntyre as he magnified the side of the car as it turned the corner, 'I don't drive with two brutes in the car.'

Then they could all see, as the car turned the corner, the bulk of two large men in the passenger seats, one in the front, one behind.'

'Back and side view,' smiled Masterton, 'all we need now is the front.'

'And we've got the reggo, boss,' said Collins.

'Collins, I love you,' said Masterton. 'Now go and get me that car. There's a black forest gateau in it for you. The rest of you, keep looking.'

Collins was back at the door to Masterton's office within the hour. 'Boss?'

'Have you got me that car, Collins?' she asked.

'Yes and no, boss,' replied Collins.

'What sort of answer is that?'

Collins placed a piece of paper in front of her.

'This is the make and reggo of the car in the tape,' he pointed out, 'but DVLC have that reggo on a white Mercedes belonging to a retired bank manager in Lincolnshire. I called the local force and they've been around to check already. The Merc is Kosher.'

'So they've forged the number plates,' mused Masterton.

'Better than that, boss.' He placed a grainy photo in front of her. 'This is the same car on Monday morning in the vicinity of Masood's place. It's another side shot unfortunately but you can clearly see the outline of our three suspects. But look here.' He pointed to the grey Honda's registration plate.

'Different number,' remarked Masterton, 'cheeky beggars.'

'They're trying to stop us tracking them,' said Collins.

'Then why not just ditch the car?' queried Masterton. 'Too risky,' responded Collins. 'They would be gifting us their DNA. This is much lower profile.'

'Get Richard in here, will you?' she said.

'Already here, boss,' said a voice from the doorway.

'Do we know anyone around here that turns out dodgy number plates on demand?'

'Not off the top of my head,' said Richard, 'but it shouldn't be too hard to find out. Do you want me to get on to it?'

'No,' she shook her head. 'I want you to stick with the NCA. We've got to get some leads on those three jokers before someone else is found bleeding or worse. Get Sergeant Craven or James on to this one. Good work, Collins. Keep it up.'

Collins was practically preening as he left the office.

'What about you, Richard?'

'Fourteen possible suspects so far,' said Richard raising his eyebrows.

'That's narrowed the field then,' replied Masterton.

'But,' added Richard, 'we've got DNA from both crime scenes.'

'They're not being too careful are they?' observed Masterton.

'They're arrogant,' said Richard. 'Probably don't think they'll get caught.'

'Or maybe don't care whether they get caught.'

Richard shrugged. 'Either way, when we do get them, we should be able to use their DNA to place one or more of them at the crime scenes.'

'Have we got all three?' asked Masterton.

'Labs still working on it,' said Richard. 'We should know later today.'

'Thanks, Richard.' Masterton glanced at her watch. 'God, it's almost five, where does the time go?' She ruffled her fingers through her hair.

'Time for a break, boss?' suggested Richard.

Masterton looked up at him with a sigh. 'The clock's ticking on this one, Richard.'

'The team is tired,' he pointed out. 'They'll start making mistakes.'

'Yes, you're right.' She thought for a minute. 'I need Craven and James to stay on those plates but tell everyone else to go and get some rest. Back in at eight.'

'Will do, boss.'

'And send her my love if she's awake,' she said quietly as he left.

Annie wasn't awake. But she was stable and resting courtesy of a cocktail of painkillers. After Richard had sworn on his dead mother's life that he would not try and rouse Annie to ask her questions, the nursing staff finally allowed him in to see her.

She was in a private room with two armed officers stationed either side of the door. Richard showed his ID as he approached and the officers meticulously recorded his name and the time he entered the room. Annie was lying on a high bed surrounded by monitors, drips, and tubes. At first, her face was obscured by the nurse tending to a narrow plastic tube that was draining pink, watery fluid from a dressing on her abdomen. Richard sucked in his breath as he saw the black and purple bruises that covered her skin from armpit to hip.

The nurse tidied Annie's gown and pulled the sheet back over her. It was then that he saw her face.

In his worst imaginings, Richard had seen Annie's face battered to a pulp, and while it was true that her right eye was black and swollen, her lip cut and her left cheek covered with a patchwork of yellow and purple bruises, the face on the pillow was still undoubtedly Annie's.

'Hello there,' greeted the nurse before scribbling on one of the charts laid out on a high, narrow table at the end of the bed.

Richard held out his hand and introduced himself, 'DI Richard Shaw.'

The nurse shook his hand warmly. Doctors might be getting younger but cops were getting better looking by the day, she thought.

'I imagined she would look worse,' said Richard.

'She hit her head on something,' replied the nurse, 'and knocked herself out. That probably saved her life.'

'How is she?' asked Richard.

'Doing well,' said the nurse smiling. 'She'll be on the mend in no time.'

'Has she woken yet?' he asked.

The nurse gave a small chuckle. 'Oh yes, almost as soon as we extubated. She practically helped us pull the tubes out.'

'Did she say anything?'

She shook her head. 'Patients often have quite a sore throat when the endotracheal tube is removed and she is still on high doses of painkillers, but she's responding well. It's just a case of waiting for the drugs to work through her system. She will be sleepy for a while but she should be with us by tomorrow.'

'Can I sit with her for a while?' asked Richard.

'Ten minutes,' said the nurse checking her fob watch, 'and no longer. I'll be back in to throw you out.'

She left the room quietly and Richard fetched a chair from the corner of the room so that he could sit close to the bed. Annie's bare arms were lying on top of the bed with intravenous infusions running into both of them. Richard could clearly see handprints on her upper arms where she had been held by her attackers. He had prepared himself to suppress the anger that he was expecting to feel at the sight of her but somehow it didn't come. All he felt at that moment was relief that she had survived.

Her left hand was still bandaged from her fall so Richard very gently took her right hand in his, careful not to disturb any of the wires and tubes that were attached to her. He held the warm hand in his and stroked the smooth skin before bending his head to tenderly kiss where he had stroked.

When he lifted his head her eyes were open.

'Annie,' he said softly, 'can you hear me?'

He stood up so that he was leaning over her, still holding her hand. 'Annie,' he said again urgently. He desperately wanted to ask her if she had seen the USB. Just one question.

Her eyes turned to meet his. She moved her lips as if to speak but the effort was too great and she closed her eyes.

'It's ok,' said Richard inwardly sighing, 'don't try to speak.'

He sat down to kiss her hand again and felt the gentlest pressure from her fingers in return. Behind him, the door opened and the nurse entered the room.

'Time's up,' she said.

Richard let go of Annie's hand reluctantly and stood up to return the chair to the corner.

'Can I leave her this?' asked Richard.

He reached into his pocket to pull out a small cream-coloured bear barely six inches high. She wore a pink dress over her long, silky, cream fur and a lace bow was perched jauntily above her shiny, black eyes. He felt slightly embarrassed as he handed it over.

The nurse smiled at the little bear. 'She's really cute. I'll put her in Annie's hand, she'll feel the texture.'

Richard watched as the bear was placed carefully beneath Annie's right hand then dutifully followed the nurse from the room.

'We were asked to log all calls about Annie,' said the nurse, 'and apart from the police we've had one other enquiry today. Do you want to see?'

'Please,' replied Richard.

The nurse fetched a clipboard and read out the details for Richard to write in his notebook. 'She said she was a friend named Helen Lacey. She called at quarter past two asking to visit. We said we would call her back when Annie was well enough.'

'Thanks, that's great,' replied Richard and he signed the book to show that he was following up.

Chapter Twenty-Eight

Richard found Andrew and Helen's Northwick house easily and was heartened to see lights behind the curtains that had already been drawn against the approaching evening. He made sure that he called in his movements to control before he left his car but declined the backup that was offered.

The small, detached house was set back behind a modest front garden comprised mostly of a slightly shaggy lawn edged by some overgrown rose bushes. Underneath the front window, the sagging faces of end of season pansies seemed to nod at him as he stepped up to the front door and rang the bell. He heard a muttering of voices and then a shadow approached and opened the door.

'Can I help you?' asked Andrew as he squinted up at Richard, assuming from his smart suit and tie that he was there to sell something. Richard held up his ID.

'Detective Inspector Shaw,' he said. 'Is your wife home?'

Andrew was suddenly conscious of his worn track pants, bare feet, and the T-shirt that his daughter had just used to wipe her nose.

'Come in.' Andrew stepped back nervously. 'It's not about her driving, is it?' he joked.

Richard shook his head and waited to be shown into the front room.

Helen was sitting with her feet up on the sofa breastfeeding her newborn son. She had pulled a shawl over her exposed breast when the door bell rang and now there was little to see but the dark hair on Jacob's head which moved rhythmically with his sucking. Andrew removed a pile of laundry and a blue teddy bear from a chair so that Richard could sit down.

Andrew made the introductions. 'This is Detective Inspector Shaw, honey. Inspector, this is my wife, Helen. Can I get you anything to drink, Inspector?' he asked.

'A cup of tea would be nice,' replied Richard. 'Thank you.'

'How do you take it?' asked Andrew, not knowing what else to do but delay hearing whatever it was this policeman had come to accuse them of.

'White, no sugar,' said Richard. 'Thank you.'

'Excuse my husband,' smiled Helen when Andrew had gone. 'Policemen always make him nervous.'

'Are you Mrs Helen Lacey?' asked Richard.

'I am,' she responded, 'and if it's about that parking ticket I got at the library last week I will pay it. I've been too busy producing this one to get round to it.'

Helen had short, brown hair that was cut into a practical bob which framed her pretty face and warm smile.

'Do you know an Annie Collings?' asked Richard.

Helen started so suddenly that she pulled her nipple from Jacob's mouth and he immediately squalled in protest.

'Sorry, bubs,' she said as she latched him on again before turning back to Richard. 'Annie is my best friend,' said Helen. She delivered my daughter and then this little one early on Friday morning. She was supposed to come and see me for my post-natal check but some other midwife arrived saying that Annie was sick. I contacted the midwifery service and her manager told me that she's had an accident and was in the hospital but the hospital wouldn't tell me anything. What's happened to her? Do you know? Can you tell me?'

Helen paused for breath only when Andrew came back into the room with a tray holding three mugs of tea.

'Something has happened to Annie, Andrew. Can my husband stay, Inspector?'

'Yes, of course.' Richard took his tea gratefully and took a few sips before speaking.

'Some time after five yesterday evening, Annie was attacked in her home by one or more assailants. She was taken to hospital by ambulance where she is recovering from her injuries.'

'Injuries? What injuries?' Helen's evident distress was enough to upset Jacob who began to cry. Andrew leaned across to take the baby while Helen re-arranged her clothing and sat up on the sofa. Her hand shook as she took her tea.

'I'm afraid I can't give you any detailed information while our investigation is progressing.'

'But was she badly hurt? Will she be ok?'

'She is recovering,' said Richard. 'We don't yet know when she will be released from hospital, but when she is, she will be given police protection until her attackers are caught.'

'Like a safe house?' asked Andrew who had placed the baby on his shoulder and was gently rubbing his back.

Richard nodded.

'But why?' asked Helen. 'What's happened? Why has Annie been attacked? Is it something to do with one of her clients?'

'I really can't give you any detailed information at this stage. But I can tell you that Annie will be ok. I have just come from the hospital and she is doing well.'

'Can I see her?' asked Helen.

Richard shook his head. 'I'm afraid not. It's safer for you to stay away from her and refrain from all contact until the men that did this are safely behind bars.'

'Are you saying,' queried Andrew, 'that if these attackers know that we are Annie's friends, they could come after us?'

Richard was quick to reassure him. 'There is no immediate threat to you or your family,' he said, 'but if these men come back looking for Annie, they wouldn't hesitate to hurt anyone that was with her. That's why she will be looked after in the interim.'

'Why would anyone want to hurt Annie?' Helen was bewildered. 'She is just about the nicest person I have ever met.'

Me too thought Richard inwardly.

'We believe that she was targeted because of a client that she came into contact with.'

'Well, I hope that client gets what's coming to her,' spat Helen.

'She's dead,' said Richard.

'Oh my God,' Helen's hand covered the expression of horror that passed over her face. 'Was it the lady in the warehouse? We saw it on the news, didn't we Andrew?'

'Yes, it was,' said Richard.

'Oh my God.' Helen repeated. 'Poor Annie. Is there anything we can do?'

'Not at this point in time,' said Richard. 'But I must ask you not to try and see her or contact her until I let you know that it's safe to do so. I'm quite sure you don't want Annie worrying about you.'

'Of course not, Inspector. We'll do whatever you say,' agreed Helen.

'What about her home?' asked Andrew. 'You said she was attacked at home.'

'Her home is secure,' said Richard, 'but I also need you to stay away from her address for the time being and not to divulge anything that we have discussed today with anyone else.'

'I hope they didn't steal anything,' said Helen. 'Did they steal anything, Inspector?'

'Not that we are aware of.'

'She has some beautiful paintings,' said Helen. 'She is an amazing artist.'

'Yes, I know,' replied Richard. 'She sketched me.'

'You're joking.' exclaimed Helen.

Richard smiled, 'I didn't break her pencil if that's what you're insinuating.'

'No, it's nothing like that,' she laughed. 'It's just that Annie doesn't do faces anymore, even though that's what she is really good at. She can draw anyone.'

'Why doesn't she draw faces anymore?' asked Richard intrigued.

Helen held out her arms for Jacob and offered him her other breast. He began to suck hungrily at once so that Richard could hear the milk being swallowed. The shawl was forgotten now and Richard did his best not to stare at the creamy curve of Helen's breast.

'She had a disastrous relationship a few years ago,' replied Helen. 'While they were together she had completed a set of four pencil studies of the bastard in question.'

'Helen. Baby listening,' remonstrated Andrew.

'Well, he was, Andrew, you've got to admit that.'

Andrew smiled ruefully. 'Yes, he was.'

'Well, not long after said bastard, sorry, Andrew, had dumped her he put the drawings up for sale. Misogynistic sod.'

'He sold pictures of himself?' asked Richard flabbergasted.

'Oh yes,' replied Helen. 'There was no end to that man's vanity.'

'He wasn't exactly the back end of a bus,' offered Andrew.

'Don't you defend him or you'll find yourself paying Child Support,' warned Helen.

'He was short,' said Andrew in appeasement.

'What happened to the pictures?' asked Richard.

'Annie bought them,' laughed Helen.

'She bought her own pictures?' Richard was amazed. 'How much did that cost her?'

'A lot,' said Helen. 'She really is talented. But she didn't want them out in the world somewhere with her name at the bottom.'

'Where are they now?' asked Richard.

'Scattered to the wind.' replied Helen.

Richard looked momentarily confused. Helen laughed again. 'We had a ritual burning in the back garden,' said Helen. 'Then we toasted marshmallows in his ashes. Very tasty they were too.'

Richard found himself laughing so much that he had to put his tea down on the coffee table.

'So, that was that,' said Helen. 'Annie knows everything there is to know about drawing faces but she said she would never draw one again and even if she did, she would never give one of her pictures away.'

'But she drew the Inspector,' Andrew pointed out.

'And she gave me the picture,' said Richard.

Helen looked at him searchingly before speaking. 'Treasure it, Inspector,' she said. 'I doubt if you appreciate the value of what you have.'

'Oh, I do,' said Richard. 'I can assure you that I do.'

'So, how can we help you, Inspector?' asked Andrew.

Richard took out his notebook and pen before he began. 'I need to know if Annie has mentioned anything unusual to you over the last week or two. Any difficult clients? Any incidents at work? Anything that was troubling her?'

Helen and Andrew both shook their heads but it was Helen that spoke. 'Nothing, Inspector. Annie has been her usual self. I've seen her every few days up to the delivery. If anything, she seemed really happy at the delivery.'

Richard suppressed a smile as he wondered whether Annie's impromptu supper at Dougie's had had anything to do with her good mood.

'So she didn't mention any difficulties with clients?'

'No,' replied Helen. 'Annie and I are good friends but she is very discreet about her clients. She would never share patient details or tell me anything about other mums. Even if I know them. Especially if I know them.'

'Did Annie seem worried about anything?'

'No, she seemed normal. I suppose she does keep things pretty close to her chest. It took her ages to tell me about the bastard boyfriend. I think she likes to keep her feelings to herself most of the time. She always seems terribly self-contained but I often remark to Andrew that she must be lonely. All she seems to do is work and paint.'

Richard closed his notebook and felt in his pocket for a card which he handed to Andrew. 'I really appreciate your time. If either of you thinks of anything, however insignificant, please call me straight away. Thank you.'

'You are welcome, Inspector,' replied Helen. 'Please keep Annie safe.'

Richard paused and smiled as he left the room. 'Don't worry, Mrs Lacey, I will be taking very great care of her.'

Chapter Twenty-Nine

Monday

Sergeants Craven and James were feeling very pleased with themselves. It was never easy integrating into a new team, especially one as established and tight knit as Diane Masterton's, but a step forward in a case was certain to produce a quick win. Masterton saw the glee plastered across their faces as soon as she walked into the office.

'You two look like my Simon when he won a bike in a Free Radio competition,' she observed.

Craven and James looked at each other and grinned even more widely. Masterton strolled over to where they were facing each other over a shared desk.

'Come on then, out with it. Put me out of my misery.'

Craven held up a mug shot in front of his face while James spoke.

'May I present Billy Lloyd,' he said with a flourish. 'Released from Hewell prison nine weeks ago after serving fourteen months of a two-year sentence for…' There was a dramatic pause during which Craven spoke from behind the photo.

'…nicking cars!'

'Go on,' encouraged Masterton.

'Billy claimed that he was working alone and went down without naming any accomplices,' continued James, 'but, someone somewhere was helping out big time.'

'In what way?' asked Masterton.

'When Billy's garage was raided he had boxes of top quality forged plates.'

'Don't tell me,' guessed Masterton. 'Random numbers?'

'Random numbers,' repeated Craven, as he removed the photo from in front of his face. 'Now tell her where Billy lives,' encouraged Craven.

'If you'll follow me, boss,' said James, leading the way to the map on the incident board.

'Right here,' he said, as he pushed a red drawing pin into a spot which formed the apex of the triangle between Masood's house and the hairdressing salon run by Kambiz.

Masterton struggled to conceal her own grin. 'Get him in here, now.' she ordered.

As the two officers left the office in a flurry of self-congratulation and back-slapping, Masterton studied the map in front of her, tracing lines with her forefinger between the various pins. Richard was next into the office and he came across to her at once.

'How's Annie?' she asked, without taking her eyes from the map.

'Off the ventilator,' said Richard, 'awake and she's holding her own.'

Masterton turned to meet his eyes and smiled. 'I am glad,' she said.

'So am I,' replied Richard with a smile that lit up his whole face. 'So what's new here?' he asked, as he positioned himself next to Masterton to study the board.

'That's a new one,' observed Richard, pointing to the red drawing pin.

'Local car thief recently released from Hewell prison. Apparently, he has an unnamed supplier of dodgy number plates.'

Richard peered more closely at the map. 'Billy Lloyd,' said Richard.

'You know him?'

'Probably nicked him about seven times when I was on the beat,' admitted Richard. 'He can't keep his hands off a nice car, but he's a harmless sort, non-violent at least.'

'And that is starting to mean a lot these days,' said Masterton. 'Anyway, Craven and James have gone to fetch him in for questioning. I want the source of those plates.'

'Good one,' said Richard.

Masterton remained staring at the board. 'What do you see, Richard?'

He answered at once. 'All the activity is confined within a tight geographical location, but,' he added, anticipating Masterton's thoughts, 'that doesn't give us the hideout of those three animals.'

'No, it doesn't,' agreed Masterton, 'but it does tell us that they are probably living locally. Think about that for a minute. They have to eat, buy petrol. Where are they going to go?'

'Not to local stores, for sure,' said Richard rubbing the dimple in his chin with the tip of his thumb. 'Three Afghan men in the middle of Worcester, they would be too noticeable.'

'Exactly,' agreed Masterton. 'They'll stick to the big anonymous shops where the staff are too bored to even look up and see if they're serving man, woman or child. How many have we got in this area?'

Richard reached over to the nearest desk and retrieved some blue pins which he placed on the map as he spoke. 'Tesco, Sainsbury's, Asda, Aldi, and Lidl. Anymore, boss? You're the shopper.'

'I never had you down as a chauvinist, Richard.'

'Quite right, too. I'm a Tesco man myself,' he smiled.

'That's it for supermarkets,' said Masterton. 'There are a few more petrol stations of course but I suspect these guys will want to limit their exposure.' Masterton turned away from the board. 'Put in a request for surveillance, Richard. They have to come out of hiding sooner or later.'

A little over an hour later, Richard strode into the interview room where Craven was seated opposite a disgruntled looking Billy Lloyd. His clothes were crumpled and he had the unshaven look of someone who had just been dragged from his bed, which in fact he had.

Craven spoke into the tape that was running at the table, 'DI Shaw has just entered the room.'

'Evening, Billy,' said Richard.

'DI Shaw,' said Billy. 'At least nicking me did someone's career some good.'

Richard chuckled as he took the seat next to Craven. 'It takes a bit more than that, Billy, but all contributions are nevertheless welcome.'

'Well, I'm clean, Dickie boy,' said Billy opening his palms to show that he wasn't concealing anything that could be construed as dirt. 'And I'm on probation. If you're charging me, I want my lawyer.'

'The only thing I'll be charging you with is an incitement to cause a riot if you call me Dickie boy again,' said Richard.

'Beg your pardon, DI,' slurred Billy.

'How many have you had tonight, Bill?' asked Richard.

'One or two pints,' he replied.

'That true, Craven?' asked Richard.

'Mr Lloyd has yet to be breathalysed,' said Craven, 'but we can do so at any minute. He appeared to be sleeping it off when we found him.'

Billy leaned across the table to wag his finger at Richard. 'Don't you try pinning no charges on me,' warned Billy. 'I know my rights.'

'Is the suspect becoming disorderly, Sergeant?' asked Richard.

'Any minute now,' answered Craven.

'What is this?' asked Billy, slumping back in his chair. 'I've been straight since I came out of the nick.'

'How many weeks is that, Billy?' asked Richard.

Billy scowled in reply.

'How about helping us with our enquiries, Billy, and you can be tucked up in bed by midnight.'

'Waddayer want?' asked Billy.

'I want to know where you get your dodgy plates,' said Richard.

'I told you, I'm straight.' exclaimed Billy.

'Funnily enough,' smiled Richard, 'I'm not actually interested in you this time. I just want to know where I would go to get a set of plates made.'

'Don't they pay you enough?' smirked Billy.

'Enough to call your probation officer and let him know that you've been picked up.'

'That's blackmail.'

Richard placed his arms on the table and leaned forward.

'A man has been murdered and a young woman beaten senseless. The men that did it are still out there and they are armed. The one thing we know for sure is that they are driving around Worcester on forged plates.'

'What's that got to do with me?'

'Where's your wife, Billy? What has she been doing today? What if she's the next one to be picked on?'

Billy rubbed his chin thoughtfully.

'Still don't get it,' he said.

'Those murderers,' said Richard, 'bought dodgy plates locally. I know that the jokers who manufacture them move all the time so they don't get caught. I also know that you can always find them.'

'If I tell you where they are I'm finished.'

'But you just told me you were straight, didn't you, Billy? Which means you are already finished.'

'Doesn't mean they won't come after me.'

'Who else knows you're here, Billy?' asked Richard.

Billy shrugged. 'No-one.'

'And that's the way it can stay, Billy. Those plates are our only lead. You give us a name and address and Sergeant Craven here will deliver you home safely. No-one needs to know that you were ever here.'

'You won't tell my probation officer?'

'Only that you have been very helpful in assisting us with our enquiries.'

Craven and Richard watched as the fight that Billy was having with himself played across his face like a movie. Finally, he spoke, 'Gary Russell. He's working out of a lock up in Dines Green. Last one on the left.'

'I owe you, Billy,' said Richard as he left the room.

Chapter Thirty

Gary Russell poured boiling water over the tea bag, added milk and sugar and then dunked the tea bag a few times before discarding it in the waste bin. He made himself comfortable on a battered sun lounger and opened up his copy of The Sun. The knock on the side door of the lock-up barely registered as he checked his horoscope for the day. A few surprises could be in store, it said.

The tall guy in the smart suit didn't surprise him. That sort were always into insurance scams. That's how they paid for the suits, half of them. The warrant card in the tall man's hand, however, was a huge surprise. Gary dropped his paper and yelled as he sloshed hot tea over his hand and struggled to his feet.

He was a small, wiry man, his face showing every wrinkle of his seventy years. He was dressed in faded trousers and a brown overall. He ran his hand through his thinning hair as he stared at Richard in horror. Gary had been kosher all his life working hard in a metal shop. It was only when he retired and had nothing but a state pension and council flat to look forward to that he turned to crime.

'Who shopped me?' he demanded.

There was no point trying to act like a shy virgin on her wedding night. There were blank plates still in their boxes stacked along one wall and several finished sets on his work bench. Richard walked over to examine one of them now.

'Nice work,' he observed, replacing it where he had found it.

'Who grassed me up?' Gary asked again.

'What's the matter?' asked Richard. 'Don't you think Her Majesty's Constabulary can't find you all by itself?'

'No, I don't,' replied Gary.

'Sit down, Mr Russell,' invited Richard.

Gary Russell did as he was told and then found himself staring up so high to see Richard's face that his neck ached.

'Mr Russell, we have a few questions we would like to ask you,' said Richard.

'Ask away,' said Russell, resigned. He would be sorry to give up his work but he had heard that they had metal workshops in the nick. And at least he would have three square meals a day and plenty of company. It had been a lonely life since cancer had taken his Vera away. They had never managed to have children, though not for want of trying, and his work mates had drifted away once he was retired. Out of sight, out of mind, he supposed.

'Can you tell me why you have a lock up full of number plates, Mr Russell,' asked Richard.

'It's me hobby. I make 'em.

'And then what do you do with them?'

'I sell 'em.'

'Who do you sell them to?'

'Whoever pays.'

'I would like you to accompany me to the station if you don't mind,' said Richard.

'Well, seein' as you asked so politely,' said Russell. 'Can I bring me paper?'

'Just make sure you lock up,' said Richard with a rueful grin.

Sergeant James had settled Gary Russell into the interview room with a mug of tea, a plate of digestive biscuits and his newspaper. By the time Richard entered the room he was feeling perfectly relaxed. Maybe it was time he retired. Again.

Richard waited for Sergeant James to set up the tape before he spoke.

'Mr Russell, do you watch the news?' began Richard.

'Depends who's reading it,' smirked Gary. 'I like that Christine Clarkson myself. Nice knockers.'

'Are you aware that a man was shot dead a few days ago?'

Gary nodded. 'Nasty business that was. Only a few streets from my place.'

'We believe,' continued Richard, 'that those same men attacked a young woman in her own home just two days ago. They left her for dead.'

Gary sucked at his teeth in disapproval.

'Fortunately, a neighbour called the police and the woman survived. Those men are armed, dangerous and still on the loose. And they are driving around the city on forged plates. We believe they are your forged plates.'

'They could be anyone's,' objected Gary. 'I don't know no killers.'

'They have several sets of plates,' interjected Richard, 'which means that they would have bought in bulk.'

'And they're running around waving shooters? What do you think I'm on?' asked Gary. 'Think I've got a death wish? Just put me inside now. I'll be safe there. Will I get me own telly?'

'We're not going to put you inside,' said Richard. 'You're going home when we've finished with you. Those men might be back.'

Richard and Sergeant James watched as Gary thought about this. 'I wouldn't mind going inside,' offered Gary at last. 'It gets lonely in me flat.'

Richard shook his head in wonderment. 'Maybe we could organise some community service for you,' offered Richard.

'Would I get a hot lunch?' asked Gary.

'We'll work out the details later,' replied Richard. 'But I'm sure Sergeant James can shout you a hot lunch after this.'

James pulled a face which Richard chose to ignore.

Gary thought carefully. If people wanted to buy his metal work it was up to them what they did with it. But murder and beating up women was just plain wrong. He scratched his head before speaking.

'A week ago last Monday,' said Gary, 'some foreign geezer came in and asked for ten sets, any old number, he said. I told him it would take a while but he just made himself at home in my seat and watched me till I was done. Took me till nearly midnight to finish. He had used up all my milk by the time I was done.'

'What did he look like?' asked Richard.

Gary shrugged. 'I'm not so good with faces. Black hair, brown skin, average height.'

'What sort of brown skin?' asked Richard. 'Was he tanned, Asian, Afro-Caribbean, Middle-Eastern?'

Gary rubbed at his chin. 'He looked like one of them Arabs.'

'What was he wearing?' asked Richard.

'No idea,' said Gary.

Richard took an envelope from the file in front of him and began laying out photos.

'Take your time Mr Russell,' he said. 'I would like you to take a look at these and see if you recognise the man that bought the plates.'

Gary Russell examined the photos with the intensity of a student sitting his finals. He paused only to drain his mug and smile happily at Sergeant James when he offered a refill.

'Don't mind if I do,' he said.

Richard had a final tally of seventeen photos from the NCA and he had to admit even to himself that some of the men in the photos looked remarkably similar. But Gary Russell was enjoying himself. He hadn't had this much fun since he forged a plate for a member of minor royalty wanting to sneak off to meet her lover in the country. He began eliminating the photos one by one until he was left with just three photos. Richard walked around the table to study the three that were left.

Two showed well-built men with dark eyes and black hair aged approximately late forties to early fifties. The third man had similar features but was scrawny and skinny. Sergeant James returned with the second mug of tea and a Kit Kat that he had been saving to eat in the car on the way home. Russell attacked both greedily as he continued to stare at the photos.

Finally, he pushed away two of the photos and prodded the one remaining picture in front of him.

'That's the one. The skinny one.'

'Mr Russell, are you sure?' asked Richard.

'As sure as I can be,' replied Gary Russell. 'Course, all these foreigners look the same to me sometimes. But this one,' continued Russell, 'has got something about his face that gives me the shivers. It's the eyes, I think. Every time I stopped for a breather those eyes were on me.'

Sergeant James told the tape which photo Gary Russell had picked.

Richard took the photo and stared at it. Gary was right, there was something sinister about that face.

'We'll need those numbers from you and there will be a bit of paperwork to tidy up before you go. Then Sergeant James will see you home.'

'And don't forget me lunch,' he reminded Richard.

'And don't forget his lunch, Sergeant,' added Richard.

Chapter Thirty-One

The debriefing that afternoon was a lot briefer than Masterton would have liked. Getting a face for one of the thugs was a step forward and sourcing the plates confirmed her suspicion that the three were based locally but little else had been achieved. She sat back as Richard addressed the team.

He pointed to the photo that Gary Russell had picked out. 'Thanks to the NCA we know that this is Abdul Farid. He is a known associate of Hajji and a week ago Monday he was here in Worcester buying dodgy number plates. You should all have a copy of the ten false plates and you will see that the plate currently on their vehicle is on that list. This confirms that we have a mug shot of at least one of our three suspects. The whole force is on the look out for those plates.'

'What about the press?' asked Spooner.

'We're keeping this under wraps for now,' interrupted Masterton. 'If these guys get wind of the fact that we're on to them they'll probably dump the plates and the car before you can blow your nose. We need to keep this quiet.'

'We've also got surveillance on the main supermarkets,' said Richard. 'If these guys so much as poke their nose in the door we'll know about it.'

'But this could all take ages, boss,' said Palmer.

Masterton moved to the front of the group. 'Right, now it's all we've got. We have to be patient and keep looking for anything that will help us find these men. We have to wait.'

'For what?' asked Palmer.

'For them to make their next move,' said Masterton.

'And you can be sure they will,' added Richard.

'Meanwhile, we will get on to property rentals in our target area and check out hotels, bed and breakfasts and guest houses. Three Afghan men are not going to find it easy to hide in this city and their actions to date suggest that caution is not top of their list,' added Masterton as she looked at her watch. 'Right, team, it's been a tough few days and you've all worked really hard. Our next move should be down the pub. First round's on me.'

The whoops of the team drowned her words as she spoke quietly to Richard.

'You can be excused from this one,' she said.

'I appreciate that, boss,' said Richard as he watched her fetch her coat and bag. 'But I don't expect any allowances.'

'You're not getting any,' she replied. 'We're going to need Annie's statement as soon as she's well enough. If she knows anything at all about the USB, the sooner we hear about it the better.'

They left the office together and walked side by side to the staff car park.

'Did I ever tell you about the time when I was a young constable and got called to a mugging?' Masterton asked.

'No,' replied Richard, intrigued.

'Oh, yes. Some low life tried to grab an old lady's bag. She was rescued by a passerby who made a citizen's arrest. I had to interview the victim and the witness.'

'And?' asked Richard.

She unlocked her car door and climbed in as she spoke.

'And when the case was over,' replied Masterton with a smile, 'the knight in shining armour asked me for a date.'

'Did you go?'

'Of course, I went,' she said as she started the engine. 'He was bloody gorgeous.'

'What happened?'

She closed the car door and opened the window so that Richard had to lean down to hear her reply.

'I married him,' she said with a smile, before driving away.

'Well, I'll be damned,' thought Richard, as he climbed into his own car and headed for the Royal Infirmary.

The route to the hospital was becoming as familiar to Richard as the drive home and he drove on autopilot as his brain replayed the facts of the case so far. The USB provided a clear motive for the thug's presence in the city and their desperation in trying to find it. With the deaths of Soraya and Masood, they were now dependent on finding Ali Haq before the three men got to work on the sole survivor of the trio. Richard was convinced that Soraya's death was a tragic consequence of her fear of the men that were chasing her. And having witnessed their sadistic handiwork it was clear that her fear was justified. It was unfortunate that the twins were born prematurely and without medical help. If either factor had not been present the outcome would have been very different and Annie would not be involved.

Richard was still having difficulty identifying Annie's entanglement in the case. Soraya had visited the Asylum Centre seeking help with her pregnancy and had seen Annie. After she gave birth, a man was at the hospital asking for Annie in the middle of the night. That must have been Masood and after parking his car he recorded a note on his phone to get mug shots taken to the hospital staff involved to confirm that it was him. He must have been looking for Annie for assistance with the babies and when he couldn't get to her, he had panicked and dumped the babies at her house. Richard felt a surge of anger at the thought of the beating she had taken simply for doing her job. The world was becoming more twisted by the day and he left his car with his jaw set firmly and a stare that challenged anyone to dare mess with him that night.

At the nurses' station, he paused to inquire about Annie's progress and was rewarded with welcome news.

'She's doing very well,' said the nurse in charge. 'Would you like a word with the doctor? He's on the ward.'

'Thank you,' answered Richard.

It was Doctor Latham who strode forward and shook Richard's hand.

'Our young midwife,' he said to Richard, 'is out of danger and well on the road to recovery.'

'How long before she can go home?' asked Richard.

'That is difficult to say,' replied Doctor Latham. 'Everyone heals at different rates but she really is a most remarkable young woman. Many patients would have been destroyed by what she has been through but she has the most amazing spirit. She seems determined not to let this get her down.'

He had reached for Annie's notes from the nursing station and was flicking through them as he spoke.

'She was sitting up in bed when I visited her earlier and she has been taking sips of fluid. Her wound is healing nicely too. Of course, it will take some time for the bruises and fractured ribs to heal and she is still in some pain but that is to be expected. Would you like to see her?'

Richard nodded and Doctor Latham indicated that they should walk to her room together.

'In cases like these,' said the doctor, 'once the patient is biologically stable, it is their psychological state that we worry about most.'

'Post-traumatic shock?' asked Richard.

'Exactly,' said Doctor Latham. 'Especially as Annie doesn't have any immediate next of kin living close by. It appears that she is an only child and her parents are deceased. She has given us the names of two friends as her proxy Next of Kin.'

'Can I ask who they are?'

The doctor consulted the notes. 'Helen and Andrew Lacey.'

'Ah, yes, I have met with them.'

'Now, Annie will need a great deal of TLC once she is discharged.'

'I understand,' said Richard, 'I can make sure that Victim Support Services are alerted.'

And I'll be there too, he thought to himself.

'That would be excellent,' said Doctor Latham as they approached the policeman at the door to Annie's room and Richard flashed his ID. 'Here you are, Inspector.'

Annie's head turned as he pushed open the door and she offered him a weak smile.

'Hello, you,' his voice caressed her.

'Hello back,' she replied, her eyes following every move as he fetched the chair to sit beside her. He saw that she held the small teddy in her hands.

She followed his gaze and waggled the teddy. 'Thank you for Alice.'

'Christened already?'

'All my bears have names,' she smiled.

Richard suddenly paled as he thought of Annie's wrecked home and recalled seeing teddy bears scattered on the floor of her front room.

As if reading his thoughts she asked. 'Are my teddies all right?'

'How many do you have?'

'Alice is my ninth.'

'Your house is still a crime scene,' explained Richard, 'but as soon as it's been cleared, I will go and rescue your bears.'

To his relief, that seemed to satisfy her.

'It's good to see you,' he said softly.

'And you.'

'How are you feeling?'

'A bit like a prisoner,' she said ruefully, 'although I can't move much yet so I don't suppose there's much chance of escape, is there?'

'None at all,' replied Richard.

Annie stroked the fur on the teddy's head as she asked the question that had been nibbling away at her since she first became aware of where she was.

'I suppose those policemen guarding me mean that the men haven't been caught?'

'No, they haven't,' said Richard. 'But we have identified one of them and we have the make and registration of their car. It's only a matter of time and, until then, we will keep you safe. You have my word.'

'Then it *was* me they were after?' asked Annie rhetorically. 'It wasn't random?'

Richard examined her critically before he spoke, wondering how strong she really was, and just how much he should tell her.

'I'm not an idiot,' she said meeting his gaze.

Richard shook his head with wonder. When he first met Annie, he thought she was kind and gentle, maybe even soft, but how wrong can a man be? She was strong and feisty and she would get through this with her spirit intact.

'I have spent my whole career interviewing the victims of crime, half of them nowhere near as serious as this one, yet you must be the most together person I have ever met.'

'Did you think I would be a wreck?' she asked.

'Honestly? Yes,' replied Richard.

Annie carefully arranged the little teddy's dress as she spoke.

'I've worked at the Asylum Centre for almost three years now,' she began. 'During that time I've treated refugees and asylum seekers from all over the world. Bosnia, Serbia, Iraq, Afghanistan, Africa. Name a war zone and I can probably name a woman that has escaped and come here. You can't imagine what those women have suffered and seen. Their families tortured and killed, their homes ransacked, perhaps destroyed, whole communities devastated. I've seen women who have been beaten and mutilated, women pregnant by their rapists, infected with HIV, so badly injured that they need caesareans to give birth.'

Richard reached out and took her hand as she spoke.

'And you can't always blame the war,' Annie continued. 'Some of those women have suffered years of abuse at the hands of their husbands. War is just an excuse for bad behaviour and women are always the victims. What happened to me...'

Her voice shook slightly and she paused to take a deep breath. Richard stroked her fingers. 'What happened to me was almost nothing in comparison.'

'It wasn't nothing,' said Richard.

'I'm here and I'm in one piece,' she replied. 'I'll get better and I'll go back to my life. The women I care for can't do that. It may sound a bit weird but I almost feel now that I will understand them just that little bit better.'

'Just don't think you can walk away from this without support,' Richard insisted. 'Disregarding what happened to you because there are others worse off does not mean that this is insignificant. If you are coping ok that's great, but I will be worried about you if you dismiss all this too lightly.'

'I won't,' agreed Annie. 'But I won't let this beat me. Except for one thing.'

'What's that?'

'I can't go back home, Richard. Never. It's not just the attack. It's the babies. I can't go back.'

'I understand.'

'Anyway,' she smiled, 'I don't suppose the landlord will let me back. And I've probably lost my deposit.'

'I think we can sort that out,' said Richard.

'I'll have to get someone to pack my things.'

'Annie, please don't worry about that now. You will have all the help you need when the time comes, I promise.'

He could see beads of perspiration forming on her forehead and she paled, breathing shallowly as if in pain.

'You're getting tired,' said Richard, standing up and releasing her hand, 'I'll go now.'

'You haven't answered my question, Inspector.'

'What question?'

'Why me?'

'It's complicated.'

'Only if you make it so.'

Richard sat down again. 'The woman who delivered the twins,' Richard began.

'Soraya?'

Richard nodded. 'When she entered Britain, we believe she was carrying some information related to an international crime syndicate. Nothing has been found. We believe that the men who attacked you were looking for it.'

'So, they think Soraya gave the information to me.'

Richard nodded.

'So, it wasn't random.'

'It wasn't random,' agreed Richard.

Annie thought for a moment. 'I think that helps,' she said.

'Annie, I must ask you. Did Soraya give you anything?'

'Like what?'

'Specifically, we are looking for a USB. Did she hand you anything?'

'No, nothing. The disturbance at the front desk must have spooked her. She was with me for a matter of minutes. When I got back to the room after checking that things were ok in reception, she was gone.'

'And she didn't leave anything behind?'

'I didn't see anything. My office is pretty sparse. I think I would have seen something like that if it was there. Was it with the babies?'

Richard shook his head. 'The babies and Soraya have been checked.'

He was about to mention Masood but stopped himself. She had enough to worry about without knowing that the men who were after her were cold blooded killers.

Richard stood up to leave. 'I need to go or Doctor Latham will have my guts for garters.'

He hesitated for just a moment before bending to press his lips gently to her forehead.

'I'll see you tomorrow,' he said. Annie's eyes were already closed, the teddy clutched in her hand. Richard replaced the chair as quietly as he could and tiptoed to the door. As he turned the handle, she spoke again.

'I can draw him,' she said.

Richard turned sharply.

'Who?'

'I can draw the man who hit me.'

A frisson of excitement buzzed in Richard's chest. This was exactly what Spooner had suggested. 'Another day,' said Richard.

She nodded and closed her eyes.

Unsettled after his visit, Richard turned his car in the direction of The Lamb and Flag, one of the nearest watering holes to the office. It is a traditional pub serving real ales and reputedly the best Guinness this side of the Irish Sea. Richard was not a great drinker but now and again a glass of Guinness fortified his spirits in a way that a glass of wine could never hope to rival. As he expected, most of the team were still there and in good humour. He ordered half a pint and made his way over to Masterton who was deep in conversation with McIntyre.

Richard caught her eye and she extricated herself smoothly.

'How is she?'

'Looking good, boss, and she says she can draw the man who assaulted her.'

'Richard, she needs time.'

'I didn't push it, I thought she was asleep and I was actually leaving when she told me that she could draw the man who attacked her.'

'Is she up to it?' asked Masterton.

'She's gutsy,' said Richard. 'I think she can handle it.'

'Go for it then,' said Masterton. 'If it's not our number plate purchaser we might end up with two out of three. But don't push her, Richard.'

Richard held up his hands in protest.

'I'm the last person that would do that,' he said.
Masterton nodded. 'I believe you.'

Chapter Thirty-Two

Tuesday

There was a thunderstorm raging over central London as the shiny nose of the Eurostar engine nudged its way into the terminal behind St Pancras Station. The rain held its breath as the train slipped under the cover of the curved roof of the station, but the rumbles of thunder followed it to the platform and flashes of lightening made the children gasp with awe. Passengers struggled to find raincoats and umbrellas amongst their luggage as they braced themselves to face the English weather, the French with cries of 'quel dommage,' the English with shrugs of resignation as if to say, 'What do you expect? This is England, after all.'

The passenger in seat 11A avoided remarking on the weather with his fellow passengers and left the train without drawing any attention towards himself. The forged European passport in his hand was, he had been assured, the best that money could buy, and so far, the master forger who had charged him the price of a Mercedes had been true to his word.

There was a long queue of tired travellers jostling to enter England and passport control waved through this citizen of Europe with barely a glance. In multi-cultural Britain physical appearance gave no clue to a person's origins. With passport in hand, you were free to roam.

Released into the concourse, he found himself amongst a bewildering mass of humanity. He struggled to find a direct route between parents with buggies, small groups of young backpackers too busy anticipating their travels to look where they were going and businessmen who miraculously weaved their way through everyone else with barely a break in their stride.

He averted his eyes from the lingerie on display in one of the shops and tried to concentrate on finding the taxi rank. Hoardings and temporary signs indicated that the usual place had been moved temporarily to the side of the terminal. He hadn't accounted for that in his plans. Now he had to stop to read the signs and try to follow the arrow. Someone bumped against his shoulder with a muttered 'sorry' and he started in fear. 'Can I help you, sir?'

It was a woman in uniform, but not police. She had a kind face and a warm smile. 'You look a bit lost,' she said.

'Taxi, please,' he muttered, as he adjusted the weight of the overnight bag on his shoulder.

'Follow me,' she said, as she turned away. 'The renovations have caught out a lot of people.' He followed for a short distance. 'There you go.' She was pointing to a set of glass exterior doors through which he glimpsed a sea of grey. Grey streets, grey sky, and grey raindrops big enough to count. He wondered how it would be living in such a dismal place. He wondered what Soraya thought of the place. He wondered how big his child had grown. Maybe he had been blessed with a son.

'Have a nice day.' said the woman and was gone.

As he emerged from the glass doors, a man was beside him at once with a large umbrella. 'Taxi, sir?' asked the voice.

'Yes, thank you,' he replied, surprised at the courteous service. He followed the taxi driver to the car keeping his head down to avoid the puddles that were collecting on the pavement. Perhaps if the sun had been shining he would have looked around him in awe at finding himself in London. Perhaps if he had looked around he would have seen the large sign further along the street that said 'Taxi' in bright blue letters behind which an orderly queue of dripping humanity had collected. But he didn't look up. He simply climbed into the taxi and gave the driver the address.

It did not take long for the taxi to leave the busy capital behind and reach the M25 motorway. The man closed his eyes, unable to believe the good fortune that had brought him here without mishap.

Since kissing his wife goodbye, Ali had been living on a knife edge of terror and uncertainty. At times, the blade seemed so sharp he felt that even the tiniest slip would thrust the point into the centre of his heart. He feared Hajji in a way that caused Masood to jeer at his older brother and tease him for having the heart of a quivering mouse while he, Masood, was a black bear.

So many times on the journey to Kabul, Ali had been close to turning back, running for Pakistan and on to Europe to start his new life with his beloved wife and soon to be born child. But Masood was his brother and Ali felt compelled to visit Hajji and plead for Masood's life. After all, who else would care about Masood? Who else would even be allowed into Hajji's inner sanctum?

Ali sighed as he thought of his brother. Even as young children, Masood had been the rebel. Always out in the street at the centre of the gaggle of young boys who would pester the foreign soldiers for souvenirs and treats then taunt them and throw stones when they were rejected. Their mother would despair at Masood's long absences and send Ali to find him. But Ali knew that Masood would take no notice of his brother and would stay on the streets until darkness fell and his stomach began to rumble. So instead Ali would rest against the trunk of a pomegranate tree at the edge of town and read one of the paperback books that he had taken from Masood's secret stash.

The books were dog-eared and in English and the truth was that at first, Ali's English was barely good enough to understand the stories of life in the West. But he persevered and by the time he was fourteen he was able to read English fluently. Masood, too, emulated his brother and despite his wayward antics he was quick and bright and had been a good student. His departure for University in Pakistan to study Computer Science had been a triumph and he had returned home with an excellent degree.

Their mother begged Masood to return to Pakistan or even travel to the West for work but Masood had already attracted the attention of Hajji. Hajji, with his henchman and his fast cars. Masood was clever and educated and his air of superiority cloaked him against his mother's pleading. Within weeks he was sitting at Hajji's right hand and masterminding the computer network that would support the growth and management of the empire of an evil man.

For several years, Ali had little contact with his brother. After graduating from Kabul University as a pharmacist, he began work at the hospital. It was there that quite by chance he met Soraya. Her mother was a patient with a complicated drug schedule and Ali found it necessary to visit the old lady often. He soon learned that the end of visiting hours was a good time for this and often he could escort this beautiful daughter to the exit doors of the hospital under the pretence of discussing her mother's case.

Arranging the marriage was not difficult. Ali was a respected professional and for once, Masood was in a position to use his connections to influence the girl's family. It helped that although her parents knew none of this, the young couple had already met and liked each other. To her parent's surprise, the normally headstrong

Soraya humbly accepted the marriage proposal and settled into her new life with great joy.

Masood, however, continued to live life with his exuberance unchecked. Even though he knew better, much better, he stole a cheeky kiss from Hajji's more than willing girlfriend, just as Hajji entered the room. While Hajji beat his girlfriend to a pulp with his bare fists, Masood ran for his life. He arrived at Ali's door in Herat quaking with the fear of the death sentence he knew would be hanging over him. Only the insurance held safely in his zipped pocket gave him any hope of survival and Ali took it from him before arranging for his brother to travel to England.

Ali knew that there would be a price on Masood's head and he was determined to try and reason with Hajji to ensure his brother's survival. His hopes were not high and he knew that succeed or not, his own future would be jeopardised by his actions in Kabul. With a child conceived, it was time to leave his war-torn land and find a life that his family could live in peace. All of them.

If only Hajji had been a reasonable man, Ali may have stood a chance, but Hajji was a human being without a heart. When Ali stood before him, Hajji simply laughed and turned away, but not before Ali glimpsed the depth of anger that glittered in his eyes like two shiny pieces of rain wet coal. When Ali tried to speak, he was dragged from the room and thrown into the street. He had no chance to plead for his brother, for himself, for his wife or for his child. He was simply a piece of litter to be tossed to the wind. So be it, thought Ali.

The days of travelling had taken their toll and in the back of the London taxi, sleep quickly overcame him. He woke as the vehicle hit an uneven surface and bounced several times before the cab jerked to a halt. Ali wondered where he was as he opened his eyes to a dim, grey light. He must have slept so long that dusk had fallen. Where on earth was he?

He rubbed his eyes with his fingers and heard rather than saw the door of the car being snatched open and rough hands pulling him bodily out of the car. He looked around him wildly and saw at once that he had been tricked. The taxi was already accelerating away, abandoning him in an old factory unit, its cavernous and draughty space empty apart from the chair in the middle of the floor. Terror enveloped him and he began to struggle as reality blasted his consciousness, but two sets of hands held him firmly.

How could he have been so stupid? After getting this far?

He was thrown into the empty chair and his arms were tied behind him with wire that bit into the skin of his wrists when he tried to struggle. Fear made him tremble and he tried to hold his knees together to control their shaking. He badly needed to pee. A rough blindfold was wrapped around his eyes and his ankles were tied to the legs of the chair with sticky tape that made a tearing sound as it was wrapped around his legs.

Footsteps approached from behind him. He moved as if to turn his head and was rewarded with a sharp slap across the face from one of the men who had tied him. The footsteps stopped and he felt warm breath on his ear. 'Hello, Ali.'

Ali knew instinctively who the voice belonged to. He also knew what the owner of that voice would do to him. He began to whimper and prayed to Allah that he would be able to endure what was to come and that his death would be swift.

Chapter Thirty-Three

Richard stopped at an art supplier on Foregate Street on his way to the hospital and asked the assistant's advice on the best material for sketching faces. He came away with a good quality sketchpad, an assortment of pencils and an eraser that looked more like a lump of blue dough than the grubby rectangles of rubber he remembered from school.

To his surprise, Annie was out of bed and seated in a chair by the window. She was wearing a voluminous pink sprigged hospital issue nightdress that made her look like a young lady from a Victorian novel. A small table was next to her with a glass, a jug of water and a call button.

'Hello, you,' he said with surprise. 'What are you doing out of bed?'

'Rehabilitating apparently,' she said. 'I have to sit here for one hour then I get a cup of tea at ten if I'm a good girl.'

Richard laughed. 'Aren't you always good?'

'If it gets me out of here even one minute earlier I will be good for the rest of my life.'

'No need to get too carried away,' admonished Richard.

'Hey, I'm on a high,' she replied and spread out her hands. 'Look, no tubes. I feel naked.'

Richard covered his eyes in mock surprise. 'I thought every well-dressed girl had at least one intravenous infusion to cover her modesty.'

'And,' she said wiggling her fingers, 'a naked hand.'

Richard took the hand so that he could examine the palm. Annie realised suddenly that she was feeling very hot.

'You can hardly see it,' Richard observed.

'Hmm,' replied Annie. 'Pity my abdomen isn't going to look that good. I think my bikini days might be over.'

'I very much doubt that,' said Richard and Annie felt a blush spreading slowly over her cheeks.

She took back her hand and pointed to the carrier bag in Richard's hand.

'You've been to PSW. I hope you asked for a discount. I'm a good customer.'

'Compliments of the Constabulary,' he said, unpacking the bag onto her table. Annie surveyed his purchases silently and Richard began to worry that he had been a little too presumptuous.

'It doesn't have to be today,' said Richard. 'There's no hurry.'

'No, it's ok. I want to do this.'

'Are you sure?'

'Is that why you haven't asked me any questions because you think I'm not up to it?'

'I just don't want to rush you.'

'There were three of them,' said Annie. 'Two held my arms while the third one hit me. That's the one I'll draw.'

Richard didn't trust himself to speak as the image of Annie being held and beaten swam before his eyes.

'Could you open the pencils for me please?'

Richard laid out the pencils on the small table and opened the sketch pad for Annie. She hesitated for just a second, closing her eyes as if to conjure the face of her attacker. But the truth was, it hadn't left her. It had been his face that she saw when she regained consciousness, and it was his face that hung behind her eyelids when she tried to sleep. The only way to exorcise the spectre was to commit him to paper so that she didn't need to remember him anymore.

She began to move the pencil swiftly over the paper, making lines that would become eyes, a nose, a mouth, a chin. Richard watched her silently. There was a connection in the room that was stronger than anything he had ever known. Annie had to feel it too.

It was over an hour before she put down her pencil and pushed the sketch pad towards Richard. He stared at the picture of the dark skinned man, the scars, and the dark eyes. Annie had drawn the lips slightly parted so that she could sketch every one of the crooked teeth that had grinned at her so cruelly. There were drops of spittle on the man's upper lip and eyes so filled with hatred that Richard felt himself go cold. He could almost hear the man breathing. He looked up at Annie, wanting to congratulate her on the picture but she was slumped back in her chair with closed eyes. Richard saw a single tear trickle slowly down her cheek.

He closed the sketch pad and leaned forward to place it on the table. She opened her eyes to look at him. 'I'm sorry,' she said. 'It was harder than I thought.'

'You've done a fantastic job,' said Richard. 'Leave the rest to us.'

'Could you call the nurse?' Annie asked. 'I need to go back to bed.'

Richard complied and stood back as he watched two nurses help Annie across the room. She leaned heavily on their arms and let out a small cry of pain as they helped her to lie down.

'Would you like something for the pain?' one of them asked.

Annie nodded gratefully. The pain she could bear, but not the memory of the stench of sour breath and sweat that filled her nostrils. She longed for the oblivion that the syringe would bring.

When she was settled, Richard placed a hand tenderly on her head. 'I'll see you tomorrow,' he whispered, but there was no response. She had already drifted away. Richard headed back to the station to show Masterton the drawing and to compare it to his collection of mug shots supplied by the NCA.

'She's bloody good,' breathed Masterton, when she saw the sketch. 'What's she doing working as a midwife? She could make a fortune doing these.'

'Enjoys bringing new life into the world I think,' Richard replied.

'Even so, she's wasted. Christ, I wish our lot were just half as good. Sometimes our artist's impressions look like a twelve-year-old has drawn them.'

She held the drawing at arm's length. 'What an evil bastard. Is he one of yours?' she asked, referring to Richard's set of NCA mug shots.

'No,' said Richard. 'I've sent this to them and they're running it through their system for me as we speak.'

'Get this out to the press, Richard,' Masterton instructed as she handed back the picture.

'Boss?'

'What is it?'

'I'd like to take in all the mug shots to the hospital, see if we can get Annie to identify the other two.'

'Do it. The sooner the better. They're still out there and we've got a darn sight better chance of catching them if the public knows what they look like.'

'I'll do it tomorrow, boss,' replied Richard.

Masterton heard the slightest change of tone.

'Did it take a lot out of her?'

'She seemed shattered.'

'Well, you're right to wait. Do it in the morning. But meanwhile, get this one out. I want it on the evening news, in the evening newspaper, and on the websites. As far as I am concerned, this guy is currently England's most wanted.'

Chapter Thirty-Four

Wednesday

The following morning Richard showered and shaved with even more care than usual. He was looking forward to spending some more duty time with Annie and he sent out a silent prayer that she had recovered from yesterday's ordeal. The truth was he was torn between leaving her to recover in peace and the driving need to get the bastards and tie up the case once and for all. Everyone on the team had been affected by the brutality and body count of the last week. Worcester was not normally a hotbed of criminal activity and the team were getting stressed and tired. They all needed a break.

As he combed his hair, Richard wondered whether he should take Annie another small gift or whether that would be over the top. The problem was that he had no precedent for the situation that he was in. For someone who prided himself on being in control, the uncertainty was unsettling.

He was tying his shoe laces when his mobile rang.

'Boss?'

'Richard, where are you?'

'At home, boss. I'm on my way into the hospital now.'

'Not anymore,' she said, 'we've got another body. Pick me up from home. And bring the mug shots.'

Masterton emerged from the front door of her large detached house like a gatecrasher ejected from a party. Her coat was half on, half off and her bag hung from her arm. She was closely followed by her husband to whom she was issuing orders as she hurried down the path to the car. Richard distinctly heard the words 'extra milk' and 'toilet paper'.

'Oh, and don't forget to pay the power bill or we'll get cut off.'

'Haven't you heard of direct debits?' asked Richard, as she settled herself in the car.

'Morning, Richard,' she said, then added, 'I don't have time to set them up.'

Richard laughed as Masterton waved merrily at the diminishing figure of her husband.

'Is it always like that?' asked Richard.

'Not always, but often,' she replied with a smile. 'And I wouldn't have it any other way.'

'So, where are we headed?' asked Richard, as he approached the junction at the end of the road.

'Take a right. M5, M42, M40 South,' said Masterton.

'Off the patch?' remarked Richard quizzically.

'Precisely. A body was discovered late last night in a factory unit just outside Oxford.'

'Murdered?'

'Eventually,' replied Masterton. 'But the victim was tortured first and for a very long time. I'll give you the details after we've stopped for breakfast. You might not want to eat for the rest of the day.'

'What's the connection?' asked Richard.

'McIntyre picked it up. He might not say much but that man works bloody hard. He must have been in at six this morning. Spotted the murder report of an unidentified male, believed to be Afghan or Pakistani. He was just off the Eurostar. What a welcome to Britain. Where are the photos by the way?'

'Backseat,' said Richard. He concentrated on joining the motorway while Masterton reached round for the manila folder behind her. She began flicking through them until she found the picture of Soraya smiling beside the man that they assumed was her husband. Richard glanced across and saw her staring at it thoughtfully.

'The body is the husband?' asked Richard, astounded.

'Looks like it,' nodded Masterton. 'Ali Haq. We'll have to run the DNA against the babies to confirm that of course, but odds are it's the father. He is the only missing piece of the puzzle.'

The Thames Valley Police Incident Room was a swarm of activity and Richard and Masterton found themselves literally dodging detectives as they wound their way towards the office of the senior officer in charge of the investigation.

'DCI Diane Masterton and DI Richard Shaw,' said Masterton as she held out her hand to DCI Alan Rowland. Almost as tall as Richard, but carrying the weight of fifteen years at a desk, he looked every one of his almost sixty years and carried the gravitas that went with it. His thick, silver hair was cut fashionably short and he wore a smart suit that Masterton could have sworn was Armani. If she had thought to consult him, Richard could have confirmed that indeed it was.

Rowland shook Richard's hand politely then enveloped Masterton in a huge and unlikely bear hug before kissing her soundly on the lips. Masterton blushed ever so slightly and Richard fought with himself not to gape.

'Well, well, well,' Rowland said, standing back to appraise her. 'Little Dee Dee. I didn't think I would get to see you again, and a DCI to boot. How are you? How are the family?'

Richard realised that he had been standing with his jaw dropped and he snapped it shut before anyone noticed.

'I'm good. How are you, Roley?' Masterton replied.

Roley thought Richard. I'll have to file that one away.

'I haven't been the same since I sent you out to interview a mugging victim,' he laughed.

'You old tease,' retorted Masterton. 'You know that you've never had eyes for anyone but Ingrid. Swedish,' added Masterton turning to Richard. 'Tall, blonde and very beautiful.'

'That gets my vote,' replied Richard.

DCI Rowland indicated that they should sit and settled into his own chair. 'Well, I was looking forward to drifting into a peaceful retirement until last night,' he said. 'I can honestly say this is the nastiest bit of butchery I've ever come across.'

'What happened?' asked Diane.

'The body was found by a security guard. He saw the door of an empty unit ajar and went over to check it out. There was so much blood in there it was trickling out of the door.'

'Jesus.' muttered Richard.

Rowland opened a file on his desk and showed them a photo. In death, the man's face was marble white although his Middle Eastern features were still discernable.

'Is this your man?' asked Rowland.

Richard placed the photo of Soraya and her husband next to the one of the corpse.

'No doubt about it. It's Ali Haq, our dead woman's husband,' said Masterton.

She quickly briefed Rowland on the course of her investigation to date. 'Was there any ID on the body?'

'There was a passport but it was a forgery. A rather excellent and expensive forgery, but false nonetheless. However, the photos match so I believe it is your missing Afghan. I understand that DNA is being matched to the dead children as we speak.'

'Was there anything significant found on the body?' asked Masterton.

Rowland handed her a piece of paper containing a list of belongings. 'No, nothing significant. What were you hoping we would find?'

'A USB.'

'No USB. No electronics at all in fact. Not even a mobile phone. If you want to see what was left of our victim, the pictures are in here,' said Rowland, tapping the file on his desk. 'They don't make pleasant viewing.'

'What do you think happened, sir?' asked Richard.

Rowland grimaced. 'He was tied to a chair, his clothes were cut from him where he sat and he was sliced to pieces like he was a Sunday roast. Practically the only skin left on him was where his body touched the chair.'

'But they didn't touch his face,' said Masterton, shaking her head. 'Why didn't they touch his face?'

'Because they wanted us to identify him,' said Richard. 'It's a warning.'

'I agree,' said Rowland. 'Whoever did this made no attempt to cover their tracks. We are already looking at two, possibly three strings of DNA recovered from the scene.'

'But who were they trying to warn?' asked Masterton. 'And why?'

'They're telling whoever has the USB to hand it over or they will get the same treatment,' replied Richard.

'Which means they still haven't got it,' added Masterton.

'If they had it they'd be long gone,' said Richard. 'There's no trace of them entering the country and I doubt if there will be any trace when they leave.'

'Oh, they're not leaving,' said Masterton. 'It ends here.'

'It does explain why we haven't had any sightings of them, though,' Richard added. 'They've obviously been off our patch for a day or two.'

'And I bet your bottom dollar they'll be back on it already,' mused Masterton. 'Roley, is there anything else that you can give us?'

Rowland shook his head. 'There were no possessions left with the body, as you can see. Not even a wristwatch. The only lead we have is a tyre track. We should have a make and model within the next few hours but it's looking like a Honda. Probably one of thousands.'

'And with a forged plate to boot,' added Masterton.

'CCTV?' asked Richard.

'No tape in the cameras,' grimaced Rowland.

'God, what a mess,' sighed Masterton, looking at the photo of Ali again. 'By all accounts, all he wanted was a quiet life for his wife and kids and now the whole family has been wiped out.'

'Maybe this will end it?' suggested Rowland.

'I wish I could believe that,' replied Masterton, 'but we've still got information out there that could bring down one of the biggest international crime syndicates since the Mafia. These guys aren't going to pack their bags and go home. If they go home empty handed, they're dead. And if they stay here without finding what they've come for, they're still dead. And the big boss will just send a new lot over. It's not enough to bring in those three thugs. We have to find the USB too. Otherwise, this will never end.'

'You need a coffee, Diane,' said Rowland.

She ruffled her hair with her fingers. 'You're right, I do. Are you coming, Richard?'

'I'd quite like to stay and have a word with the team if that's all right with you, sir?' asked Richard.

'Of course, I'll take you out and introduce you,' offered Rowland. He indicated the file on the desk. 'Do you want the photos?'

Richard grimaced. 'Maybe just the mug shot. I'll pass on the others if you don't mind.'

'Wise man,' said Rowland. 'Come through and you can meet the team before I whisk your boss away.'

Richard raised his eyebrows to Masterton before he followed Rowland out of the office. She mouthed 'thank you' to him as he left.

Chapter Thirty-Five

There was a restless silence in the car as they drove back to the station, both of them occupied with thoughts of the case. The motorway was busy and Richard was grateful for a dry, sunny day as he pushed his way through the traffic.

'Penny for them?' asked Masterton eventually.

'I was just going to say the same thing,' replied Richard.

'No, you weren't. Anyway, I asked first. Boss's prerogative.'

Richard smiled briefly before becoming serious as he replied, 'I was just wondering who they are going to kill next.'

'You don't think they've already had a bellyful then?'

'Not by a long shot,' replied Richard. 'These are men that kill for a living and probably still manage to sleep at night. They won't stop until they've got what they want.'

'I agree with you there,' mused Masterton. 'It's starting to feel a bit crowded in my office the way the bodies keep piling up.'

'We're on the back foot all the time, boss,' said Richard. 'We're reactive. They kill someone, we react. We need to change our approach.'

'We've already got a large part of their suspected locality under surveillance,' she pointed out.

'It's not enough.'

'Go on then,' replied Masterton with a smile. 'Impress me.'

'Suppose we find the USB.'

'And how do you propose we do that?'

'Through Soraya.'

'I hate to remind you, but she's dead, Richard.'

'Exactly. She was only on the loose for a matter of days and she was heavily pregnant. She probably didn't go far. If she carried the USB into the country ahead of her husband she could easily have hidden it somewhere. The police pathologist found nothing on her body. These guys, these animals, are not going to give up their search and their actions to date suggest that Soraya was a prime target. We know the USB wasn't at the house because they are still out there looking and going by the state of Ali, we can assume he didn't give much away. Probably because he genuinely didn't know.'

'Poor sod,' said Masterton. 'Do you think they told him his wife and babies were dead?'

Richard shook his head. 'I doubt it. He probably would have given up if he'd known that. I think those thugs would have wanted him to think she was alive and in danger. That's the only way they would get him to talk.'

'So you reckon we track Soraya's movements?' asked Masterton returning to her previous question.

'I do,' agreed Richard. 'We find out every place she visited and every person she came into contact with. Basically, we retrace her steps from the time she entered the country till the moment she was found in the warehouse. And we search everything and everywhere she touched.'

'So we beat them to the evidence, hand it over to the NCA and we have three now very disgruntled thugs on our hands.'

'You've forgotten the ancillary plan,' added Richard.

'What's that?'

'We draw them out,' said Richard, 'and the sooner the better. We need the men and we need the evidence and we need it yesterday.'

'You must know that I agree with you, Richard, but you are making it sound just a little too straight forward.'

'Are you suggesting we sit back and wait for their next move?'

Masterton smiled and shook her head. 'I am suggesting that you work up a plan and it had better be a bloody good one.'

Richard dropped Masterton at the station and headed to the hospital. He was surprised and delighted to find Annie in her chair by the window again. Her crazy curls were completely out of control and a patchwork of multi-coloured bruises decorated her face but her eyes were bright and her smile broad.

'Hello, you,' he said, as he entered the room.

She started slightly at the sound of his voice then relaxed as she recognised him.

'Hello back,' she replied with a smile that warmed him down to his toes.

'You're looking better,' he remarked.

She pulled a face as she spoke. 'Sorry about yesterday.'

'You've got nothing to be sorry about,' said Richard, as he fetched his chair to sit across from her. 'You've been amazing and if you refuse to believe that I might have to arrest you.'

'What's the charge Inspector?' Her eyes were twinkling as she joined in the game.

'Stubbornly refusing to believe a police officer,' Richard shot back.

'And the sentence?'

'I will have to discuss that with the judge,' he replied loftily.

'You can't think of anything,' she accused.

'Oh, believe me, I can,' he assured her. 'It's lucky for you that you're convalescing.'

'With my own personal protection officer right outside the door,' she pointed out.

'You're pushing your luck you know that, don't you?'

She laughed so much she had to put a hand on the scar on her abdomen. Richard laughed with her, amazed at how happy she made him feel even in the midst of the worst case of his career to date.

'Can you do something else for me?' he asked.

'Of course, anything,' she replied.

'We have faces for two of the men who attacked you,' he explained. 'We need the third. Can you look through some photos for me, see if you recognise anyone?'

Annie felt a hollow open up inside her stomach and Richard saw the colour drain from her face, but she nodded anyway. However she felt about the attack, she would do anything for this man. And she would not be beaten down by what had happened to her. As she recovered from her injuries, Annie was shocked to find herself imagining the revenge she would take on her attackers if only she could be given the opportunity. She wanted them wiped from the face of the earth. Annie realised that the events of the last few days had changed her in ways that went against her previous placatory approach to people.

Richard handed her the pack of photos and she began to look through them, studying each one carefully before putting it to one side and picking up the next.

The man already identified by Gary Russell, Abdul Farid, was the fifth photo in the pile. He saw Annie's eyes widen and her hands begin to shake as she stared at the face in front of her. She held out the photo to Richard.

'This one.'

'Are you sure?'

'I'm certain. He was one of the ones holding me,' she said. 'He has an unusual profile.'

Richard reached into his jacket pocket for his pocketbook and made a few notes while Annie continued to sift through the photos. Today she was wearing hospital scrubs a size too large which made her look more vulnerable than ever. Richard looked away, fearful that his own face might reveal his feelings. When he turned his head back, he saw that Annie had reached the end of the pile. She held the photo of Ali and Soraya in her hands and she was studying it intently.

She opened her mouth as if to say something then closed it again with a little shake of her head.

'What is it?' asked Richard.

Annie ignored his question. 'Could you pass me my sketch pad and pencils?' she asked. 'They're on the locker beside the bed.'

Richard brought them over and Annie began sketching furiously, glancing occasionally at the photo of Soraya and Ali.

'We know that this man is not one of the suspects...' Richard began, but Annie shushed him so sharply that he closed his mouth in astonishment. Her concentration was total as she worked on the sketch. Richard resigned himself to sitting back and enjoying the opportunity to commit every centimetre of her face to memory. Annie's wild curls fell forward as she drew and he was sorely tempted to lean forward and tuck them behind her ear. Somehow he sensed that the gesture would not be appreciated right now.

'There.'

She turned the pad around to face Richard and he sat up in astonishment.

'What do you see?' asked Annie triumphantly.

'A man,' began Richard, 'who looks like Soraya.'

'Exactly,' said Annie. 'Soraya's brother.'

Richard was flabbergasted. 'Are you sure?'

'When I first saw that photo,' said Annie, indicating the picture of Soraya and Ali, 'at first glance, I almost thought it was him. The photo is quite formal and posed and probably taken a year or two ago. Soraya's features have softened since then which is why I didn't pick up on the likeness before. But the bone structure of the face and the eyes are exactly the same. They may be siblings or even half-siblings, but I'm absolutely certain they're closely related.'

'Are you telling me that the third thug could be Soraya's brother?'

'Or half- brother,' Annie pointed out.

'Are you really sure?' asked Richard.

'I can't be one hundred per cent certain,' said Annie, 'but I am reasonably confident.'

A dozen thoughts were chasing themselves around inside Richard's skull.

'So, Soraya does a runner with her husband Ali and brother-in-law, Masood and her own brother gets sent to bring her back. How bizarre is that?

'It's probably a family honour thing,' suggested Annie, 'or maybe it's a test of the brother's loyalty?'

'You are in the wrong job,' smiled Richard.

'Either way,' replied Annie, 'it's a good enough likeness. Now, will you do something for me?'

Richard returned the photos to the folder.

'Just ask.'

Annie pointed to her scrubs with a look of total disgust on her face. 'Your lot took away every stitch of my clothing. I need something to wear,' she said. 'Can someone fetch some clothes for me?'

'I'll have to check that your place has been cleared but I don't see why not.'

'Shall I ask a friend to call round?'

'No,' replied Richard remembering the upturned drawers and blood-spattered walls in Annie's bedroom. 'It's better left to the police for security reasons. It's still a crime scene. We have to log everything we take and have it witnessed. Write me a list, I'll go myself.'

'I don't want you sorting through my undies,' remarked Annie.

Richard chuckled. 'If it makes you feel any better,' he said, 'I'll take a WPC to get your things.'

'Thank you,' replied Annie as she started to write her list.

Chapter Thirty-Six

Richard was back at the station later than he would have liked but he was thrilled to have pictures of the three men. Abdul Farid had already been identified, there was the thug that Annie had initially drawn and now a third man believed to be Soraya's brother. Richard knew that taking Annie's word on this was more than a little tenuous but his gut told him that she was right.

It could explain the links between the hunters and the hunted and why the whole mess had materialized on their doorstep. If both Ali and Soraya had a brother working for Hajji, there could be a great deal of honour and loyalty at stake. As well as no amount of jealousy and double-crossing.

Every new piece of information brought them closer to catching the thugs and he sent the third drawing through to the NCA as soon as he reached the office.

Masterton had begun a new incident board focusing on the three Afghans with Masood, Ali, and Soraya shown as associates. The revelation from Annie demanded a re-ordering of the relationships.

'Is she quite sure about this?' questioned Masterton.

'It's only her opinion,' admitted Richard, 'but she does seem to know a lot about faces. I think we can trust that this is a good likeness of the third man and the resemblance to Soraya is uncanny. It's definitely a lead worth pursuing.'

'Ok,' agreed Masterton. 'We'll go with it for now, but treat it as supposition only until we have more information. Meanwhile, get Collins back out to the hairdresser first thing in the morning with these pictures.

See if he can give us anything else on these three and anything on Soraya's movements.'

'Will do, boss. Can I borrow one of the WDC's?'

'Where are you off to?'

'Annie's place. Forensics have finished and she needs some clothes.'

'Yes, go for it. I'm assuming that nothing was found there? No USBs or anything of that nature?'

'Nothing, boss.'

'Pity,' said Masterton. 'We're in dire need of a breakthrough on this one.'

WDC Palmer was happy to escape from the station for an hour or two, especially as it meant overtime. Her boyfriend was taking her to Cyprus in January and the extra spending money would come in handy. Working with DI Shaw was an added bonus. You always knew where you were with him. There was none of the chauvinistic banter that the WDC's still had to put up with even though it was supposed to be against the rules. Of course, these days, the women gave as good as they got, but with the DI it was always strictly business. She wondered if the rumours flying around about him having a thing for the witness were true. Well, good for him if they are, she thought. He deserves to have someone in his life.

They pulled up outside Annie's house just as the early evening light bathed the front garden in a pink glow.

'What a gorgeous house,' remarked Palmer.

'You might not say that when you see inside,' replied Richard.

'Even so,' Palmer replied, 'it's really cute. It's the sort of house kids would draw.'

Richard had the key in his hand as he walked to the front door. He wanted to be in and out as quickly as possible. The place was spooking him.

The front door opened directly into the front room which the thugs had begun searching so that the cupboard doors hung open, their contents spewed across the floor. The sitting area was relatively unscathed but when Richard looked through to the kitchen it looked as if a tornado had rushed through and upended every item onto the floor.

'I can see it's a mess,' said Palmer, 'but it's still a lovely home.'

'She won't be coming back, though,' said Richard. 'There are too many bad memories. She doesn't want to come near the place.'

'Oh, that's a shame.' Palmer looked genuinely sorry for the unwanted house.

'Do you have the list?' asked Richard.

'Yes, boss, it's here.'

'Let's get on with it then.'

Upstairs in the bedroom, Richard had to avert his eyes from the sight of Annie's blood which stained the walls and carpet. He was glad that she didn't want to return to the house. She didn't need to see this.

'Can you get the toiletries, boss? I'll do the clothes.'

Palmer was already lifting items of clothing from the bedroom carpet and examining each of them before placing them on the bed in orderly piles. Richard went next door to the bathroom where he had to stop and close his eyes for a moment as he breathed in the scent of Annie.

He found a sponge bag in the cabinet beneath the sink and filled it with most of the open bottles around the bathroom, shampoo, conditioner, cleanser, moisturiser, toothbrush, and toothpaste. He turned to take the robe hanging on the back of the door and his foot crunched on broken glass. A bottle of perfume had been smashed there and it was this scent that had filled the air. Richard examined the remains of the bottle and committed the name of it to his memory.

Back in the bedroom, he handed the items to Palmer who was ready to pack a small suitcase that she had retrieved from the top of the wardrobe. She called out each item for Richard to jot down so that they had a record of all the items removed. When they had finished there was still room in the case.

'If she's not coming back boss, we might as well fill this up. It's all going to have to be packed for her at some point.'

Richard concurred and they filled the case with track pants and tops that Palmer thought would be cool and comfortable in the stuffy hospital. Downstairs Richard retrieved a large plastic bag from his pocket and filled it with teddies.

'Special request,' he offered in response to Palmer's quizzically raised eyebrows. 'Right, let's get out of here.'

Richard was feeling increasingly uncomfortable in the house, unsure whether it was the fact that it was Annie's home or because of what had happened there. He was grateful that the last evening light had not faded before they left. The suitcase and bag of teddies were deposited in the back seat of the car and Richard started the engine with relief.

'I'll drop you at the station so that you can knock off,' said Richard. 'I'll take these things to the hospital in the morning.'

'Sure, boss,' responded Palmer. She seemed to be obsessed with Annie's home and was still raving about the décor and paintings when Richard realised that he was being followed. The vehicle three cars behind him was a grey Honda.

'Palmer!'

She stopped babbling as he snapped out her name and she flushed. 'Sorry, boss.'

'Palmer, listen to me,' he interrupted. His tone of voice was severe and he immediately had her attention. 'Whatever you do, don't move unexpectedly and please do not turn around.'

Palmer immediately froze in her seat.

'Are we being followed, boss?'

'I believe we are,' replied Richard with a reassuring air of calm.

He reached forward and pressed the speed dial on his phone.

'Richard.' Masterton's voice was clear over the speaker.

'Boss, I'm returning to the station with WDC Palmer. I am being tailed by a grey Honda. Repeat. I am being tailed by a grey Honda.

'Where are you?' she asked sharply.

Richard gave his position.

'What's your ETA?'

'Ten to twelve minutes,' he replied.

'Keep driving, Richard, and get back here as quickly as you can without arousing their suspicion. I'm sending out all of the available unmarked response cars now. Keep the line open.'

She was back on the line in minutes sounding breathless but controlled.

'Richard, can you hear me?'

'Loud and clear, boss.'

'Unmarked cars have been despatched and the armed response unit is gearing up. Drive directly to the station where you will find the car park gates open for you. Do not engage these men in any way. Do you understand, Richard?'

'Understood, boss,' he replied.

'Where are you now?'

Richard gave his position and he could hear Masterton giving directions to the unmarked cars. It was taking all of his concentration to maintain a steady speed when he knew that his Audi could outrun the following car easily. He also knew that a chase in an urban area was unwarranted and dangerous. The last thing he needed was to be responsible for killing a child.

'Are they our suspects?' asked Palmer.

'Questions later, Palmer,' said Masterton over the speaker. 'Help the DI to focus.'

'Yes, ma'am.'

Richard was an expert driver and he handled the Audi smoothly. The grey Honda was holding its position three cars behind and Richard felt sure that the men did not know he was aware of their presence. A background voice crackled over the speaker and Richard heard Masterton issue a short command before returning to the line.

'Richard, we have a silver Ford at the next junction. He has a visual on you.' Richard looked ahead and saw the car.

'Got it, boss.'

Richard accelerated slightly to give the Ford an opportunity to pull out behind his Audi. He knew that the officers in the car would be armed and he immediately felt some of the tension in his shoulders ease. Almost at once he caught sight of a second unmarked car ahead of him.

'Ok, Richard,' said Masterton, 'we've got you covered. Pull ahead and get to the station. The others will try to hold him.'

'I can draw them out, boss,' said Richard, 'just tell me where you want them.'

Palmer looked at him fearfully.

Masterton's voice was authoritative. 'DI Shaw, you are in the company of a WDC and you are both unarmed. You have seen what these men can do. Now get back here at the double.'

Richard sighed but complied with the order. 'On my way.'

The traffic lights ahead were on amber. Richard eased his car forward and just as they turned red he shot around the corner. The cross traffic blew their horns as they were forced to break but Richard executed the move smoothly and accelerated away. The grey Honda had little chance of escaping the traffic amongst the congested Worcester City Centre roads.

Within minutes Richard was parked in the station car park where he ushered a shaken Palmer inside.

'Go and get yourself a cup of tea,' he advised, before rushing up to the Incident Room where Masterton was still barking orders into the radio mike.

'You find them and you pull them in. Use whatever force is necessary.'

'Where are they?' asked Richard.

'Heading for the M5 motorway by the sound of it.'

'They've aborted?'

'The minute they lost you at the lights they executed an illegal U-turn and headed in the direction of the motorway. By the time our dozy lot had turned round they were out of sight.'

They both listened anxiously to the radio calls as the pursuit cars searched for the Honda. It soon became clear that it had disappeared into thin air.

Masterton slammed the desk with her hand. 'Jesus bloody Christ! We had them in our sights. How could we lose them like that?'

Richard placed a hand on her shoulder.

'Like you said, boss, these men are professionals, we know what they are capable of. It wouldn't surprise me if they were using a scanner.'

'Even so,' Masterton shook her head. 'We shouldn't have lost them that easily.'

'I don't think we did,' said Richard.

'I can't see them being brought in,' replied Masterton.

'I think they just wanted to watch where I was going. As soon as they saw me turn towards the station, they scarpered.'

'Where have they scarpered to for God's sake?'

'Somewhere really close,' guessed Richard. 'A garage, lock up, old shed. Somewhere they could run and hide. And it has to be close for them to disappear so easily. They must have been watching Annie's house and followed me from there.'

Masterton was on her feet, her spirit at least partially restored.

'I'll get onto McIntyre and make sure he's in first thing. He can set up a search grid. It's time for a bit more house to house. Or shed to shed more likely.'

'We'll need a cover story for the door knocking,' Richard pointed out. 'If we find these guys they won't be keen on opening their doors to visitors.'

Masterton paused to think.

'We can say we are looking for a runaway teenager,' she said. 'House to house, anybody seen anything.'

'We'll need a mug shot, boss.'

'You can use David Beckham for all I care, half the population say no without even looking anyway.'

'I'll get McIntyre to sort us something before he starts the grid.'

'Right, you do that,' she sighed. 'I'm going home.'

Chapter Thirty-Seven

Wednesday night

It was late when Richard left the station and he took great care to scan the streets all the time he was driving. On an ordinary night he would be home and in his flat in less than ten minutes, but that night he spent over an hour cruising the streets of Worcester as he constantly checked his rear view mirror for an unexpected grey shadow. Only when his car was secure in the underground car park and he was safe behind the double locked door of his flat did he begin to relax. He thought of Annie, attacked in her bedroom, and tried to imagine even a fraction of the fear she must now have at the thought of living there again. It was time those men were put away and the sooner the better. He almost wished that they would come for him so that he could batter them to kingdom come.

Perhaps it was the adrenaline of being followed or the horror of Annie's invaded home, or maybe both, but sleep eluded Richard for much of that night. He plugged in his iPod and turned up the volume as high as he could bear in an effort to drown out the noise of the case in his head. When Meatloaf didn't work he tried Adele but her lyrics tightened his throat and blocked his sinuses with emotion. Even the little-used TV failed to distract him and he found himself staring blindly at the screen barely able to discern whether he was watching an ad or a feature. Finally, he gave up distraction as a tool and let his mind free to roam over all the ridges and furrows of the case. The men were so close he could feel them, and as he paced across his living room floor, a plan began to form in his mind. He fetched paper and pen and began to write.

There is a period of the morning, sometime around four am, when even the most hardened night shift worker begins to droop a little. It's the time when accidents are more likely to happen when workers who sit too comfortably in a chair are likely to feel their eyes droop and their minds wander towards the very small nap that will tide them over till morning. That's the time when the strong coffee is made and consumed, the smokers light up or the dieters succumb to a quick sugar fix. That was also the time when the night sergeant decided to step out into the car park in the hope that a blast of cold air would sharpen up his senses.

His hand was just reaching out to the keypad that opened the door to the outside when an enormous roar followed by a screeching crash shook the building. Instinct made him drop to the floor before his brain had engaged enough to bring his eyes up to the window so that he could look outside. Instantly the alarm sounded in the building and he could hear shouts and running feet.

His jaw dropped as he looked outside and saw the giant earthmoving monster that had driven through the security gates of the car park as if they were matchsticks. Reversing into the car park next to it was a tow truck and the sergeant knew at once which car they were after. Two officers came panting towards him, ready to run outside but he held up his hand and reached out to switch off the light that would be illuminating them all like bulls eyes at a fairground.

'What the…' began one of the men but the sergeant shushed them and pointed outside. His two colleagues froze as they saw the driver of the earthmover with his back to the tow truck and a Kalashnikov pointed at the station.

'Just go and make sure those cameras are running,' he instructed and one of the men ran to the CCTV room, happy not to have to be a hero.

Richard picked up his mobile on the first ring.

'Can't you sleep either, boss?' he asked.

'I've been sleeping very well thank you,' replied Masterton, 'but our three friends must be suffering from insomnia.'

Richard was instantly alert.'What's happened?'

'They've ram-raided the station car park with an earth mover and a tow truck.'

She paused, waiting to see if Richard would identify the target.

'Annie's car,' said Richard.

'Precisely.'

'So, they're still looking.'

'And getting desperate,' replied Masterton. 'It wasn't exactly a subtle move.'

'Caught on camera?'

'They had better be or someone's for the high jump.'

Richard was already leaving his flat as he spoke and Masterton heard him closing his front door.

'It didn't take you long to get your clothes on,' commented Masterton.

'I didn't take them off,' replied Richard. 'I couldn't settle tonight.'

'Well, if that happens again make sure I'm the first to know,' she said. 'Your instincts have always been spot on. I'll see you at the station.'

Chapter Thirty-Eight

Thursday

Masterton and Richard watched the tape through several times at normal speed before slowing it down and enhancing sections that interested them, like the face of the driver as he climbed from the cab of the earth mover waving his Kalashnikov and the tow truck emerging from its shadow with Annie's car hooked up like a fish caught on a line. As soon as Annie's car was clear of the car park, the driver climbed back into the cab of the earth mover and trundled it slowly forward, effectively blocking the exit to and from the car park.

'Those things are not easy to drive,' commented Richard.

'Well, he seems to know what he's doing,' observed Masterton. 'It could be another clue to his identity. I wonder how many earth mover drivers there are in Afghanistan?'

'Quite a few, I would imagine,' said Richard. 'I hear there is a lot of rubble.'

Masterton turned to the night sergeant who was sitting next to them drinking a huge mug of strong, sweet tea. 'Do we know where they got it?'

'Railway station, boss. They're putting in a new shunting yard. It's like a box of Tonka toys down there.'

'And not much security, I presume?'

'The machinery was all in a locked compound,' replied the sergeant, 'and there were regular security patrols but that was it.'

'Regular patrols, well, we all know what that means don't we?'

'Hourly drive by,' offered Richard.

'Absolutely. On the other hand,' said Masterton, 'it was probably just as well. It looks as though this lot were prepared to shoot anyone that got in the way. Has the tow truck been recovered?'

'No sign of it, boss,' replied the sergeant. 'We couldn't get our own vehicles out to follow quickly enough so had to call in the few cars that we had mobile. They were well gone by then.'

'They've definitely got some sort of lock up, boss,' said Richard. 'And it's so close. I can almost feel it.'

'I think you're right,' nodded Masterton. 'It's still our next best move. What time is it?'

'Just after five.'

'Ok. Sergeant, you can return to your duties. Get this written up before you knock off and get Collins out of bed and on to CCTV. I want him to scan the surrounding area and everything between here and the railway station. Richard, I want you to see Annie as soon as she's awake. Find out what was in that car. And somebody get me some coffee.'

'I don't think there was much in the car,' replied Richard. 'I checked it myself when I brought it here. There was just her midwifery bag which I put into my boot.'

'Check anyway,' said Masterton, then paused. 'What is it?'

She had seen the expression on Richard's face suddenly change.

'It's Annie. I think we should move her.'

'What are you talking about? She's perfectly safe. She's got an armed guard on her door.'

Richard shook his head vehemently. 'These men are getting desperate. I think she's in danger. It's obvious she's their target.'

'Not to me it isn't.' Masterton placed a hand on his arm. 'Richard, I think you're over-reacting. Perhaps you have got too close.'

'No, boss.' Richard was adamant. 'Why would they take Annie's car now? And so blatantly. Those guys didn't even bother to cover their faces.'

'They took the car because they could and clearly it's another place they need to search. I would imagine they have been looking for her car for a day or two. It's possible that they were following you when you drove it here.'

'So, why haven't they targeted the landlady, or the hairdresser, Kambiz? Soraya may have had contact with them too?'

'Supposition, Richard.'

Richard began to pace around the table. 'And what about me?'

'What about you?'

'I drove Annie's car to the station. Clearly, I was followed. If they were watching the station they may have seen me searching the car. I could be a target too.'

Masterton nodded as she thought about this.

'Or what if Ali did talk before he died? What if he pointed the finger at Annie?'

'He didn't know Annie.'

'But he must have talked to Soraya on the phone or via Skype or something. His wife was pregnant, he would have asked her how she was, where she was, whether she had seen a doctor.'

Richard swung round to face Masterton.

'Is Annie's house under surveillance?'

Masterton shook her head. 'We don't have endless resources, Richard, you know that.'

'If they have been back there,' said Richard, 'do you agree that Annie should be removed to a place of safety?'

Masterton stared at him for a moment. His eyes were burning with passion and his jaw was set so firmly she imagined his teeth might start to crack. She was afraid that his feelings for Annie were affecting his judgement. As always, Richard seemed to read her mind.

'If we catch these men, Annie is going to be a key witness for the prosecution. She has already been beaten, traumatised and suffered God knows what else. She has a right to be protected by us and we can't afford to lose her. My friendship with her has nothing to do with those facts and you need to accept that as the truth.'

Masterton's instinct was to retort back, annoyed at being spoken to like that. But she recognised that there was indeed some truth in his words. She was assuming that Richard's decisions were based on emotion when the points he was making were actually logical.

'Ok, Richard. I'll send out a patrol. Meanwhile, you've got some thinking to do because even if the doctors agree that we can move her, I have no idea where she could go.'

'Oh, I know the perfect place,' replied Richard, calmly. 'There has to be some purpose to siblings.'

Masterton raised her eyebrows at his proposal. 'I can't get clearance for that.'

'The Super can,' answered Richard.

Masterton shook her head as she stood up to leave the room.

'It takes very little to surprise me, Richard, but you seem to manage it all the time.'

'You're welcome, boss,' he quipped and reached for the phone.

Richard was in the canteen tucking into toast and muesli when Masterton came to find him. She held her right hand out to Richard and said, 'put it there.'

'Boss?' he asked, as he allowed her to shake his hand.

'When I'm wrong I say I'm wrong.'

She sat down opposite him and Richard put down his spoon.

'Annie's house,' he said with a feeling of dread.

'Completely done over.'

Richard felt himself go cold. Finding himself proved right brought him no pleasure.

'They finished what they started.'

'They haven't yet,' said Masterton. 'Go and get her.'

Chapter Thirty-Nine

Annie was sitting in a wheelchair swathed in blankets and looking totally bewildered when Richard arrived at the hospital. Her little teddy was clutched in her hand. All she had been told was that she was being transferred. All she could think was that Richard should know that she was being moved. Richard should be there to say that it was ok. She relaxed visibly as she caught sight of him striding into the ward looking calm and confident. Her stomach turned a flurry of somersaults.

'Hello, you,' she smiled with evident relief. 'Where are we off to?'

'We have to get you out of here,' he said without pleasantries. 'I'll explain on the way.'

Annie nodded, recognising the professional persona that she had witnessed at the Asylum Centre. Her questions could wait.

'Inspector Shaw,' Doctor Latham had entered the room. He handed Richard a bulky folder. 'Medical notes, charts, prescriptions, and nursing plan. Her drugs are in the blue bag.'

'Thank you, Doctor,' said Richard. 'I realise this has been a bit of a rush for everyone.'

'I can't say I am entirely happy about it but I understand completely,' reassured the doctor.

'Thank you for all that you have done, Doctor.' Richard shook his hand and nodded to the armed officers still guarding Annie

'Let's go,' he ordered.

A nurse led the way pushing Annie's wheelchair before her. To Annie, the labyrinth of corridors seemed endless but it didn't take them long to reach what looked like a storage area piled with flattened cardboard boxes and abandoned trolleys. They squeezed into a dusty service lift with a rutted vinyl floor and stared at the closed doors while the lift bumped down to the basement of the hospital. As the lift doors opened onto a dim underground area, two further armed police officers signalled the all clear to Richard. An ambulance was waiting with its back doors open. Annie was quickly installed while Richard checked out the two paramedics. He was pleased to find that he recognised both of them but still checked their IDs thoroughly. He joined one of the paramedics who introduced himself as Peter with Annie and the two armed officers in the back of the ambulance. It was a bit of a tight squeeze but no-one complained.

'The world,' exclaimed Annie, as the ambulance emerged into the street outside the hospital. She smiled at Richard. 'I'd forgotten what it looks like.'

'I'm afraid you don't get to see much from in here,' apologized Peter, indicating the small window next to Annie's stretcher. 'These beasts are built for privacy.'

'It doesn't matter,' grinned Annie. 'I'm outside, it's a beautiful day and I won't have to eat another hospital sandwich.'

Richard was reluctant to spoil Annie's joy but he believed that bad news was best delivered as soon as possible. 'Annie, I have some bad news.'

Annie's smile froze and Richard leaned across to take her hand.

'We have to move you to a place of safety because your house has been broken into and searched. We believe it was the men who attacked you.'

Annie was bewildered. 'They came back? Why did they come back? They must know I'm not there?'

'The first time they came to your house they were disturbed by the arrival of the emergency services,' explained Richard. 'At this stage, we can only speculate, but they obviously haven't found what they are looking for so they came back.'

'Do you think they are looking for the USB?' asked Annie.

'We think so,' replied Richard. 'Are you sure you haven't seen anything like it?'

Annie shook her head. 'But they obviously think I might have it'

Richard rubbed his chin and regarded Annie thoughtfully. 'As far as we are aware, you are the only person known to have had direct contact with the dead woman.'

'But she didn't give me anything,' said Annie. 'I would remember.'

'There is a possibility that she concealed the USB somewhere. She didn't necessarily have to hand the thing over. She was clearly very frightened. And these men won't stop until they find it. So until we find them, we are going to keep you safe.'

Annie nodded but said nothing more. Visions of her cosy home upturned and vandalised were almost too much to bear. She marvelled that one minute her life was pottering along with nothing much to worry about beyond a difficult case or a bill to pay and the next she was embroiled with dead babies and international terrorists. Life suddenly felt very unfair and she wondered if she would ever feel safe again. Annie closed her eyes and wished for sleep that refused to come.

With judicious use of the blue light they reached the police station quickly and were waved through into the car park by armed officers. A small crane was removing the mutilated gates and Annie could see new ones already waiting to be installed. She saw the devastation through the window of the ambulance and glanced at Richard, but he was already occupied discussing her arrival with Peter. Once again, the ambulance was backed right up to a ground floor doorway so that she could not be seen as she was transferred into the station.

As she was wheeled through the station, Richard once again found himself breaking the bad news to Annie.

'Annie, there was a break in at the station last night. Did you see the damage to the gates as we came in?'

Annie nodded. 'What happened?'

'I'm sorry to have to tell you but our three friends came for your car.'

'Did they get it?'

'I'm afraid so. Were you attached to it?'

Annie shrugged and shook her head. She wasn't particularly attached to the little Toyota that had served her well for the last three years. But even if she had been, with everything that had happened over the last few days it barely mattered.

'Annie, I have to go upstairs. I'll see you shortly,' said Richard and before she could even say goodbye, she had been whisked into the bowels of the police station.

'Where is the Inspector going?' asked Annie.

'Back to the hospital,' explained the paramedic. 'He'll leave by the front door and drive back here in his own car. He wants to make it look as if you're still there.'

'I see,' said Annie. What else was there to say? Whatever was happening was outside of her control and right now she was too sore and far too tired to think of anything beyond the oblivion of a good sleep.

She was installed in the station's tiny windowless first aid room that was the closest thing to a prison cell she had ever experienced. Peter checked her temperature, pulse and blood pressure and examined her wound before declaring her satisfactory and settling himself into the corner of the room with a paperback. Although the door was closed Annie could hear the quietly murmured conversation of the police officers guarding her door.

She closed her eyes hoping to rest but the conversation in the ambulance was replaying itself over and over in Annie's head. Now that she was ensconced in the police station, the reality of her situation finally began to sink in. She was largely responsible for the death of two babies. She had been violated in her own home which was now wrecked and tainted by the men who had attacked her. Her car was gone and her life was in danger so that now she felt like a prisoner.

A feeling of dread settled itself inside Annie's guts and she could sense the panic that was creeping up to join it. She didn't know what was going to happen to her. She didn't know if she would get through this. And she didn't know how she could ever hope to return to any sort of normal life. Most of all she wished that Richard would come back and make her feel safe again.

She tried to hold back the tears but a small sob escaped and Peter was on his feet at once.

'Hey, are you ok? Are you in pain?'

Annie shook her head. 'Just a bit overwhelmed by everything.'

Peter made all the right noises to reassure Annie, but his platitudes were useless. The truth was she felt absolutely terrified. It was the sedative that finally helped her to fall asleep. She was unaware of Richard peeping round the door on his return to the station or Peter's whispered, 'She's ok.' The short ride in the ambulance had left her exhausted and she didn't wake until a knock on the door heralded the arrival of her food, a bowl of soup, a tuna sandwich and a melting lump of vanilla ice-cream. Annie grinned.

'I thought I had escaped institutional food,' she commented to Peter.

'Not yet,' he replied. 'You are still officially a patient I'm afraid.'

'That's the problem,' said Annie. 'I don't think I'm very patient. I'd give anything to have my life back right this minute.'

Peter patted her arm. 'Hang on in there, Annie. I'm sure it will all be over before too long.'

'If only,' thought Annie, with a touch more premonition than she would have liked.

Chapter Forty

Richard found the Incident Room buzzing with activity. As well as the extra officers, Masterton had managed to secure some additional clerical staff to handle the telephone lines, emails, and social media. There was a dedicated press officer and an experienced officer liaising with central agencies in an attempt to identify the three thugs. To date, only Abdul Farid had been named and Richard knew how important it was that they identified the two others as soon as possible. The good news was that Thames Valley had provided them with DNA from three unidentified males and he felt confident that once the elimination work was complete they would be left with the three thugs.

What interested him most was the drawing that Annie had made suggesting that one of the men was related to Soraya. At this stage, it was no more than supposition but Annie's conviction and Richard's own gut made him believe that there could be a connection. If Soraya and one of the three Afghans were siblings, it would explain how Soraya and her husband had got involved with Hajji in the first place, and with Masood's help, it might also explain how they had accessed Hajji's computer. The more Richard thought about it, the more sense it made.

'Can I have your attention everyone?'

Masterton was at the whiteboards ready to brief the team and Richard took to the floor to explain the plan that he had hatched during the night. Masterton had been busy in his absence and everything was arranged.

'I will be taking Annie to a place of safety as soon as it's dark this evening. You will not be told her destination except that it is off our patch. First thing in the morning, we will issue a press release to say that Annie has been discharged from hospital and returned home to the care of relatives.'

'But the suspects know her house is wrecked,' interrupted Spooner. 'Why would they believe that she would go there?'

'We have a team tidying up as we speak,' said Masterton. 'We'll include that information in the press release. Continue, Richard.'

'We use a decoy police officer who will leave the hospital as Annie,' continued Richard. 'She will be taken into the house by paramedics who will then leave.'

'Who will be the decoy?' asked Palmer.

'I think it should be McIntyre,' suggested Collins. 'He doesn't get out much.'

'You're the screen star, Collins,' countered McIntyre.

'I'm not on it,' retorted Collins. 'I just watch it.'

'The decoy will be armed,' continued Masterton, 'with a wig, blankets and a few dressings to the face. We should be able to affect the transfer without his or her face being visible.'

'This is a high-risk operation,' said Richard. 'There will be an armed response team in the house. If these men are as desperate as we think they are, they won't waste any time breaking in.'

'What do we do, ma'am?' asked Carter.

'We continue our search of the locality,' said Richard. 'If the decoy plan doesn't work…' Hoots and catcalls went around the room. 'If the plan does not achieve the desired result,' continued Richard, 'finding their base of operations is going to be our next best option. We believe that they are holed up somewhere in this locality.'

Richard turned to point at an enlarged map showing Annie's house and the nearby streets. As he gave details of the operation, Masterton silently prayed that Richard's sting would work. Apart from the growing body count, she had been hauled over the coals that morning by the Super demanding to know why the most expensive operation in the County was producing nothing but corpses. You've got to the end of the week, he had told her, and Masterton had vowed to put that time to good use.

It rained during the afternoon and Richard spent much of it checking the weather forecast and traffic updates on his computer. His ability to focus under pressure made him a confident and competent driver. But that was without Annie in the car and definitely not with the complication of greasy roads and a possible tail. The images on his screen assured him that the roads should be dry by the time the evening rush hour was underway and he prayed that they would be right. Meanwhile, he concentrated on memorising his route and ensuring that he had suitable backup available in the areas where he felt he would be most vulnerable. There was also one more phone call to finalise arrangements for their arrival. He picked up the receiver and dialled.

It had been a long day and would be an even longer night but Richard was already beginning to feel the effects of the adrenaline rush that would carry him through the operation. Good detective work was about persistence, patience and attention to detail, all characteristics that Richard had by the bucket load. But there was nothing like the thrill of some concrete action to get him fired up and ready to get those tossers once and for all. And the beauty of this case was that thanks to modern forensics, they had enough evidence to put the three thugs away for life. Finding the missing data would be the icing on the cake, but from Richard's point of view, that was currently secondary to getting those murdering bastards off the streets. There was nothing worse than catching a criminal only to watch him walk free due to a lack of evidence, a talented lawyer, or even worse, some cock up from the prosecution. But not this time, thought Richard. Catch them and they will be canned. His thoughts were interrupted by the appearance of Masterton beside his desk.

'It's time, Richard.'

'I'm ready.'

'Radio silence unless absolutely necessary. We are reasonably confident that they are scanning our radio signals.'

'Yes, boss,' replied Richard calmly.

'I'm not going to wish you luck because you don't need it, you're well prepared and the backup is all in place.'

'Thanks, boss.'

'Just make sure you get some rest before you drive back.'

Already on his feet, Richard nodded his thanks and was gone.

Masterton watched him leave, so confident and in control. I wish I could clone him, she thought.

Chapter Forty-One

Despite her delight at being released from her enforced imprisonment, Annie felt sleepy and befuddled as Peter bundled her into the wheelchair once again. This time, she was to be taken to Richard's car.

'I can't stay awake,' she complained.

'It's the drugs,' explained Peter, 'but you need to be comfortable for the journey. The Inspector won't want to stop until you reach your destination.'

'Where are we going?' asked Annie.

'I'm not going anywhere except home,' explained Peter. 'My shift is over. You, however, are going somewhere safe. I understand there will be medical staff there when you arrive, but to be honest you are recovering really well.'

'Where's there?'

Peter shrugged. 'Persistent aren't you? But I'm not allowed to know. It's all top secret. Some sort of safe house, I think.'

Annie was intrigued but unworried. Richard made her feel safe and she was looking forward to escaping her cell and spending some time in the car with him. And anything would be better than having to go home.

Peter wheeled her to Richard's car and she was made comfortable in the front seat. She waited for only a moment or two before the driver's door was opened and Richard slid into the seat behind her. She smelt his aftershave and was close enough to him to see the weave of his suit. He was uncomfortably close and her heart fluttered as he turned to smile at her.

'Ready?'

'As I'll ever be,' she replied.

Richard started the engine and they slipped away from the station, the unmarked backup car a safe distance behind.

Annie sat quietly until they reached the M5 motorway, aware of Richard's concentration as he scanned the streets for anything remotely suspicious. As he accelerated into the outside lane, Annie saw him visibly relax. She knew that they were travelling far in excess of the speed limit but decided that she would rather not know just how fast they were actually going. She would be more than happy to stay in the car with Richard for a very long time. She could see the hairs on the back of his wrist and wondered how it would feel to touch his skin.

For his part, and despite his concerns about Annie's safety, Richard was enjoying the journey. His obsession with cars had been with him for even longer than his obsession with being a police officer. Now he had the best of both worlds, driving an extremely nice car very, very fast and with no worries about a ticket from the law because tonight he was the law. The Audi had been a present from Debbie along with his wardrobe of designer suits and he had held on to both after her death. Annie saw the trace of a smile cross his face and in that moment became acutely aware of how she must look with her injuries and fading bruises. She felt sure that Richard liked her but was afraid that the case and her beating had ruined any future relationship that they might have had.

Listen to yourself, she chided silently. Weren't you the woman that swore off all relationships, not more than a year or two ago? What sort of about-face is this? She sighed in exasperation.

'Are you ok?' asked Richard.

'Just thinking.'

'Penny for them?'

'Can you tell me where we're going?' asked Annie. Not quite what was on her mind but an impressive response, she thought.

'Not till we're there,' replied Richard with an enigmatic smile.

'I know,' she joked. 'If you tell me, you'll have to kill me.'

Richard looked serious. 'I think someone already tried that.'

Annie had no response to this and Richard was immediately contrite. He reached across to take her hand.

'I'm sorry, Annie. I shouldn't have said that. Please forgive me.'

She fought the urge to stroke the back of his hand with her thumb.

'It's the truth. Don't ever be afraid to tell me the truth,' she said.

Richard returned his hand to the steering wheel and Annie stared ahead. A light drizzle of rain had begun to fall and the windscreen wipers flicked across in front of her. Richard silently cursed the Met Office for getting it wrong again. He was driving fast, constantly checking his mirrors and concentrating on the traffic around him. Even so, he detected an uncertainty in the atmosphere inside the car. Annie's stillness seemed to emphasise rather than hide her restlessness.

'Are you comfortable?' Richard asked.

'I'm fine,' Annie replied.

Yet another good enough response, she thought, but Richard already knew her too well. He could almost hear her brain working.

'You must have a lot of questions,' he said matter-of-factly.

'A few,' agreed Annie.

'I can't answer them all now,' he explained, 'but I will be able to in the next day or two.' He glanced across and saw Annie nod but there was a shadow across her face that he hadn't seen before.

'How are you holding up?' he asked.

'I'm fine, really I'm fine.' But there was a crack in her voice which she knew that he heard.

'You don't have to be brave all the time,' said Richard.

'It's not a case of being brave, or not being brave,' explained Annie. 'It's about being lost.' She turned slightly in her seat so that she could look at Richard as she spoke. 'This time last week my life was actually ok. I had a job I loved, a nice home, good friends, I knew where I stood. Everything was in order, but now?' She raised her hands and let them fall to her lap. 'It's as if my whole life has been taken away from me and what's left is some sort of bad TV show. There's no normal for me now and I don't know how there ever will be again. I don't know where I'll live so that I'll feel safe, I don't know if I'll ever be able to go back to the Asylum Centre again and put myself at risk in that way. I don't know if I'll ever be able to go out on call again without looking over my shoulder all the time. I don't know where to go or what to do. I don't think I even know who I am anymore.'

'Annie, that's completely normal. You've suffered a trauma and it's going to take time to get over that. But you will, I promise you. And you will get all the help you need.'

'A psychologist do you mean?'

'Talking to someone can really help and I can vouch for that.'

'You mean you've been to a psychologist?' asked Annie intrigued.

'Twice,' admitted Richard. 'Once when my wife was killed and once after a house fire.'

'What happened?'

'I was first at the scene but the fire was too fierce for me to be able to do anything. I couldn't get near the place. The heat was incredible but the noise was even worse. The flames were roaring and things were cracking and splintering in the inferno. But much, much worse than that were the screams of the children trapped inside as they burned. Two boys and their little sister, aged six, eight and nine. They had been left alone in the house. Their mother was drinking at the local pub.'

'What caused the fire?' asked Annie.

'It was an electrical fault. The house was in a state. That's why it went up so fast. No smoke alarms, of course.'

'Richard, that's awful.'

'I had nightmares for a long time after that.'

Annie reached across to place a hand on his arm, concern softening her voice. 'I am so sorry.'

'It goes with the job,' said Richard. 'You do toughen up over time but there are some cases that just get to you. The force offers counselling after something like that and it really does help.'

'I just need time to sort things out,' said Annie. 'Everything feels like a bit of a blur at the moment.'

'I can imagine,' said Richard, 'but it will soon be over.'

How wrong can a man be?

Chapter Forty-Two

It happened just as they joined the M50 motorway. They heard a loud crack that seemed to echo behind them, followed by a screeching of tyres.

'Shit!'

Annie saw Richard stiffen a fraction before the expletive escaped from his lips. His eyes were darting between the road in front and the rear view mirror and she felt rather than saw the mixture of comprehension and horror that clouded his features. She tried to turn in her seat to look behind her but was surprised to find how stiff and sore she had become from sitting in one position for so long.

'Shit. How the bloody hell…?'

Richard knew immediately what had happened. He just couldn't understand how it was possible.

Annie managed to turn round just enough to peer through the gap between the two front seats. Behind them, the headlights of the backup vehicle were strobing in and out of sight as it went spinning erratically across the motorway before juddering to a halt on the hard shoulder, its nose facing the oncoming traffic. Its place behind Richard's Audi was taken by a grey car driven menacingly close. Annie felt fear grip her insides at the certain knowledge that the car contained three men whose faces would be imprinted on her mind for all time.

'Tell me what's happening,' she asked.

'I need to focus, Annie,' said Richard. 'Keep your head down and hold on tight.'

As Annie clung to the sides of her seat, the radio sprang to life and above the crackles and shouts she heard a voice from the backup vehicle calling into control.

'We have been shot at. I repeat, we have been shot at. Officers unharmed but our vehicle is disabled. We are no longer in pursuit.'

Radio silence was broken but given that the thugs were practically hanging off the Audi's bumper it was academic. The bad guys knew where they were. The details of the vehicle that had shot them from the motorway were relayed to control but Richard already knew what they would be and who would be inside it. Even so, he continued to listen intently, his face a mask of concentration. The steps he needed to take to evade the gunmen were already slotting into place like the last few pieces of a jigsaw puzzle. Annie felt the surge of acceleration as Richard pushed the car forward but although the gap between the two cars widened slightly, the car behind held its position frighteningly close.

Richard spoke with only the slightest edge of tension to his voice.

'Brace yourself as best you can, Annie, this is going to get bumpy.'

Annie lifted her feet up onto the dashboard so that her ribs and wound were cushioned between her thighs and the blanket that had been tucked around her. She grabbed onto the handhold above the passenger window with both hands. Her heart was beating painfully behind her ribs and when she tried to swallow her mouth was as dry as sandpaper. The world that had been whizzing past them in a blur of spray shifted back into focus.

They were slowing down.

Annie turned to Richard to ask what he was doing but she could see that her question would be useless. Right at that moment, his world was the motorway, the pursuers and the power of the vehicle that he had under his control. His focus was absolute and Annie understood that she must surrender completely to whatever was about to take place.

As they approached and then passed the next exit from the motorway, Annie saw the lights of the following car loom large in the wing mirror as Richard brought the pursuers closer to him. They were still in the outside lane of the motorway overtaking everything in front of them when the slightest shift in Richard's weight in his seat indicated to her that he was ready for action. With no other warning, he pulled on the handbrake with one hand while the other controlled the wheel and he executed a perfect handbrake turn across two lanes of traffic. While the pursuing car was still thinking about braking, Richard was racing down the hard shoulder against the oncoming flow of traffic. Cars blared their horns and flashed their lights at the temerity of the law breaker and Annie half smiled at the thought of all the drivers who would be on their mobile phones calling in their misdemeanour to the local police.

When they reached the bottom of the slip road Richard proved that the first handbrake turn had not been a fluke by executing a second as tightly controlled as the first so that they were heading off the motorway into Herefordshire. As they crossed over the motorway, Annie saw the grey car reversing wildly back down the motorway with approaching cars swerving to avoid what could only be a madman on the loose. And then it was hit from behind by a large white van which shunted the car into the central barrier in a blizzard of sparks. The bonnet crumpled and as Richard accelerated away Annie saw three men climbing from the car and dodging the traffic to run across the motorway.

'They've crashed,' she informed Richard. 'I saw three men get out and run.'

The car veered to the left as Richard turned off the main road and headed into the heart of the countryside. Away from the street lights Annie now closed her eyes against the blur of hedgerows and fences that flashed past the windows. She was still rigid in her seat and was finding it difficult to breathe. She tried to force oxygen into her lungs and threw off the blanket as prickles of sweat began to crawl away from her scalp and worry her body. Richard was still driving fast using the gears and handbrake to throw the car around corners and bounce through puddles. A wall of water rose on each side of the car as they aquaplaned through a ford and slid onto a muddy lane.

Richard's mirrors remained dark but he kept his foot on the accelerator knowing that their only chance was to remain undiscovered in the twisting lanes of his childhood.

Annie was fighting off waves of nausea, desperate not to let Richard down, but as sweat began to trickle down between her shoulder blades, she knew she needed to vomit.

'Richard, please stop. I'm going to be sick.'

He was about to refuse when he glanced over and saw the colour drained from her face so that her lips looked an eerie blue in the darkness. He switched off his lights as he pulled over into a gateway. Annie threw open the car door and leaned out to empty the meagre contents of her stomach onto the grass. Richard reached over to hold back her hair and rub between her shoulders as she retched repeatedly but his eyes did not cease their surveillance of the countryside for a second.

When she had finished, Annie sat back and pulled the car door closed.

'Go,' she gasped, as she searched in her pocket for a tissue.

The car was moving before she had even managed to refasten her seat belt.

They had been driving through the dark country lanes for a further twenty minutes before Richard began to believe that they might actually be safe. He slowed the car just a fraction to try and ease the jolting and jarring for Annie. Her eyes were tightly closed and her breaths were short gasps as she prayed that the journey would end soon.

'Almost there,' said Richard, as if reading her thoughts.

Annie opened her eyes. Her healing ribs were throbbing, her abdominal wound was sore and she felt sicker than she had ever felt in her life. But when she spoke it was from the heart.

'I'm not afraid,' she said.

Richard heard in her voice that it was the truth. He reached over and squeezed her hand.

'We're here. At Credenhill. SAS Headquarters,' he said.

They turned towards an army guard post and Richard showed his ID and spoke to one of the soldiers who waved them through onto a concrete road. The seriousness of her situation finally hit Annie solidly in the stomach.

They passed through a second guard post where Richard was given directions towards a single storey building set amongst mature trees and lawns. Someone had obviously alerted the base to their arrival as an army Colonel was descending the steps to greet them before their car had pulled to a halt.

'Looks like you've undergone some endurance training on the way,' he remarked, as he surveyed what little of Richard's car was still visible beneath its covering of mud.

'Camouflage,' laughed Richard, as he stepped from the car and, to Annie's surprise, embraced the Colonel. When the hugs and back slapping were over, Richard opened the passenger door to introduce her.

'Annie,' he said, 'I would like you to meet Colonel Patrick Shaw.'

Shaw. Of course. She saw the likeness at once. The Colonel was an inch or two shorter than Richard but significantly broader. Whereas Richard was lean, the Colonel was solid and muscular and his sandy hair was razored into a marine cut. But the eyes, when he leaned down to smile hello at her were the same rich caramel as Richard's. Only the absence of the gold flecks separated them.

Annie undid her seatbelt and Richard took her arm as she stood up but the journey had taken its toll and her exhausted body failed her. She stumbled forwards and would have fallen if Richard had not caught her in his arms and lifted her off the ground. She clung to his neck, too weak to even mumble the apology already formed on her lips but still able to lean her head against his chest and smell his delicious scent. It made her think of laundry fetched in from outside at the end of a hot summer's day.

Richard was shocked at how light and frail she felt in his arms as if she were a fledgling scooped from a hostile nest. Her complete surrender told him more about her condition than any words and he indicated with his eyes that he was ready to follow his brother. Inside the military clinic, they were led to an airy two bedded room. Here Richard and Annie were introduced to Sam, the patrol medic, who would help her to settle into a bed and freshen up.

Patrick indicated to Richard that he should follow him and they turned left down the corridor to a small sitting room cum kitchen where Patrick offered Richard a much needed strong black coffee. The briefing was short and to the point.

'Your backup car had its tyres blown out but fortunately only some pride was injured. The thugs have not been apprehended, however. Their car was hit and disabled and three men got away. We can assume that they are currently on foot and will head back to their base. Presumably, they will help themselves to a vehicle on the way.'

'Let's just hope no one is in it at the time,' said Richard. 'These guys don't take any prisoners.'

Patrick's response was to raise an eyebrow.

'I presume you still remember our old rally routes,' he said.

'Saved my life,' replied Richard.

'I spoke to DCI Masterton about half an hour ago. She wants me to call in your safe arrival and your orders are to rest here tonight. She'll speak to you in the morning.'

It was almost midnight and Richard was too tired to think through the implications of the evening. Now that Annie was finally safe and he had relaxed, his body was craving sleep.

'Thanks, bro,' he said to Patrick. 'I think I need to get some sleep.'

'There's a bed in Annie's room or you can come across to my quarters with me,' offered Patrick.

'I'll stay here if that's ok,' replied Richard. 'Can I catch up with you at breakfast?'

'Sure thing, I'll have it sent over.' Patrick gave his brother a hug and wished him goodnight before leaving. Annie was already fast asleep and the patrol medic was just leaving as Richard went into the room.

'I'll be right next door, sir,' he said. 'Just call if you need anything. Anytime.'

'Thanks very much,' answered Richard, who wanted nothing more than to feel the pillow under his head and his feet off the floor. A clean T-shirt and shorts had been placed at the end of his bed and he slipped gratefully into them before falling almost instantly asleep.

Chapter Forty-Three

Friday

The face of the Afghan man was so close to Annie's that she could smell his foul breath and feel its heat on her face. She wanted to struggle, to get away, but her legs and arms refused to obey her stricken brain. All she could do was beg repeatedly, no, please, no. Hands were holding her shoulders, shaking her and suddenly she was awake and it was Richard's hands that were shaking her, and Richard's warm breath that she could feel on her cheek.

'Annie, wake up, it's just a dream.'

She stared into his eyes, bewildered for a moment and then the tears of relief began to flow as she clung to him.

'I thought…' she began, but he shushed her and rocked her and kept repeating that it was just a dream until her pulse had stopped racing and she was breathing normally again, her soft breath caressing his neck.

Richard became acutely aware of the small amount of fabric separating their skin and as he felt his body begin to respond to her proximity he forced himself to pull away from her.

'Can I get you anything?' he asked.

Annie shook her head, wanting desperately to ask him to hold her again but afraid that he might refuse. Instead, she stared at him, drinking in every feature. She had so much that she wanted to say to him but not the words to express her feelings. Richard was lost in her gaze and returned it unashamedly. He had never felt as close to anyone as he felt to Annie at this moment and yet he barely knew her.

She shivered, breaking the spell.

'You're cold,' he said as he went to pull the covers over her but she pushed them away.

'Will you stay with me?'

There, she had said it. After all, what did she have to lose? Richard's face seemed to soften as he smiled at her and without a word he climbed carefully onto the narrow bed. Annie moved over as far as she dared and Richard placed a protective arm around her as he placed his head on the pillow next to hers.

It was enough. Annie was asleep in seconds.

Fingers of light were creeping around the sides of the curtains when Annie woke with a start. She was alone in her bed but Richard's regular breathing told her at once that he was nearby. Despite her aching limbs, the thought that had woken her was so urgent she forced herself to leave the warm bed. She shivered as her bare feet hit the cold floor and groaned as her wounds and bruises objected to the sudden movement. She hurried over to where Richard was sleeping peacefully in the next bed, one arm flung above his head and his hair ruffled against the pillow. She tapped on his shoulder.

'Richard, wake up.'

He sat upright, instantly alert. 'What is it?'

'My midwifery bag. I left it in my car.'

Her face was anxious.

'It's ok,' he reassured her. 'I took it when I left your car at the station. It's in my boot. It's safe.'

'Is it here?' Annie asked, agitation flushing her cheeks despite the cool of the morning.

'Yes, but...'

'You have to fetch it, Richard. You have to fetch it now.'

'Annie, what is it?' Richard reached for his sweatshirt and pulled it over his head as he spoke.

'I left my bag in my room at the Asylum Centre when Soraya was there. When I came back into the room she was gone, but my bag was still by my desk. There is a possibility that it may have been moved. I think Soraya could have put the USB in there.'

'Christ Almighty.'

Richard hopped to the door pulling his trousers on over his shorts as he went. He rushed out of the medical centre in bare feet only to find that his car was not where he had left it. The soldier on the door was regarding Richard with some amusement as he rushed back up the steps and demanded to know where his car was. The soldier directed Richard to the parking bays at the side of the building and he flew to the boot ignoring the gravel that cut into the soles of his feet making him wince and curse as he hopped along.

Annie was sitting on her bed pulling at the fingers of her hands as she waited for Richard to return with her bag. He dropped it onto the bed next to her with a flourish and Annie immediately began ransacking the contents. The bed was soon covered with packets and instruments and lotions and there were dressings and swabs spilling onto the floor. Finally, Annie upended the bag to show that it was empty with a look of total devastation on her face.

'It's not here,' she said.

Richard had been standing watching her search but he now stepped forward and took the bag from her so that he could check every compartment.

'Look again,' he said, but his own spirits had already sunk from the high of just a few minutes ago.

Annie went through everything again before shaking her head.

'Nothing.'

Tears of disappointment pricked her eyes. 'I thought it was going to be over,' she said.

'It will be.' Richard's words were spoken with kindness but she saw her own feelings reflected in his eyes.

'What? Kit check already?' came Patrick's cheery voice as the Colonel strode into the room dressed and ready for inspection. He smiled at them both but faltered as he sensed the atmosphere in the room. Annie wondered if Richard's unusually impeccable turnout was anything to do with his military sibling or whether it was a family trait. Either way, there was nothing shoddy about the Shaws, she thought. The thought cheered her slightly and she began to repack her bag.

'A bit of a fruitless search I'm afraid,' said Richard to his brother. 'We thought we were going to find a much sought after USB but unfortunately, it's not here.'

'I'm sorry I got your hopes up,' Annie apologised to Richard.

'No matter,' he replied, lifting his hand as if to touch her, then withdrawing it sharply as he remembered his brother. 'By the way, I have a family of homeless bears on the back seat as well,' he said, 'remind me to leave them before I go.'

'Oh, thank you so much.' Annie was touched that he had remembered and her eyes shone with pleasure. 'They were really the only thing I wanted to be rescued.'

'Anytime,' said Richard, holding her gaze.

Patrick cleared his throat. 'If I may interrupt, breakfast will be ready in the small mess room in ten minutes. Turn left, fourth door on the right.'

'I'll join you now,' said Richard. 'I need to discuss a few things with you.'

An array of fruit, juice, and cereals were laid out on a table at the side of the room with hot plates of bacon, eggs, mushrooms, and tomatoes. Richard suddenly realised that he was ravenous and he filled his plate.

'Hungry work this case, is it?' asked Patrick with a touch of irony in his voice.

'We don't get fed like this in the force if that's what you're referring to,' countered Richard. 'And come to think of it, I can't actually remember when I was last fed at all.'

'Why do you think I joined the military,' laughed Patrick. 'Don't you know a man marches on his stomach?'

'God help you when you retire.'

Patrick grinned. 'I won't be doing that in a hurry. Besides, I was not referring to the size of your appetite.'

'What were you referring to then?'

'Are you dense or in denial?' asked Patrick.

'What are you going on about?'

'You can't fool me, little brother. There was definitely something going on back there.'

Richard swallowed before he spoke. 'We thought Annie might have had the USB in her bag. We both had our hopes up for a few minutes.'

Patrick snorted and shook his head. 'I'm not talking about that. I'm talking about what was going on between you two. Or should I say what *is* going on between you two.'

Richard lowered his knife and fork to stare at his brother. 'Nothing is going on, as you put it. Annie is a witness and a victim in this case.'

'And you don't get involved. Am I right?'

'Absolutely,' replied Richard.

Patrick regarded his brother thoughtfully before he spoke. 'You might be trying to fool your boss,' he said. You might even be trying to fool yourself, but you can't fool me. I haven't seen you so doe-eyed over a girl since your wedding day.'

Richard opened his mouth to protest but Patrick held up his hand.

'I'm your big brother, Richard. I know you too well.'

'There really isn't anything going on,' said Richard, shaking his head.

'Oh, that may well be true,' said Patrick. 'But give it time. The look on her face was as soppy as yours.'

Richard was stunned into silence and used a mouthful of bacon as an excuse not to speak. His first thought was to wonder who else had noticed. His second was to marvel at the thought that Annie might feel the same way that he did. He was about to ask his brother exactly what he thought he saw when Annie came into the room. Patrick was on his feet at once helping her to her seat and fetching her cereal and fruit before settling down with his own breakfast.

It was obvious that the two men had a good rapport with each other and Annie found herself enjoying the banter that pitched backwards and forwards across the breakfast table. Still only half dressed and with his hair uncombed, Richard appeared relaxed and happy and more handsome than ever. When Patrick made some comment about a cousin that caused Richard to throw back his head and laugh out loud, her stomach lurched uncomfortably and she had to put down her spoon. She was unable to eat another bite.

'Not hungry, Annie?' asked Patrick.

She tore her eyes away from Richard with such obvious reluctance that Patrick had to struggle to hide his smile.

'I still haven't got my appetite completely back,' she replied.

'Ah, of course,' said Patrick. 'You look so well I had completely forgotten that you've had a bit of a rough time of it lately.'

The shrill notes of Richard's mobile phone cut off her reply.

'Boss?'

He listened intently and silently. Annie and Patrick both watched as his expression and posture shifted instantaneously from brother and friend to professional detective.

'I'm on my way,' was all he said and he snapped his phone shut.

'I have to leave at once,' he told them, already rising from his chair.

'Finish your breakfast, bro,' said Patrick.

Richard shook his head. 'My destiny was never to eat three sit down meals a day,' he grinned, 'but the taster was excellent.'

Annie followed him to their room and watched as he pulled on his socks and tied his shoes. 'Something's happened, hasn't it?'

Richard smiled. 'The National Crime Agency has identified the second man you drew. You were right. He is Soraya's brother and he is the Chief Lieutenant of our bad man in Afghanistan. So Soraya and her husband both had brothers working for the same villain. It's joined a lot of the dots for us.'

He stood up so that she had to step back to look up at him and was dazzled by his smile.

'And,' he added, 'the hideout has been found.'

Annie gasped. 'The three men?'

'The very same,' said Richard.

'Are they there?'

Richard grinned. 'That is what I am about to find out. And God help them if they are.'

He kissed her on the forehead and was gone.

Chapter Forty-Four

A quick stop at his flat for a shower and change of clothes was all that Richard allowed himself before rushing to the police station. As he pushed open the doors to the Incident Room, he was almost stopped in his tracks by the wall of noise that greeted him. He felt a grim sense of satisfaction at the level of activity that pervaded the room while wishing that none of it was necessary. Before he had even had a chance to sit down, Masterton was beckoning him from her office as if she had been waiting for nothing but his arrival.

'You missed the briefing so I'll give you a quick update and don't apologise,' she said, as Richard opened his mouth to do just that. 'You can't be in two places at once. How's Annie, by the way?'

'She's getting stronger every day.'

'Good. I need everyone fully focused today.'

'We've definitely got them?' asked Richard.

Masterton indicated that he should sit down and she settled herself behind her desk. Richard noticed the dark smudges beneath her eyes and realised just how much this case was affecting everyone. He wondered when Masterton had last spent a relaxing evening with her family. Or even just spent a relaxing evening. Her gaze, however, was unaffected as she studied Richard.

'They are under surveillance as we speak.'

'How?'

'Pure luck,' she replied as she opened a folder on her desk. 'Apparently, two nights ago the key holder from a tyre dealer's in Sherriff Street got a call to say that the burglar alarm had been activated. Do you know the area?'

Richard nodded. 'Industrial units, car repairs, light engineering, that sort of thing. The place is a bit run down and not well lit. It's a prime spot for drug deals.'

'That's it. When the key holder arrived there, he couldn't find any sign of a disturbance, no break in, no vandalism, no one around. So he reset the alarms, checked the locks and prepared to go home.'

'But?'

'But he had his dog with him. It's not much of a guard dog, more a family pet, but it looks ugly so he takes it as a deterrent. Apparently, the dog was unsettled and whining, wouldn't get back in the car and kept trying to pull our key holder towards a unit across the way. It's a unit that is supposed to have been empty for several months.'

'What did he do?'

'He let the dog have a sniff round the door. He said that he thought there was probably a rat about but there was nothing to be seen. He knows the unit well and he was just about to pull the dog away when he saw that there was a brand new padlock on the door. But he was spooked. The landlord normally informs all of the tenants on the estate when a unit is being let but this time, he had heard nothing nor had he seen anyone during the day. As you say, Richard, the area is a popular spot for drugs and he thought someone might have been setting up a lab. So, last night, he decided to bed down in his own unit with his dog and keep watch.'

'That was a bit foolhardy.'

'He didn't want anything going on that would deter his customers. Business is bad enough as it is, apparently.'

'So, presumably, he saw our suspects?'

'These two jokers.' Diane pushed the photos across the desk to Richard and he stared at the brutal faces on the desk. The two that held her, he thought.

'Several times during the night, they came out of the unit and patrolled around. Our witness described them as…' Diane searched through the folder until she came to the witness statement. '...big, bloody bandits with machine guns. Mind you, he also said he thought they were Mexicans.'

'Do you think he alerted them?'

'Doesn't look like it. We would be scraping another corpse off the concrete if he had. He stayed put until the staff arrived to open up and then he legged it down here. He's pretty shaken up and worried about his staff but we've got plain clothes surveillance in place down there and we're just watching at the moment.'

'When are we going in?'

'That's the problem.' Diane closed the file with as much of a bang as the cardboard would allow. 'We've got the authority to deploy firearms officers but they're tied up this morning on some drugs bust at the airport. I'm waiting for the number one Specialist Firearms Officer to contact me and I'm hoping we'll be ready to go in later today.'

Richard sucked air over his teeth. Waiting was not something that he was good at. Especially when he felt like ringing the necks of all three of those bastards with his bare hands.

'To be honest, it's probably the best thing,' continued Diane. 'We can't clear the area without alerting them and by evening the place is pretty much deserted. If there are any stragglers, they'll be called and told to evacuate because of a suspected gas leak. So dusk would be the ideal time to go in. Now, there's a press blanket in place on this and I've grounded the team for the duration. I need you to go over the logistics for me and then we'll start the operational briefing.'

'I'm on to it, boss.'

Her words stopped him as he reached the door.

‘It’s funny, isn’t it?’

‘What, boss?’

‘The way we can slave away getting nowhere and then one single stroke of fate can change everything.’

‘In more ways than one,’ agreed Richard.

Chapter Forty-Five

At Credenhill, Annie was lying on her bed with her abdomen exposed to Sam the medic who was carefully removing her stitches. He had been shocked at the extent of bruising to Annie's torso. She looked like a soldier lifted from the field of battle and he found it hard to believe that this could happen to someone in the safety of their own home.

'I'm sorry this has happened to you.'

Annie shrugged. 'It's not your fault. I was just in the wrong place at the wrong time.'

Sam shook his head. 'I would say working at an Asylum Centre is pretty much the front line these days.'

Annie was thoughtful for a moment. Helping a woman to deliver her baby was a privilege that Annie cherished. Every new life was precious and Annie loved her job. But she had come to realise that the greater the need of the woman, the more satisfaction she got from helping her. It was true that many of the women she cared for disappeared before they could be identified and thrown out of the country and sometimes it troubled Annie to think that some of the women were not genuine refugees. Occasionally she had delivered a baby and the mother had returned to her safe and comfortable home as soon as the baby was registered. Without paying her NHS bill. Equally, some of the genuine asylum seekers settled and stayed and Annie loved to see them coming to the child health clinic looking well-nourished and happy and, most of all, safe.

'It's incredibly rewarding,' Annie told Sam now. 'Sometimes I think we all have so much that we take everything for granted. Even the right to live our lives without oppression, torture, and murder. I can honestly say that this is the first time I have ever been hurt because of my job.'

'Has it put you off?'

'That's a difficult question to answer,' said Annie. 'I'm going to need some time to think about that one. I would like to think that I can be brave and fearless and help the oppressed against the odds. But the truth is, I'm just an ordinary woman doing an ordinary job. I don't intentionally take risks. I don't even jaywalk.'

'I would say that bringing new life into the world is a pretty extraordinary job,' observed Sam, 'and pretty rewarding too.'

'It is,' said Annie. 'I haven't been put off that.'

'Well, just make sure you think about your safety. You are no good to anyone if you can't work.'

'So, when do you think I will be able to go back to work?'

'This has healed really well,' Sam said, 'and the scar will fade quite a lot over time.'

Annie squinted down at the ugly red mark laddered across her abdomen. 'There's a way to go yet.'

'It's a war wound,' said Sam, 'wear it with pride.'

'I am not quite sure about that.'

'I'll give you some oil to massage into the scar when you feel able, that will help to reduce it as well. And the bruising should fade completely over time.' He held the last stitch up in his forceps to show Annie. 'There you go, all done.'

'Thank you, that feels better already.'

Sam sprayed a plastic dressing over the wound and left it to dry while he tidied away his trolley.

'If you get any soreness or tenderness, or any discharge, you need to tell a medic straight away. But I don't think you will have any problems. You had a good surgeon by the looks of things.'

'I guess it helps to be in a proper operating theatre and not in some tent in a battlefield.'

'Fortunately, that is one thing I haven't had to experience,' said Sam. 'But I had a tour of duty in Iraq which wasn't pleasant.'

'War never is, is it?'

Sam sat down to write up Annie's notes. 'So how are you in yourself?'

'What? Do you mean am I falling apart?' asked Annie with a smile.

Sam's face was serious as he spoke. 'Post-traumatic stress disorder is a very real condition and you have suffered severe trauma. It would be abnormal if you didn't feel some effects.'

Sam was watching her closely.

'Bad dreams,' said Annie. 'I keep dreaming that I'm back at home and those men are in my room.'

'Anything else?'

Annie shook her head. 'Not really. I work at an Asylum Centre with men and women who have suffered so much in their lives. I can't help comparing myself and thinking that in some ways that I got off lightly. I do think, why me? But then I think, why not me? I am grateful that I'm alive and recovering and that I have my job and friends. It doesn't mean that I'm not scared shitless, though. And I think my days at the Asylum Centre are probably over. I don't feel like putting myself on the front line again.'

'That's fair enough. It sounds like you've done your bit. Are you having some counselling?' asked Sam.

'The police are organising it, I think.'

'Make sure you go,' said Sam. 'It is important after what you've been through.'

'I promise.'

'Ok, I'll leave you to get some rest. Press the buzzer if you need anything and I'll see you later.'

'Thanks, Sam.'

Annie rolled over onto her side to face the window so that she could watch the tops of the distant trees rustling in the breeze. The world outside looked so benign today, it was hard to comprehend that there were terrorists loose in her home city. She tried to clear her mind and relax, but her disloyal brain refused to be quiet. It was like asking an over active toddler to sit quietly and not make a sound. Impossible.

Despite her reassurances to Sam, every time Annie closed her eyes she found herself replaying the last few days over and over again. From meeting Richard at Dougie's, finding the babies and then being beaten senseless. But most of all her thoughts kept straying back to Soraya and the USB. Annie wondered if Soraya really could have concealed something in her bag while she was out of the room. She got up from the bed and started emptying her bag again. This time, she examined every pack and package and piece of wrapping, even feeling along the lining inside the bag. Nothing.

Once again Annie repacked the bag before lying back down on the bed, her brain buzzing. With everything that had happened over the last week, she had not had the presence of mind to think back to her first meeting with Soraya. She closed her eyes and took herself back to the day that Soraya had walked in.

Chapter Forty-Six

It had been another long clinic and Annie was weary and ready for a cup of tea. When Malcolm knocked on her door and asked if she could manage one last client she had wanted, more than anything, to say no.

'She's a walker,' Malcolm said, meaning someone who had walked in off the street. Annie reluctantly agreed to see her. The residents at the Asylum Centre were a captive audience and if Annie missed them one day she could always see them the next. The walkers were often the people who needed care the most, those who had no permanent address, no access to health care and who had probably been plucking up the courage for days to face what they would see as authority.

So, Annie had been doubly surprised when Soraya was pointed out to her in the waiting room. Her initial appearance was so far removed from the refugees that Annie normally saw that she had hesitated for a moment before calling her name. When there was no response Annie approached and greeted the well-dressed and very pregnant woman before her. Annie noticed at once the good clothes, gold jewellery, and expensive looking bracelets. The young woman was extremely beautiful and the tasteful makeup only enhanced her looks. As Annie leaned forward to shake the woman's hand, she smelled expensive perfume. Soraya could not have looked less like a refugee if she had tried.

'Hello, I'm Annie.'

The woman had taken her hand and met Annie's gaze. 'I am Baseera,' she said, without any hesitation.

Annie shook her hand and led her through to her room where she indicated a chair. 'Please sit down and tell me how I can help you.'

When Baseera spoke her voice was heavily accented. 'I am new to this country,' she began.

'How long have you been here?' asked Annie.

'A few days only.'

'Can you tell me where you have come from?'

This time, there was a momentary pause. 'I am from Pakistan.'

Annie had nodded and looked at the woman carefully. Her gift with faces had always served her well and this woman looked uncannily like a young refugee from Afghanistan who had stayed at the Asylum Centre the previous year. This was not the same woman but the similarities in their features were enough for Annie to challenge the woman. 'But you are Afghan, aren't you?'

Baseera's eyes had widened slightly before she nodded and Annie saw her face tighten with fear. 'How do you know this?'

'That's ok,' said Annie quickly. 'No-one else needs to know. Everything that happens here is confidential.'

After a brief hesitation, Baseera indicated her swollen stomach which she was stroking tenderly. 'I need help with my baby.'

'When is your baby due?'

Baseera shrugged. 'A few months, maybe.'

Annie looked at Baseera's bump and thought that was an optimistic estimate. A few weeks more like. Annie wondered how the woman had managed to reach Britain in such an advanced state of pregnancy. Most airlines refuse to carry women after twenty-eight weeks. But those questions would have to wait. The woman was fine-boned and fragile, reminding Annie of a cornered animal preparing for its fate. She packaged her curiosity for the moment and reached for a blank maternity record.

'Have you seen a doctor at all during your pregnancy?'

Baseera had shaken her head and Annie tried not to sigh. In time she would find out more but she felt irritated that a seemingly intelligent woman could progress through pregnancy without seeking any care.

'Ok, Baseera, I will need to ask you some questions about your pregnancy and your health. Then I would like to examine your tummy and listen to the baby's heart to check that all is well. After that, we will need to talk about where you want to have your baby and also…'

Annie had been cut off by raised voices drifting through from the reception area. A man's voice was shouting, angry, and Malcolm was saying, 'Ok, calm down and we can talk about this.' Then she heard the sound of glass breaking.

If it was possible Baseera seemed to have shrunk even further into her chair. Her head had dropped and she was wringing her hands in obvious distress.

'Don't worry,' reassured Annie. 'I'll go and see what's happening. You wait here.'

Annie closed the door of her room behind her to try and drown out the sounds of the heated argument that was coming from the reception area. It was not unusual to have disturbances at the Centre, especially when the residents received bad news or were removed by the authorities, but more often than not things could be calmed down.

By the time Annie had reached the reception desk Malcolm and his colleague had already subdued the man who had presumably kicked the glass door that led from the hallway to the reception room. A gaping hole was all that was left of the lower panel and shards of broken glass littered the ground on both sides. The culprit was a thick-set, muscular man and Malcolm was struggling to hold him even with a colleague's help. They led the man to a chair and sat him down.

'Now, are you going to calm down or do we need to call the police?' asked Malcolm.

The man visibly relaxed. 'No police,' he said.

Malcolm and his colleague had let go of the man's arms but stood close ready to grasp him again if needed.

'Everything ok, Malcolm?' called Annie.

The man had looked up at Annie's voice and she saw immediately that he was an Afghan. He stared straight at Annie and the look on his face made her feel unaccountably afraid. His eyes were narrowed and there was a sneer on his face as if he was making sure that he would remember her next time they met.

'All sorted, thanks, Annie,' said Malcolm.

Annie had turned away, grateful to be dismissed. She felt shaken, almost as if the man had spoken to her unpleasantly. When she returned to her room to find the door ajar and no sign of Baseera she was not the least surprised. She had gone to the back door and looked out but there was no-one to be seen. Oh well, she thought, she'll be back. No-one wants to give birth alone.

Annie opened her eyes with a start and sat up on the bed. From what the police had told her, Soraya had not been seen by anyone else in the few days between arriving in Britain and dying in childbirth. She was also trying to hide something that so far had not been found. When Annie had emptied out her midwifery bag she had been convinced that she would find the USB. Why? Because Soraya had no one else to give it to. If the Afghan man at the centre had been after Soraya, and the USB was in her possession, she would have dumped it and run. It had to be in the consulting room. She was absolutely certain.

Annie pressed the buzzer for Sam. 'I need to see Patrick.'

Sam looked at his watch. 'He'll be over in his office working by now.'

'It's really important. I have to see him now. Please.'

'Can you tell me what it's about?'

'It's about the case. I think I've remembered something important.'

Sam hesitated. Disturbing the Colonel was not an action that he undertook lightly but Annie's agitation was enough for him to take a risk.

'Ok, I'll call him.'

Annie began to pull on her socks and trainers and had just finished packing away her few possessions when a voice caused her to whirl around.

'Going somewhere?' asked Patrick.

'That was quick,' smiled Annie. 'Thank you so much for coming.'

Patrick sat down on Richard's bed and regarded her thoughtfully. 'You know you can't leave.'

'Am I under arrest?'

'No, of course not.'

'Patrick, I have to. I think I know where the USB might be.'

Patrick raised his eyebrows. 'Where?'

'At the Asylum Centre. In my office.'

She began to tell Patrick about Soraya's visit, the shouting in the reception, the Afghan man, and Soraya's flight.

'She must have left it there, Patrick. It was the only chance she had to get rid of it.'

Patrick was calm. 'Then we should alert the police and get them to search the place. '

'It's an Asylum Centre, Patrick. The manager would never allow a police search without warrants. How long will that take? And what if those three thugs get there first? Just the sight of a uniform can freak those people out enough to erase months of work spent building trust. Besides, I know that centre like the back of my hand. We're looking for something small. If it's there, I'm the one that will be able to spot it.'

Patrick shook his head. 'Annie, you need to be kept safe and that means you must stay here where you can be protected.'

Annie went over to Patrick. 'I'm not safe as long as those men are on the loose because they will keep looking for the USB and they think that I have it. That means I won't ever be safe again unless they are caught.'

Patrick moved as if to say something but Annie held up her hand.

'It really doesn't matter if the men are caught. If the data is still out there, they'll just send more men. I know how these things work. But if the data is found, then the whole bloody lot of them can be put away for good.'

Patrick was staring at her thoughtfully. He could see the sense in what she was saying and he had nothing but admiration for her courage and tenacity. But he was sure that his brother was in love with this woman which gave him both a duty and an obligation to protect her. He shook his head.

'I can't let you go.'

'You said I'm not under arrest.'

Patrick smiled. 'I did.'

'Then you can't stop me.'

'I can refuse to help you.'

Annie folded her arms. 'So you would have me call a taxi and walk all the way to your main gate to be picked up?'

Patrick was shaking his head in what looked like the beginnings of surrender.

'And what use will some taxi driver be if I need protection? I need you to help me, Patrick.'

Patrick sighed. 'I'll have to call Richard.'

'No, you won't. He's got enough on his plate.'

'You know that he will try and talk you out of it.'

'He can waste his time trying if he wants to. He wants that USB as much as anyone and I want to find it for him.'

'So, are you telling me that you are doing this for him?'

Annie felt her cheeks flush slightly. 'I am doing it for him. But I'm doing it for me too. And for the families of everyone who has already died. And for all those people who are still to die. We all deserve our lives back. And we all deserve to feel safe.'

Patrick stood up and placed his hands on Annie's shoulders. His face softened as he spoke.

'My brother told me you were something pretty special and I can see what he means.'

Annie's spirits lifted. 'So you'll help me?'

Patrick stepped back and gave Annie a mock salute. 'Be ready in half an hour.'

It never occurred to Annie to wonder why Patrick had capitulated quite so easily.

Chapter Forty-Seven

It was almost lunch time before Patrick returned to Annie's room where he found her pacing up and down as fast as her aches and bruises would allow.

'I thought you had reneged,' accused Annie.

'I thought you would be resting.'

She was angry. 'Why would I rest for only half an hour? If you had told me you would be this long I might have tried. I honestly thought you were just playing along and weren't coming back.'

He clenched his fist to his chest. 'I am nothing if not a man of honour.'

'I should hope so considering the uniform you're wearing.'

'Sorry, Annie. I had things that I needed to deal with here and getting permission for something like this is not easy. I have also organised some back up for us.'

'What sort of backup?'

'A second car with an armed escort.'

'You know you won't be able to go into the Asylum Centre, you'll frighten them all half to death.'

'We go with backup or not at all.'

Annie opened her mouth to protest then closed it again. It was enough that Patrick was helping her at all. And if she was honest, she was more than a little scared.

'Ok,' she agreed.

'And my second condition is that we have some lunch before we go. You are still convalescing.'

'I'm still not very hungry.'

'Then it won't take long, will it?'

Annie began to laugh. 'You Shaw boys are good guys, do you know that?'

'Oh, and there is a third condition.'

'Go on.'

'We have to inform West Mercia Police.'

'What?'

Patrick held up his hand to stop her. 'Sorry, Annie, but there are procedures to be followed. I'm stretching things as it is. I can't take you to the Asylum Centre without informing the police. Take it or leave it.

Annie's eyes narrowed as she regarded Patrick but she knew when she was beaten.

'I take it. Where's that lunch?'

The return journey to Worcester was far less fraught than the journey down with the M50 no more than a benign rural motorway. And while the traffic picked up when they reached the M5, the sunshine, and normal fellow travellers made for an almost relaxing journey.

Annie sat in the passenger seat wondering what the hell she was doing. She had been safe at SAS Headquarters and yet she had willingly left to go back to the place where she could be most at risk. Yet some basic instinct was urging Annie back there. She silently cursed herself for not thinking of her office before the trauma of her attack, but the post-operative drugs and her flight from the hospital had temporarily drowned any logic and reasoning that might have led her back earlier. Please let it be there, she thought.

Patrick drove very like his brother, fast and controlled and she said so now. Patrick snorted his reply.

'I can assure you I am a far better driver than that wannabe.'

'No sibling rivalry then?'

Patrick shrugged and smiled but Annie sensed an almost imperceptible cooling of the atmosphere in the car. She hurriedly tried to restore the mood.

'You guys seem to get on well,' she observed.

'We get on well enough though we don't see much of each other these days. Richard has always been a bit of a loner. Done his own thing.'

'A loner? But I thought he was married?'

'If you can call it a marriage. Did Richard tell you about Debbie?'

'Briefly,' admitted Annie. 'But it wasn't something I wanted to quiz him about. I thought it might be a sensitive subject. He did say it wasn't a great marriage.'

Patrick's jaw was set in a hard line that made him look even more like his brother.

'That's a bit of an understatement.'

'Why?'

'Debbie was gorgeous,' Patrick continued. 'Absolutely beautiful and heiress to a property portfolio that would make your eyes water. But given that she had eyes only for my brother she was probably not too bright.'

'Why do you say that? Richard seems like a good guy.'

'Richard is a good police officer there is no doubt about that. But good husband material? Nah. I don't think he gave a damn about Debbie. She was at home giving him the life of Riley and he was working shifts on the beat trying to make detective. He could have done anything he wanted but he wouldn't do the one thing his wife wanted.'

'Which was?'

'To give up the force. Debbie was sick of the shifts and the overtime. She offered to set him up in any business he wanted but he refused.'

'Why?'

'God only knows. Maybe he loves his job more than he loved his wife. Maybe he didn't want to live off his wife. I can't answer that. Of course, he inherited everything when she was murdered but he insisted on remaining a cop.'

'So, Richard is rich?'

'My baby brother is stinking rich but don't ask me what he does with the money because he sure as hell doesn't seem to spend it.'

'Did Debbie have family?'

'Only child,' answered Patrick. 'There were three old codgers that ran her Trust Fund until she was twenty-five and a few distant cousins but there was no-one else. I think that is one of the reasons she rushed into marriage with Richard. They were so unsuited it's not true. God knows what she saw in him.'

I know, thought Annie.

'She deserved better.' There was a slight catch in Patrick's voice that startled Annie. 'You sound as if you were very fond of her.'

'I was,' Patrick admitted. 'I was in love with her.'

Annie glanced across at Patrick but he refused to meet her gaze.

'Did she feel the same?'

'Yep.'

Annie fell silent as she processed all she had heard. What a mess the brothers had got themselves into. She realised Patrick was still talking and brought her attention back to his words.

'When Richard agreed to divorce Debbie she and I were over the moon. We planned to marry as soon as the divorce was finalised and we were going to travel for a year while we decided what we would do with our lives. Then she was killed.'

'Did Richard know?'

'About Debbie and I? I can't be sure but I think he must have done. He is a bloody good detective. And Debbie was pregnant when she died.'

A dawning realisation caused Annie to half turn in her seat and face Patrick.

'Were you the father of Debbie's baby?'

'I was. It's why she pushed for a divorce.'

Annie did not reply. Her words had slipped away with the shock of the revelations. By the time she did manage to speak they were leaving the motorway.

'Patrick, why are you telling me this?'

'Because I need to get it off my chest and you need to know.'

'Why do I?'

'Because I can see that you have feelings for him and you seem like a good person. Getting mixed up with Richard might not be such a good move for you. My brother is a cold fish. He didn't love his wife and I am not sure he has loved anyone since our parents died. Richard was an Oxford scholar. He inherited all the brains in the family. But when mum and dad died he walked away from everything. He just gave up without a thought for anyone but himself and disappeared. I fetched him home from Egypt two years later and told him to get his act together.'

'Two years? What had he been doing?'

'God only knows. Grieving, finding himself, wallowing in self-pity maybe.'

'What about you?'

'I was already in the Army and going for SAS pre-selection. I got on with it. I couldn't afford to be self-indulgent.'

'You sound as if you resent him?'

'I think Richard is extremely selfish and also thoroughly self-contained. He doesn't seem to need anyone, or at least he hasn't up until now. But he actually seems to have feelings for you and if those feelings are reciprocated, you need to know what he is really like.'

Annie wanted to ask why Patrick kept up the façade of brotherly love when he seemed to resent Richard so much. Was it because of Richard's money? Or was there some other reason? At Credenhill she would have sworn that the two brothers were best friends. She wondered if Richard knew how his brother felt. It was true that she had thought Richard cold at first. But in the last few days, she had seen a different side of him. However much she tried she could not reconcile the man she knew with the person that Patrick was describing. They were approaching the centre of Worcester by the time Annie spoke again.

'Patrick, I still don't understand why you have told me this. If Richard didn't know about you and Debbie, aren't you afraid that I will tell him?'

Patrick smiled. 'I can assure you I am not afraid of my brother. But maybe you should be.'

'Right now, Richard is the only person that makes me feel safe. Why would I be scared of him?'

'Because Debbie was pregnant with my child when she asked Richard for a divorce. They had a prenup because of her wealth. Within weeks she was dead and Richard inherited everything.'

'Are you telling me he was involved?'

'I'm telling you to be careful, that's all.'

Chapter Forty-Eight

It was well past three by the time they reached the Asylum Centre and Patrick parked the car a few houses away from the building on the opposite side of the road. Annie glanced behind them and saw that the backup vehicle was a few hundred yards further down the road. Patrick turned to Annie.

'Now for my fourth condition.'

'You're coming in with me,' replied Annie, secretly pleased. Now that they were here her earlier feelings of anticipation were being eroded by a creeping dread.

'That's my fifth condition.'

'How many are there?'

'As many as we need to keep you safe.'

'The fourth then.'

'We phone Richard and tell him what we're up to.'

Annie began to protest but Patrick was already dialling Richard's mobile phone. In the proximity of the car, Annie could hear the ringing and then Richard's distorted voice through the receiver, 'DI Shaw.'

'Hey, bro.'

'Patrick, what's going on? Is everything ok?'

'An update on manoeuvres for you. Unless you have already heard the news?'

Richard's voice was sharp. 'What news, what manoeuvres?'

'Annie and I at the Asylum Centre.'

'What? You had better repeat that and change your location. Annie is safe in Herefordshire.'

'Annie and I are at the Asylum Centre. She thinks the USB might be here.' He looked smug as he spoke.

'That was not the plan, Patrick. Annie should be kept on base. That was the whole point of risking both our necks to get there.'

Patrick sighed. 'She wants this over, Richard. She's convinced the USB is here.'

'It doesn't matter what she wants. She has to be kept safe.'

'You mean a prisoner?'

'I mean safe.'

'It's her choice, Richard. We go into search and then we head straight back to base.'

'Patrick, please don't do this. I can get down there in no time and search the place. Just wait!'

'Don't worry. I have armed backup with me. And my bosses have informed your bosses. The Armed Response Unit should be on their way as I speak. We'll be in and out in no time. Hold on a minute.' Annie's hand was on his arm.

'Let me speak to him.'

Patrick was about to refuse but the resolve in Annie's eyes and in the set of her jaw changed his mind. He handed her the phone.

'Richard?'

'Annie, what the hell do you think you're playing at?' His tone stung her but she was determined to try and explain.

'Richard, I have to do this.'

'It's not safe, Annie.'

'Well, I'm here now, and everything looks quiet. I'll be in and out in no time. It's the only place that no-one has searched. I'm sure the USB is there, Richard. I have to look. It's the only way to end this.'

'Even if it puts you at risk?'

'That's the whole point, though, isn't it? We're all at risk until that data is found. Me more than anyone. You must see that surely?'

She heard Richard sigh at the other end of the phone and when he spoke his voice was tinged with ice. 'Come straight to the station as soon as you've finished. And you can tell that brother of mine that I'll deal with him later.'

The phone went dead and Patrick took it with a grimace. 'I heard. Come on then.'

Annie steeled herself to get on with what she needed to do. There was no doubt that she was afraid, to be brutally honest she was terrified, but having Patrick beside her gave her more than enough protection. His aura of invincibility and confidence was settling along her shoulders like a gossamer shawl, light and airy for sure but tangible and very real.

More than that, slivers of anger were beginning to pierce Annie's tattered feelings. She was angry that Soraya and her babies had died needlessly, she was angry that the tiny bodies had been left on her doorstep, she was angry that she had been attacked in her own home. Once again, Annie felt an overwhelming urge to seek revenge, to get back at the men that had caused so much harm and to prevent them from causing any further tragedy. She was ready to do what needed to be done and she would do it willingly.

She nodded at Patrick. 'I'm ready.'

They climbed from the car and Patrick took her arm as they crossed the road. Annie was aware of the soldiers from the backup car creeping like shadows behind them. She did not look back.

Chapter Forty-Nine

Earlier that day, the Incident Room had once again been alive with concentrated activity. When Masterton strode in and clapped her hands, the silence was instantaneous. 'We go in this evening', she said.

Applause broke out around the room and there were a few muted cheers. Masterton waited for silence before she resumed.

'The unit at Sherriff Street is under surveillance. The area is busy during the day and any attempt to go in at this time could end up in a siege, a blood bath or even a hostage situation. At the present time, we believe the three assailants are inside the unit and that's where we want them to stay. I don't need to tell you that we have a total press blackout. Even the smallest leak could lead to a direct loss of life. Please remember that we are not just concerned with the local picture here. We know that these three men are connected to the largest crime syndicate operating out of Afghanistan. It is an organisation that is responsible for a great deal of misery and suffering around the world. So, while we want these men banged up for murdering on our patch, there is a lot more at stake both for Britain and the rest of the world.'

Masterton paused to survey the faces around the room. The team was subdued and serious, already focusing on the task ahead.

'You all know what you need to do so get to it and make sure you are prepared. We'll have a final briefing at five for a six pm departure. The Armed Response Team will already be in place. They'll get the signal to go in as soon as the area is cleared. All set?'

'Yes, boss,' reverberated around the room like a Mexican wave.

Masterton gazed at her team with satisfaction. She felt immensely proud of every one of them. 'This is our chance to nail these bastards so let's make sure we do a good job of it. If anyone is not sure of anything then ask. With a bit of luck, most of you will be home for dinner.'

It was then that Richard's mobile phone vibrated in his jacket pocket. He glanced at the number before he took the call. During the short conversation his features had set so firmly, a chisel would not have made a single mark.

'Shit.' Richard swore as he threw his mobile phone onto his desk and ran his hands through his hair. 'Shit, shit, shit.'

'Got an attack of Delhi belly?' called Collins.

'Told you there was a real person in there somewhere,' added McIntyre. 'Mr Cool has finally melted.'

'Shut it.' snarled Richard as he headed for Masterton's office followed by cries of, 'ooh, temper, temper.'

He knocked on the door but strode in before she had answered. Masterton sensed his mood at once.

'What is it, Richard?'

'The best of the SAS have left base and taken Annie to the Asylum Centre.'

Masterton's jaw dropped. 'What? Why?'

'She thinks the memory stick is there.'

'Of course,' nodded Diane. 'Clever girl. We should have thought to search the place ourselves. That is my error.'

'No, not clever. Pretty stupid, actually. As long as she's on the street, she's in danger.'

'As long as that data is on the street, we are all in danger.'

Richard knew better than to waste time arguing.

'I'd like to go over there.'

'She's with the SAS. They will look after her, you know. Or do you think you can do better?'

'She's a target.'

'She's protected. You stay here.'

'But boss...'

'That's an order, Richard. Now, get back to work.'

Richard gave Masterton a look of such disgust that she dropped her eyes back to the operational plan on her desk. The last thing she needed was an argument with her right-hand man. Richard had started silently cursing his boss before he had even left her office.

'Sticks and stones,' said Masterton so quietly that Richard stopped and turned his head to look back at her. Diane kept her eyes fixed on her papers but a smile played at the corners of her mouth.

'What was that?' asked Richard.

'Psychic powers,' she said. 'I get them from my Auntie.'

Richard couldn't help the faintest smile that crept across his own face. 'Sorry, boss. I'm just worried.'

'Just make sure that mobile phone still works after you've finished chucking it around the office,' said Diane.

At that moment, her thoughts were interrupted by the insistent ringing of her own phone. Masterton listened in disbelief to the voice at the other end of the phone as it relayed the news that Annie was being taken to the Asylum Centre. 'A bit bloody late telling me now,' she thought as she slammed down the receiver. 'It's only my case after all.' She was about to call Richard back to her office when the phone rang again. 'DCI Masterton,' she answered while she continued to write.

'What did you say?' she asked, as her face paled and the pen fell from her grasp then, 'Thank you.'

She redialled without replacing the receiver and yelled out Richard's name as she began talking hurriedly into the receiver. Richard was at her doorway at once.

'Boss, what is it?'

'An apology from me for starters,' she said, as she covered the mouthpiece of the telephone.

'What…?'

Masterton flapped her hand to shush him while she continued firing orders down the phone before slamming it down onto her desk as she ended the conversation.

'Richard, listen carefully.'

'Fire away.'

'I've just had a call from the surveillance team at Sherriff Street. Two of our suspects have just left the unit in one hell of a hurry. They're heading in the direction of the Asylum Centre.'

Richard didn't answer straight away as he absorbed what he had just heard.

'I'm sorry, Richard. The Armed Response Unit have already been mobilised and are on their way and the SAS have been informed.'

Richard was staring at her as if the English he had just heard was a foreign language.

'They're monitoring everything.' It was a statement, not a question. 'Phone calls, radio, the lot.'

'Without a doubt. Explains why they've been on to people so quickly.

Richard shook his head in wonderment.

'Go,' said Masteron, 'I'll be right behind you with back up. And for God's sake, be careful.'

He didn't even stop for his jacket.

Chapter Fifty

Annie chose to enter the Asylum Centre through the back door, afraid that she would be delayed by the residents if they caught sight of her. Her office was locked but she had her key ready in her hand and slipped inside with Patrick close behind her. She heard him muttering into his radio as she began to search the room carefully and methodically.

She searched every square inch of the office and found nothing. The journey back to town and the effort of searching the office had made her wound throb and her ribs ache. 'I can't understand it. I felt sure my bag had been moved. She must have been looking for a hiding place.'

'Would she have gone anywhere else?' asked Patrick.

'I don't think she had the time,' mused Annie. 'She left by the back door and there was nowhere else that she could have gone without me seeing her.'

Annie paced behind her desk for a minute before going and sitting in the chair that Soraya had occupied.

'Could you look under the desk for me Patrick?'

Patrick obliged and squeezed his large frame beneath the furniture. 'All clear here,' came his muffled voice as he struggled out and back onto his feet. 'I'll just check that all is quiet outside and radio our back up. Don't leave this room until I come back.'

Annie was imagining herself in Soraya's place. Trying to see what she would have seen. Annie had already checked all around her desk and the chair that she was sitting on.

Where could it be? Where could it possibly be?

Her eyes began to check the room systematically from the point where Annie herself would have sat in ever widening circles to the brightly coloured posters on the wall. Annie looked at these too, wondering if Soraya had been able to read English as well as she spoke it. Annie's favourite poster showed a mother with a new baby cradled in one arm and a toddler holding the other hand. It encouraged parents to bring their under-fives to the well child clinic for checks and advice. Annie loved the happy, smiling faces of the mother and the toddler while the baby gazed serenely from its shawl. It was written in several Asian languages including Hindi, Urdu, Arabic, Chinese and the Afghan languages Pashto and Farsi. Annie assumed that Soraya would have been able to read it and wondered if she had imagined herself coming to the clinic with her own baby.

Annie looked at the toddler's feet clad in soft boots with socks that tumbled around his ankles. She saw that one of the boots was wrinkled at the corner of the poster and was annoyed that someone had been in her room and damaged the picture while she was away.

But her room had been locked.

As if in a dream, Annie walked toward the poster and ran her hand over the glossy surface. The Asylum Centre was an old building with uneven walls that had been buried over the years beneath layers of wallpaper. Annie's room currently had a heavy woodchip on the walls painted a sunny yellow. The lump behind the poster that she was feeling now was much bigger than any piece of wood chip. It was about the size of a USB.

With a small cry, she pulled the corner of the poster away from the wall and caught the USB before it fell to the floor. She turned it over in her hand, scarcely able to believe that it was real. She closed her fingers around it and kissed them.

'Annie.' Patrick was back at the door. 'We need to get out of here. Two of the Afghans are on their way.'

His manner was suddenly clipped and the urgency that she heard in his voice scared her. As she hurried from the room locking the door securely behind her she said 'I've got it,' but Patrick seemed not to have heard. His firearm was braced and he was muttering into his mouthpiece. He indicated that she should be quiet but when Annie stepped into the corridor there was still no-one around. Knowing how busy the Asylum Centre was at times she marvelled at their luck at not being seen. They moved quickly and quietly towards the back door. Annie didn't see Patrick nod to the soldier concealed by the dumpster across from the door.

Just as he turned the corner of the building Patrick stopped suddenly and stepped back so that Annie bumped into him almost dropping the USB. She thought of Soraya and secret hiding places and pushed it down inside her bra. It was cold and scratchy against the soft skin of her breast but the USB was safe and her hands were free.

'Annie, go back.' Patrick hissed.

His tone was enough. Annie retraced her steps to the back door but Patrick motioned her to keep moving past it. At the next corner, he pulled her to a stop. motioning towards a wooden gate.

'Where does that lead to?'

'An alley at the back. It takes you down to City Walls Road.'

'Go,' he ordered. 'Quickly.'

Annie slipped through the gate. Patrick, who had paused to signal to the waiting soldier, was close on her heels as she hurried to the end of the alley. City Walls Road was a busy dual carriageway and the traffic spewed dust and exhaust fumes as it rushed past them. Patrick concealed his firearm and linked arms with Annie, setting a brisk pace as they dodged the traffic and followed an alley leading to New Street. They passed silent flats caught in their last moments of slumber before they were woken by the chattering of children home from school and the weary feet of adults returning from a day's work. There were few pedestrians and they ducked through the cobbled pavement of Reindeer Court to reach the Shambles.

As they walked, Patrick spoke urgently into his radio to the soldiers in the backup car. The euphoria at finding the USB was draining away with every step that Annie took. If she had momentarily dared to forget that she was recovering from trauma, her body was now seeking its revenge. She was already short of breath and her legs felt as if they belonged to a twenty stone woman.

'I need to slow down,' she gasped.

'Sorry, Annie, we can't.'

'What happened at the Asylum Centre?' asked Annie., 'Who did you see?'

'Richard,' he said.

Annie stopped suddenly.

'Exactly,' said Patrick, urging her forward.

Annie was confused. 'I don't understand. We don't need to hide from Richard.'

'We need to hide from the reason that he was there.'

As they reached the end of Reindeer Court, Patrick finally stopped to look around before they crossed the Shambles which was crowded with shoppers. Annie concentrated on her breathing, trying desperately to calm her complaining heart which was thumping against her aching ribs. Patrick pulled her across the road. They were now walking along the pedestrianised street dodging slow-moving pensioners and parents with pushchairs.

'What reasons?' demanded Annie. 'Surely he came looking for us?'

'Richard told us to go to the station when we had finished,' said Patrick. 'He wasn't planning to come to the Asylum Centre. Something must have made him come after us.'

'You don't know that for sure.'

Patrick turned to look at her without breaking his stride. 'I do know,' he said. 'He is my brother. I know how he thinks.'

They cut through Marks and Spencer, weaving in and out of rails of the latest fashions to reach the High Street. Patrick steered her towards Boots and led her to the very back of the store where they finally came to a halt. Annie was seriously short of breath and her head was thumping painfully. She sank down gratefully onto the edge of a shelf and rested her head in her hands and asked. 'What now?'

Patrick was standing at the end of the shelves so that he could watch the store. 'We wait.'

'What for?'

Patrick indicated the radio in his hand. 'The all clear.'

Annie massaged her temples, just glad to be still. She realised that it is easy to feel well and recovered when you don't have to exert yourself. Keeping pace with Patrick had pushed her to her physical limits. She was happy to wait for a very long time.

Chapter Fifty-One

By some miracle and the occasional use of his blue light, Richard reached the Asylum Centre in ten minutes flat. He parked in the street and hurried from the car to the bottom of the drive that led up to the house. He took a quick look around but saw no signs of anything amiss. As he walked up the drive looking up at the windows of the house he failed to see the faintest movement at the far corner as Patrick pulled back from his line of sight. There was no sign of the Armed Response Unit although Richard knew that they could be only minutes away.

He climbed the steps to the front door which was held open by an ancient piece of rusty iron and walked into reception. A young woman sat at what looked like an old dining table tapping away at a computer. She had the mellow skin of an Eastern European and her long hair was pulled up into an untidy ponytail. She looked up as Richard approached and he hesitated at the sight of the stitches laddered across her right cheek.

She pretended not to notice his reaction and smiled. 'Can I help you?'

'Is the midwife here? Annie Collings?' he asked.

'No,' said the girl, in slightly accented English. 'She is away for some weeks.'

'What about the manager?' asked Richard. 'Is Malcolm here?'

The girl smiled and nodded at Richard's use of the manager's first name and she got up from her chair and disappeared through a door. While Richard waited, he looked at the stand of leaflets, What to do if you are Unwell, Find help with Housing, Legal Services for Asylum Seekers.

'Detective, how nice to see you.' Malcolm held out his hand and Richard shook it warmly but spoke quickly and without preliminaries. 'Has Annie Collings been here?'

'No, of course not.' Malcolm looked perplexed. 'She will be away for some time yet, I imagine.'

'Can we check her room?' asked Richard.

'Of course, follow me. Can you tell me what this is about?'

'Annie was on her way here this afternoon to look for something,' explained Richard, 'but we think she may be in danger.'

'I see.' Malcolm quickened his step and unlocked the door to Annie's consulting room. It was empty. Richard stepped inside. 'Can you tell if anyone has been here?'

Malcolm looked around briefly before shaking his head. 'Not that I can see. But this is really Annie's domain, Detective. I wouldn't know what to look for.'

'How many people are in the building at the moment?' asked Richard.

'It's hard to tell. We have people coming and going all day. Staff and visitors as well as residents. It could be anywhere between twenty and forty people although it's quiet today. Most of the residents are out.'

They had returned to the front reception. The young woman was back at the computer.

'Do you know what happened to Annie Collings?' Richard asked her.

'Of course, it was in the papers. We could not believe it when we heard. Annie has been of much help to us here. I cannot think who would want to hurt her.'

Richard turned to face Malcolm. 'We think we know who hurt her, but we haven't caught them yet. There is a chance they may come here looking for her.

There is a possibility they are on their way here right now.'

The colour drained from Malcolm's face and he began to look wildly around the reception area.

'What should I do?'

'There are police on their way but we need to get everyone together as far away from the entrances as possible and we have to lock all the doors.'

'We can go to the basement,' said Malcolm.

'Do it,' said Richard. 'And take a mobile phone with you.'

The young woman at the reception desk who had been listening attentively was already running from the reception area calling out in a language that Richard did not understand. He heard voices replying and the sound of running feet.

'I'll lock the back door,' said Malcolm. 'You get the front.'

Richard hurried to the front door and bent down to pull away the piece of cast iron. As he bent his head he heard the screech of tyres on the drive and cars doors opening. He straightened and saw the doors of a grey Honda swing open and the muzzle of a weapon rise into the air. Sirens sounded outside as the Armed Response Unit and several squad cars raced along the street but rather than distract the two gunmen, the noise caused them to move faster. As Richard slammed the door he saw the men running towards the front steps.

The door was old and solid with bolts top and bottom that Richard slid into place. The gunmen were already banging on the door outside and there were cries from the Centre's residents as they emerged from various parts of the ground floor to run down the stairs.

Malcolm re-appeared. 'The back is secure.'

'Get downstairs. Keep everyone away from the windows,' ordered Richard.

Outside the soldiers who had been observing the building were now watching the two men banging on the doors. Their weapons were aimed with deadly accuracy. Behind the soldiers, police officers were cordoning off the street and running from house to house, advising people to stay inside and keep away from the windows. Radios were crackling into life and the Armed Response Officers poured out of their van and hurried into position around the building. Richard checked the bolts one last time before heading for the stairs. He had taken the first step when a noise behind him made him falter. The young woman was back at her computer gathering papers and CDs into her arms.

'No,' shouted Richard, 'leave them.'

The woman ignored him and began to move the mouse. 'Leave it,' shouted Richard again and hurried to the woman intending to get her downstairs even if it meant doing so forcibly. He was half way across the hall when a shout outside warned the Afghans to drop their weapons and lie face down on the ground. Their response was to turn their weapons on to the door and try and blast their way inside. Over the deafening percussion of the shots, Richard heard screams of terror from inside the building and a waterfall of shattered glass flooded onto the floor. Richard threw himself and the young woman to the floor with his hands over his head. The shots seemed to go on forever as Richard lay immobile, waiting for them to stop. He hadn't realised that he had closed his eyes until he opened them and found himself staring directly into the terrified, tear-filled eyes of the young woman.

'It's ok,' whispered Richard and she nodded silently. The sound of muffled crying was still coming from inside the building and Richard wondered briefly what terrors some of the residents had been reminded of. He also wondered why the banging on the door had stopped. All he could hear were orders being barked outside. He did not yet know that the two Afghan men had signed their own death warrant the minute they pulled the triggers on their weapons, nor that they now lay dead on the other side of the door that he had closed only minutes before.

A sudden thump on the door startled him before he heard the shouts of 'all clear' from outside. He pushed himself up from the floor then fell down again as an agonising pain tore through his left shoulder. It took him several deep breaths before he was able to roll onto his back and push himself into a sitting position with his right arm. His left arm hung uselessly by his side. The young woman beside him had also moved and she gave a faint cry as she saw Richard. He looked down at the blood soaking his shirt and knew that he had been shot.

Thank God he had left his jacket at the station.

Chapter Fifty-Two

Masterton's arrival had coincided with that of the Armed Response Vehicle, a fact that gave her huge comfort. She was also pleased to see that the squad cars had arrived and officers were already moving quickly from house to house. As the Armed Response Officers moved into position, Masterton waited in the designated area until the all-clear could be given. Even if detectives were still issued with guns, Masterton would have been happy to sit this one out. Not for the first time in her career, she gave thanks for the special squad.

She watched as the squad moved into position. In their helmets and body armour, they reminded her of a movie where she had seen a race of aliens invade a quiet, suburban street. Mind you, she thought, it doesn't get more alien than this. The movements of the squad were slickly executed in a choreography of short runs and positioning that covered the target and the men in the squad. Within minutes, Masterton heard the challenge followed by a burst of automatic gunfire answered immediately by the guns of the officers. Two sharp retorts. There were two men. That would do it, thought Masterton. Sure enough, the all clear was soon signalled and she hurried along the street.

The driveway of the Asylum Centre was swarming with officers and Masterton had to push her way through a pressure cooker of testosterone and adrenaline to reach the steps at the front door. The two crumpled bodies of the men who had been terrorising her patch for far too many days had tumbled to the foot of the steps. Both men had red patches of blood seeping from the left side of their chests which was beginning to trickle down the drive. She stepped over the bodies to join the officer who was banging on the door and calling the all clear. She heard the bolts being drawn back and the door opened slowly. The white face of the man that she would learn was the Centre manager opened the door cautiously and peered out. Masterton thrust her ID into his face.

'DCI Masterton. It's all clear out here now. Mind if we come in?'

Malcolm's voice trembled as he spoke. 'We need an ambulance, the detective has been shot.'

A look of disbelief fell over Masterton's face even as she pushed past Malcolm into the reception area. She was already pressing the buttons on her cell phone. Richard was lying slumped against the leg of a table, the front of his shirt an ugly red and his left arm hanging by his side. A young woman with a scarred face was holding a scarf against Richard's shoulder with one hand as she tried to loosen his tie with the other. Masterton's shock was tempered a little when she saw that Richard was conscious and talking to the young woman. But her concern for him went too deep to let her relax. She practically shouted into her cell phone.

'This is DCI Masterton calling from the Asylum Centre. A police officer has been shot. I repeat, a police officer has been shot. We require a paramedic urgently.'

Then she was on her knees beside Richard, ignoring the rough floorboards that snagged her tights and scuffed the toes of her shoes. She took over from the young woman to remove Richard's tie. Richard turned his head to look at his boss and smiled when he saw her.

'I always knew you were dying to undress me, boss,' he joked.

'If I wasn't so bloody relieved to find you alive and full of cheek I might have something to say about that remark. As it is, you've probably got until the paramedics arrive to get away with blue murder.'

'Think someone's already tried that,' he grimaced, 'didn't work, though.'

'Oh, yes it did,' she smiled, 'at least from our point of view.'

'You got them?'

'Two of them.'

Richard looked down at his shirt. 'That was worth ruining a shirt for.'

'Claim it on expenses, Detective.'

Richard smiled but his expression was becoming pinched with the effort of talking and he leaned back against the table and closed his eyes. Masterton touched the young woman on the arm. 'Thank you for taking care of him.'

The young woman shook her head. 'No. He was taking care of me.'

'What's your name?' asked Masterton.

'I am Tania.'

'Thank you anyway, Tania.'

'Ok, let us at him,' said a male voice behind her and both women were relieved to see the green overalled paramedics striding towards them. Masterton rose to give them room but as she moved away Richard called her.

'Boss. Do you know where Annie is?'

'I don't,' replied Masterton. 'But she's not here which is a good thing.'

'But she's with that brother of mine. That could be a bad thing.'

'Do you think so?'

'Not for a minute,' said Richard, 'but I'd like to know.'

'I'll find her,' promised Masterton.

Outside the Asylum Centre, Masterton was simultaneously shouting orders down her mobile phone whilst giving instructions to the officers manning the cordons to look out for Annie and Colonel Shaw. She had already learned from the soldiers present that Annie and Patrick had entered the building but then left from the back and disappeared into the nearby streets. She was certain that the Colonel had somehow been alerted to the danger and was equally positive that he would be back. Even as she snapped her mobile phone shut, one of the soldiers was at her side.

'We've just made radio contact with the Colonel, ma'am. They are on their way back.'

'Can you take a car and fetch them?' asked Masterton. She wasn't absolutely sure that she was authorised to give the army orders but it was their own senior officer that they were retrieving after all.

'Certainly, ma'am.'

'I wish my lot were as disciplined as that,' she muttered under her breath, as she watched the soldier's smartly retreating back.

Chapter Fifty-Three

In Boots, a radio crackled to life causing the browsers in dental care and first aid to stare suspiciously at the soldier and the fragile young woman with him. Patrick remained focused on the doorway throughout the brief conversation with his back up before visibly relaxing.

'It's ok, Annie, we can go back.' He held out his hands and helped Annie to her feet. 'We can take it easy this time,' he said. 'Lean on me.'

As they reached Cornmarket, Annie was beginning to think that she might have to ask Patrick to carry her when a car slid to a halt beside them a sharp, 'Sir.' causing Patrick to stop.

'Ah, the cavalry,' he smiled to Annie as he opened the car door for her. She sank gratefully into the back seat and, as she fastened her seat belt, she felt the pressure of the USB. The thought that so much evil was against her skin suddenly repelled her and she fished it out and handed it to Patrick. His jaw dropped in surprise.

'Where was it?'

'Behind a poster.'

'Thank you, Annie.' Patrick took the USB and placed it in his pocket. 'I'll keep it safe.'

The car turned the corner towards the Asylum Centre and slowed to pass the police cordons that blocked the way to the building. She gasped as she surveyed the scene that greeted her and turned to Patrick. 'My God, what on earth has happened?'

'Apparently, there has been a visit from two rather unpleasant characters. And not a friendly type at all.'

'You mean the terrorist type.'

'Precisely so.'

The car stopped outside the Asylum Centre and Annie saw DCI Masterton approaching the car. Something about the grim look on her face as she caught sight of Annie made the hairs on Annie's arms stand on end. Masterton opened the car door and helped Annie out. Patrick hurried around from his side of the car and offered Annie his arm. They both looked at Masterton expectantly.

'Two of our thugs turned up here not long ago,' Masterton began.

'They were after me,' said Annie.

'Possibly,' replied Masterton. 'Why they came is not important. Fortunately, we were close behind them and they have been apprehended.'

'They've been arrested?' asked Patrick.

Masterton paused. 'Apprehended permanently,' she said.

Annie understood that this meant they were dead. She felt a grim sense of satisfaction. 'I hope they suffered.'

'Too quick for that,' said Masterton, 'although I entirely understand your sentiments.'

'Is everyone at the centre ok?' asked Annie.

Masterton looked from Patrick to Annie before speaking and her hesitation unnerved both of them to the extent that they instinctively took a step forward. Masterton held up her hands and touched them both on the arm to stop them.

'Richard was here,' she said.

Annie gave a small cry and leant heavily against Patrick who had visibly stiffened. Masterton hurried on.

'He's conscious and talking but I have to tell you that he has been shot.' Annie closed her eyes to try and still the spinning of her head and take away the nausea that was rising in her throat. Masterton's voice came to her from a long way away. 'The paramedics are with him now. They'll be moving him to the hospital very soon. Annie, are you ok? Do you need to sit down?'

Annie shook her head and opened her eyes. She had to hold it together or they would cart her off in an ambulance as well. She forced herself to speak in the steadiest voice she could muster. 'Can we see him?'

'Of course.'

Masterton led the way up the driveway that was now almost as familiar to her as her own and skirted the two bodies that had been covered with a forensic cloth. Annie climbed the steps as if she were entering a totally unknown world which was indeed what this had become.

Inside the reception hall, she saw Richard's long legs sprawled beside the table that held the computer used by the residents, but two paramedics obscured her view of him. What she did see was the equipment spread around them which she recognised as the stuff of serious trauma. She began to tremble so badly that Patrick was virtually holding her upright, then one of the paramedics moved aside and she saw Richard's face.

He had the grey pallor of shock and his eyes were closed but his shirt had been cut away and her trained eye took in his condition. She saw the regular, even movement of his chest as he breathed normally and the large dressing that was applied to his shoulder. No major organs, she thought.

The paramedic still squatting beside Richard was inserting a cannula for an intravenous infusion while the second man was organising oxygen. Annie felt her strength returning and she released Patrick's arm to go to Richard. The paramedic inserting the cannula glanced at her as she kneeled beside him and she recognised the man who had helped her after her fall at home. He nodded in recognition and Annie smiled in return.

While the paramedic strapped the cannula into place, Annie sat on her heels and gazed at the face that had come to mean so much to her. In the instant that she had heard he had been shot, she knew without a doubt that this man meant more to her than anyone who had ever touched her life. The paramedic hooked up the infusion and stepped aside to organise his equipment ready for Richard's transfer. Annie slipped into his place and laid her hand on Richard's good shoulder which she began to stroke with the lightest touch.

'Hello, you,' she whispered.

Richard's eyes sprang open. 'Hello back,' he replied. 'Thank God you're safe.'

'Thank God you are.'

There didn't seem to be anything else to say to each other. They simply smiled and devoured each other with their eyes. As he observed the two of them, Patrick had to stamp down sharply on the pang of envy that he felt emerge as he recognised the connection between these two people. Then he thought of Debbie and had to turn away at the unfairness of the world. Richard did not deserve this and he did not deserve Debbie's money. He liked Annie though. It was a shame she was caught up in all this.

The paramedic's hand was on Annie's shoulder indicating that she needed to step away. She stood up and moved towards Patrick. She thought he would be upset about his brother but the look she saw in his eyes chilled her. Following her with his eyes, Richard noticed his brother for the first time.

'Thanks, Patrick.'

'Anytime,' replied Patrick and he put his arm around Annie's shoulders to move her away so that Richard could be lifted onto the chair and carried down the steps to the ambulance. It was all Annie could do not to shrug his arm off as she felt Patrick's hostility. She found it hard to believe that Richard could have had anything to do with his wife's death. If he had wanted her money so badly, surely he would have done something with it by now. Surely he wouldn't be doing the job he did, as well as he did it, and taking gun shots in the process? Was it possible that Richard knew about Patrick and his wife? Could he have known that Debbie's baby was fathered by his own brother?

The thoughts swirling around in her head were making it ache and Annie tried to shake them away. She could not even begin to judge a man that she hardly knew and she could not deny the strong connection she felt with him. All that mattered right now was that he got better quickly so they could spend time getting to know each other. Anything else could wait.

Masterton was waiting at the doors of the ambulance as Richard was made comfortable on the stretcher inside.

'One of you can go with him,' she said, as Annie and Patrick approached.

Annie looked up at Patrick but he was already squeezing her shoulder. 'You go. I need to brief my men and make a few phone calls. I'll catch up with you later.'

Annie smiled her thanks at Masterton who waved them away.

'And if he asks,' Masterton said, 'tell him I'm going back to get the third one.'

Annie climbed the steps into the ambulance and the paramedic showed her where she should sit opposite Richard's stretcher. His eyes were closed again but there was the faintest hint of a smile on his lips and as the ambulance began to move he reached out his good hand for Annie's.

Chapter Fifty-Four

Masterton was talking into her phone as she drove herself back to the station. Just once, she thought, just once it would be nice to make a journey with her iPod or Free Radio for company rather than a raft of urgent phone calls and the worry of the current body count. Crimes of this nature were just not meant to happen on her patch and she would be glad when this one was over.

The raid on the industrial unit was still scheduled to go ahead and she was determined that it would be perfectly executed. She rubbed at the skin between her eyes and sighed. Richard's shooting had carved out another furrow to add to the sorrows she had accumulated during her years in the force. She thanked God that he was going to be ok and swept up the anxiety that was littering her thoughts. Richard would recover and the team would bring down the last villain if she had to do it with her own bare hands. Only one man still standing, she thought to herself, but not for long. She glanced at her watch. Just over an hour till kick off.

News of the shooting had already reached the Incident Room and the mood was remarkably subdued when Masterton walked in but she sensed at once that it was concentration and tension that controlled the atmosphere. The team was more determined than ever to finish the job and finish it well. Every officer fell silent as she walked to the incident board and swung around to face the room. She had learned from experience that there was no point setting scenes and issuing provisos because every person in the room was waiting to hear only one thing. She cut to the chase.

'DI Shaw has been involved in an incident at the Asylum Centre and was shot by one of our three suspects. However, he is not critically injured and should make a full recovery.'

The collective sigh of relief that swept the room was almost a physical force. For once, she was not bombarded with questions and comments as everyone listened attentively.

'Annie Collings was escorted to the Asylum Centre by an army officer. It appears that a mobile phone call between the army officer and DI Shaw was intercepted by our suspects because they left Sherriff Street within minutes of the call being placed and headed directly for the Centre. Fortunately, Annie and the Colonel had already left. DI Shaw was first on the scene and managed to secure the premises. Unfortunately, he was caught by a stray bullet as he was trying to remove one of the residents to a place of safety. He was shot in the shoulder and has been taken to hospital.'

'So he will definitely be ok?' asked Palmer.

'I'm not sure about ok,' smiled Masterton. 'I only tried to loosen his tie and he accused me of trying to get his kit off.'

'He's ok,' laughed Collins. 'What about the shooters, boss?'

'The two suspects were shot dead at the scene.' Masterton turned to the incident board to indicate the two men who had been killed as mumbles of approval filled the room.

'However,' she continued, as she turned back to face the team, 'we still have our third suspect out there. He is under surveillance and up until now he has remained at Sherriff Street. The operation goes ahead as planned. Any questions?'

'It doesn't seem the same without the DI,' said McIntyre.

‘He may not be here,’ said Masterton, ‘but it doesn’t mean that anyone lets him down. Or me, for that matter. Let’s get this case tidied up and finished. Enough people have died already.’

At Sherriff Street, the workers were leaving for the day and heading home. While the shutters were closed and doors and windows secured, Armed Response Officers were once again taking their places with the stealth of a big cat moving in for the kill.

Chapter Fifty-Five

Richard was settled quickly into the trauma room at the Accident and Emergency Department and assessed by the on-call surgeon. The x-ray examination showed that there was no skeletal damage and the doctor was pleased that the pressure bandage had stemmed the bleeding. It was decided that Richard would require surgery to have the wound cleaned and repaired and while he was waiting to be taken to the operating theatre, Annie was allowed to sit with him.

As she approached the bed he held out his right hand to her which she took gladly, careful not to disturb the cannula that was drip feeding life-giving blood into his veins.

'How do you feel?' asked Annie.

'Better than you look,' he smiled.

Annie immediately ran her free hand through her hair and Richard squeezed her fingers. 'It'll take more than that,' he said and his voice softened. 'You look exhausted.'

'I bet I look better than you do right now.'

'You want to make this a competition?' Annie laughed and shook her head. 'Then go and get some rest.'

'Do you want me to leave?' asked Annie.

Now it was Richard's turn to shake his head. 'No, not ever.'

'That's settled then,' said Annie.

'But you still need to get some rest.'

'Later. I will later.'

The room was suddenly invaded by nurses and orderlies and a bustle of chart collection and re-arrangement of equipment.

'Time to go,' said one of the nurses.

Richard let go of Annie's hand and she immediately felt bereft. Her clinical head told her that Richard would be fine but her heart was screaming for him to stay with her. Without a moment's thought she leaned forward and brushed her lips against his but by the time she had stepped back he was already being wheeled away and Annie snuggled into her blanket of worry.

Despite the exhaustion that laid heavyweights on every muscle in her body, Annie paced the waiting room unable to sit still, let alone rest. It was a long time since she had been to church but she found herself whispering prayers for Richard's recovery. By the time Patrick arrived with a steaming cardboard cup of takeaway coffee she could barely put one foot in front of the other. He was shocked at the lines of exhaustion that had settled around her eyes.

Patrick put the coffee down on the small table in the corner and led Annie to a seat. 'Come on,' he said, 'this is not helping anyone. You need to rest.'

Annie sat down but she hung her head, unable to meet Patrick's eyes. 'It's my fault.'

'What is?' asked Patrick. 'What's your fault?'

Her voice was heavy with guilt and resignation. 'Richard was shot because of me.'

'Don't be ridiculous.' Patrick grabbed her shoulders and turned her towards him. 'Look at me, Annie.'

Annie raised her eyes to meet Patrick's concerned gaze. 'None of this is your fault. Have you forgotten that you are the victim, here as much as anyone else? It's you that got beaten up. It's you that almost lost her life. And all because of the good work you do trying to help unfortunate people. How on earth can this be your fault?'

'If I had stayed at the base,' she said, 'if I had done what he wanted, this wouldn't have happened. They came after me, didn't they? They were following me. And Richard got hurt because of me.'

A single tear rolled down her cheek and Patrick pulled her towards him so that he could put his arm around her shoulder.

'Annie, because of you, two of the most evil men to walk the earth of this country have been taken off the streets – permanently. Because of you, they can't hurt or kill anyone else. If you drew them out of their hiding place, that's the best thing that could have happened. All I can say is that I wish all three of them had turned up. Getting the hat trick would have made my day.'

'He's still hurt.'

'Yes, Annie, he's hurt. But that's not because of you. He was hurt trying to save some woman who refused to move downstairs when she was told. He was hurt saving her life and that's the sort of person my brother is.'

Annie swallowed her tears and shifted slightly so that she could turn to look at Patrick.

'Do you really mean that?'

'I do.'

'He'll be all right, won't he?'

Patrick squeezed her shoulder. 'He's as tough as old boots underneath all those fancy suits he wears. Mind you, he might falter when our aunt turns up and gives him a piece of her mind. She's always telling him to be careful. My God, her tongue can slice through you like a razor blade through butter.'

Annie couldn't help laughing. 'That's better,' said Patrick. 'Now, drink your coffee, unless you think it will keep you awake.'

Annie took the cup gratefully and had swallowed her first mouthful when the door of the waiting room opened and a young nurse walked in. 'Mr. Shaw is back from the theatre,' she said. 'You can see him now.'

Patrick and Annie looked at each other and both mouthed, Mr Shaw. 'That was my father,' whispered Patrick and Annie laughed again.

They were taken to a single room at the end of the surgical ward where Richard was settled into bed. He still had the intravenous infusion in his right arm but the dressing to his left shoulder was a neat gauze rectangle. He looks so well, thought Annie, and was surprised to find tears pricking her eyes again.

'Here he is,' said the nurse unnecessarily. 'The doctor will be along shortly to see you but everything went well. He is still a bit groggy from the anaesthetic but he's going to be fine.'

Patrick and Annie stood on opposite sides of the bed. Annie was on the right so that she could take Richard's hand in hers, and Patrick on the left, to get a closer look at the dressing.

'Beaten the record, do you think?' were Patrick's first words to his brother.

Richard moved as if to shrug but winced in pain and lay still. 'Certainly feels like it.'

'What record?' asked Annie.

'The family record for whoever has the most stitches,' replied Patrick.

'And currently held by our sister who fell off a horse and cut her leg open. Seven,' said Patrick.

Annie placed her hand on the wound across her abdomen. 'I had nine.'

'Show off,' replied the brothers in unison.

They were interrupted by the doctor who checked Richard's dressing and surveyed his chart before smiling at his patient.

'The surgery went really well. We've cleaned the wound and stitched everything up for you. You'll need antibiotics and pain medication and you'll need a course of physiotherapy but otherwise, you should make a full recovery.'

'How long will I be here?' asked Richard.

The doctor glanced at Richard's chart again. 'If you remain stable overnight and tomorrow morning you should be able to go home around midday. We can arrange for someone to change your dressings at home and you can have your stitches removed as an outpatient. Will there be someone at home to look after you?'

'Yes,' said Annie and Patrick in unison and Annie flushed.

The doctor nodded at them both. 'Ok, then I'll see you tomorrow.'

Patrick and Richard both looked at Annie with the same questioning looks on their faces.

'I-If you need me, that is,' she stammered.

'Annie, you need looking after yourself,' said Richard, and when he smiled at her the gold flecks in his eyes were caught by the overhead lights so that she finally understood what was meant by the term twinkling eyes.

'You both need looking after,' interrupted Patrick, 'and I know just the woman.'

Richard groaned. 'Don't tell me you called Aunt Sarah?'

'What was I supposed to do? You could have died and I would never have been forgiven if I hadn't called.'

'Annie, take me home,' pleaded Richard.

'I don't have a home if you remember. Besides, your aunt can't be that bad. Can she?'

'Let's just say she likes to make a fuss,' explained Patrick, 'which can be a little overpowering at times.'

'She probably just loves you both to bits.'

'Well, I'm going to love you and leave you, Richard,' said Patrick. 'Do you need anything?'

'A shirt.'

'Army or Armani.'

'Very funny.'

'Are brothers always like this?' asked Annie.

'Always,' replied Patrick. 'Annie, can I give you a lift?'

'Can I stay here?' She was looking at Richard.

'Course you can.'

'Are you going to be his nurse?' asked Patrick.

Annie just smiled in reply and watched as Patrick took his leave from his brother, the affection between the two men obvious but puzzling. Patrick was almost schizophrenic in his dealings with his brother and it left Annie feeling bewildered and confused. Something was going on with Patrick but she had no idea whether it was anger, jealousy or something more sinister. Whatever it was, she had determined that Patrick could act his socks off.

'Actually, I haven't anywhere to go,' said Annie, shrugging her shoulders.

'You mean I'm the last resort?'

'You'll never be that.'

'Annie, you are very welcome to use my flat or I could call the station and get you somewhere to stay.'

'No, thank you. I'd like to stay here.'

His eyes were searching her face again and Annie felt her stomach contract as she gazed back unashamedly. 'I can't believe how well you look.'

'These things often look worse than they are. Besides, I was lucky. The bullet went straight through without hitting anything important. It's basically a flesh wound.'

'There was a lot of blood.'

She was biting her lip and Richard could feel her tension in the hand that was holding his.

'What's on your mind, Annie?'

'I want to apologise.'

'For what?'

'For not staying at the base. For causing all this.'

'You didn't, Annie, those bastards did. You did us a favour. At least we've got two of them and we've got enough forensic evidence to put the last one away for good when we catch him.'

'That's enough work talk you two.' It was the young nurse back to check Richard's vital signs and tuck him in for the night. She turned to Annie. 'Would you like to stay?'

'Yes, please,' said Annie. 'If that's ok.'

The nurse pointed to the Laz-E-Boy chair in the corner of the room. 'The chair is really comfortable. I'll fetch you a pillow and a blanket. But the patient needs his rest and if you don't mind me saying you look like you could do with a good night's sleep yourself.'

'It has been a long day,' agreed Annie.

When they were both settled the nurse dimmed the lights and Annie's whispered good night had barely left her lips before she had slipped into a deep and dreamless sleep.

Chapter Fifty-Six

The sun had slipped away to leave a warm, dry twilight that softened the ugly corners and contours of the industrial units in Sherriff Street. During the day the bustle of workers and visitors brought life to the faded buildings and battered concrete. But once the crowds had gone home it was not a place to linger. It was a sad and sorry part of the cathedral city and in much need of refurbishment.

A small mongrel dog cloaked with wiry hair and coloured like a faded sheepdog was padding silently between the darkened units of Sherriff Street, twitching its whiskers at the scent of rats. It paused to sniff at something in the space between two of the units, moving cautiously forward before turning tail with a wounded squeal and scampering off with its tail between its legs.

Then all was still.

No-one walking past would have seen the black-clad officers pressed back into the shadows unless they had literally tripped over one of them. So when the command to go was finally given and the door to the unit rammed open the last of the trio of murderers still breathing was caught hunched over the dials of a radio receiver. His look of shocked surprise was almost comical. His arms twitched as he moved to lift the Kalashnikov in his lap but before he could raise the sights a single shot to his chest exploded through his heart. His mouth dropped open and his eyes widened as the Kalashnikov clattered to the floor closely followed by the gunman's corpse. He died without even a sigh.

The Unit was small but bristling with hi-tech surveillance and computer equipment. When the all clear was called and Diane Masterton walked into the unit to see the man who had so much blood on his hands, she felt an overwhelming sense of satisfaction. In a strange way, these final moments had been almost too easy. She had expected some sort of stand-off or struggle. Maybe even an exchange of gunfire, like that outside the Asylum Centre. Instead, there was just the last breath of a murderer who had been gifted an easier death than those suffered by his victims.

'Good job,' she said to the team. 'Very well done, everyone.' And despite a heart that weighed a little heavier than it had that morning, she walked away with just the faintest trace of a smile.

Chapter Fifty-Seven

Saturday

Annie was already awake when the rattle of a trolley outside the room and the cheery good morning of the orderly who was dispensing cups of tea to the patients heralded the start of the day. She had been surprised to open her eyes at seven am to broad daylight and realise that she had slept deeply and, more importantly, dreamlessly.

'Good morning.' Her heart told her it was Richard's voice before her brain had even absorbed the words.

She looked across to see him sitting up in bed with his hair ruffled and a huge grin on his face. 'What are you looking so pleased about?' she asked suspiciously.

'It's jail break day.'

'Excuse me?'

'Parole, Annie, we get to go home.'

She feigned indignation. 'You've only been here one night. You should try a stretch of five.'

'You're right.' He glanced at his watch. 'I'll do five more hours then I'm off.'

Before Annie had a chance to think up a smart reply a nurse had appeared to take Richard off to the shower.

'I'll go and find myself some breakfast,' said Annie. 'Don't break out without me.'

Annie went to the canteen where she ate scrambled eggs and toast and drank a huge mug of tea. When she had finished, she strolled the full length of the long hospital corridor to the maternity unit. Patients in wheelchairs were being pushed by porters to various destinations, office staff scuttled along with arms of folders and the occasional laptop and the first members of the public were drifting in for their outpatient appointments. For several minutes, Annie stood and stared at the doors of the maternity unit before turning away and retracing her steps. She didn't need to go in there, she just needed to know that her world was still intact, unchanged and waiting for her return. She was on home turf and felt normal for the first time in what seemed a very long time.

By the time she had wandered back to the ward, Richard was dressed in surgical scrubs and was having a sling fitted by the nurse. Annie regarded him thoughtfully.

'I hadn't realised surgical scrubs were the in thing for detectives these days.'

Richard tried to shrug then grimaced as a stab of pain reminded him why he was sitting on a hospital bed being strapped up by a nurse.

'I don't think I'll be squeezing into a suit for a day or two, even one without bullet holes. But the doc has been in and signed my release. I'm on my way home.'

Annie smiled to show that she was pleased for him, but at the same time, she felt a stab of envy. She didn't have a home to go to. In fact, she had no idea where she could go. She thought briefly of asking Helen and Andrew if she could stay with them but a new baby and a toddler would not be conducive to a good night's sleep.

The nurse finished tying the sling and stepped back.

'All done, Inspector. I'll just go and fetch your drugs and outpatient's appointment and you'll be ready to go.'

Richard was still grinning. 'Thank you, Nurse.'

'You're welcome. I'll need to sort you out some transport as well.'

'That's all sorted, I can transport him wherever he wants to go,' said Masterton as she strode into the room.

'Boss, what are you doing here?'

'Visiting my favourite…' she paused and looked him up and down, 'I was going to say detective but it looks as though you're going for a change of career.'

'I couldn't get my shirt on, boss.'

'I don't need to know that.' She turned to Annie. 'Good morning, Annie, how are you?'

'I'm feeling very well, thank you.'

'Enough already,' interrupted Richard. 'Just tell me how it went?'

'What?' asked Masterton, feigning innocence.

'Innocence is one coat you can't wear, boss. How did the operation go?'

Now it was Masterton's turn to grin.

'We got him.'

'Got him where?' asked Richard. 'Cell or coffin?'

'Bodybag, actually.'

Richard punched the air with his good arm then winced as the movement tugged at his sore shoulder.

'Fan-bloody-tastic. That's it then.'

'Well, it is as far as capturing villains go. Three murderers in twenty-four hours is not bad going. It's just a shame we didn't get the intelligence to blow the whole operation. God knows they need bringing down.'

'What do you mean by intelligence?' asked Annie.

'We didn't get the USB. It's still out there somewhere.'

Annie was perplexed. 'But we did get it. I found it hidden behind a poster in my office. I gave it to Colonel Shaw.'

'When?' asked Masterton sharply. 'When did you give it to him?'

'While we were in the car on the way back to the Asylum Centre yesterday.'

Masterton was punching numbers into her mobile phone. She looked angry and Annie felt sure she had done something dreadfully wrong.

'I don't think you can use those in here, boss, it interferes with…' began Richard, but she cut him off with a single glance before barking into the phone.

'Did I do the wrong thing?' asked Annie.

'No, of course not,' reassured Richard. 'He's an Army Officer and my brother but the USB should have been handed to the police straight away. We've lost a good few hours of analysis time. Masterton will need to find it. Don't worry. She will sort things out.'

But Annie was worried and tears were gathering at the corners of her eyes.

Richard pulled a tissue from the box beside his bed and went over to Annie. She took the tissue and blew her nose while Richard returned to sit on his bed. After a few deep breaths, she plucked up the courage to look at him. His eyes were on her but she couldn't read his expression. All she could think was that she had let him down. Disappointed him, when all she wanted to do was please him.

'Richard?'

He spoke quietly. 'Come here.'

She took a step towards him.

'I really am so sorry, I can't…'

'Shush.' He reached forward to place his fingers to her mouth and he felt her lips quiver beneath his touch.

'Please stop saying you are sorry or I may have to arrest you for annoying behaviour.'

She waited for his anger but he smiled at her with a look of unadulterated wonderment.

'You risked your life yesterday to recover that USB. If it's what we've been looking for you will have prevented more crimes than most officers could even dream about. Now come here.'

Annie took another step towards him, so close that she could feel his breath against her hair. He reached forwards with his good arm to cradle her face in his hand. Annie felt her skin melt into his and her eyes closed.

'Look at me, Annie.'

She did, even though meeting his eyes caused her throat to constrict and her heart to thud against her ribs.

'Annie, this is a bit of an about face for me, but I can't live another minute without telling you.'

Annie raised her hand to his and brought his palm to her lips. Richard seemed to shudder and when he spoke his voice caressed her.

'I love you, Annie. I've loved you since the first moment I saw you in that café. I've loved you every day since and it's nearly killed me not being able to tell you. I want you in my life, from today, for always.'

Annie stared into his eyes and any doubts she may have had about him melted away. It was true that she had many questions to ask him and there was much that she needed to learn about this man, his life, and his past. But she was good with faces and this one was trustworthy. Sometimes in life, you just have to go with your gut and this is what Annie would do.

She kissed his hand again before speaking. 'I love you too, Richard. And it's an about face for me too. I always told my friends that love, at first sight, is a fairy tale. But it's not, is it? It's real. This is real.'

'Annie, will you come home with me? Now? Today? You can stay in the spare room, have your space, take your time, whatever you need.'

Annie hesitated and Richard's jaw stiffened with anticipated disappointment. It made Annie's heart leap. 'I will come home with you,' she smiled, 'I would love to come home with you.

Richard returned her smile.

They were interrupted by Masterton who ended her call and made to leave.

'I've got work to do. I'll be in touch. You two look after yourselves and for God's sake, Richard, will you give the woman a kiss already. The case is over.'

She was gone and Richard and Annie faced each other. Richard smiled.

'Boss's orders,' he said as he pulled Annie towards him.

Epilogue

It took several days of telephone calls, shouting and even a little swearing before Masterton found herself speaking to the Commander of the SAS. Colonel Shaw had not returned to base. He had not made contact with the base or with any of his known friends or colleagues. No-one knew where he was and no-one knew anything about a USB. An investigation was underway and Colonel Shaw's computer had been transferred to GCHQ because the level of encryption was too sophisticated for the Army to decode. So far, all they had found was a Swiss bank account in the name of Hajji.

A Note from the Author

Thank you for taking the time to read my debut novel and I hope that you enjoyed it.

Writing is a solitary occupation. It can be very difficult to know whether readers have enjoyed getting to know your characters and if they would like to find out what happens next.

Let me know!

I would love to hear from you via my Goodreads page, my blog, or a review on Amazon.

Thank you for your support, it is hugely appreciated.

Wendy Williams
September 2016
www.mylifewitheyecancer.com

Lightning Source UK Ltd.
Milton Keynes UK
UKOW04f1908191016

285704UK00017B/514/P